Project Anthro

PROJECT ANTHRO

By

Dallin Newell

Printed by Lulu

First Printing, 2017

ISBN-13: 978-1542866873

ISBN-10: 1542866871

CreateSpace
4900 LaCross Road
North Charleston, SC 29406
USA

www.createspace.com

1

Three UH-1 Iroquois helicopters flew in formation over the vast expanse of the lush, green Vietnamese jungle as they turned around to make another pass over the battle raging below. In unison, they all released their payload of tow missiles and fired their machine guns at the enemy troops' position.

One of these helicopters broke away from the formation, flying low toward the spot where Kay, an anthropomorphic cougar, flagged it down. As the now vulnerable helicopter landed, Kay fired at the charging enemy with his M16 rifle.

We had been stuck in that valley for hours, after being ambushed unexpectedly by nearly a hundred VC troops, which was about double the number of troops we had.

I, an anthropomorphic fox and the only other anthro in the unit, was firing on the enemy with my rifle as I felt Kay grab me by the shoulder.

"Chance," he yelled over the deafening gunfire. "Get your ass over there and tell that radioman to call in an artillery strike!"

I nodded in compliance and began running over to where the radioman, along with another young private were stuck behind a mound of earth, gripping my rifle tightly. I aimed my rifle and unleashed a hail fire of lead on the oncoming Viet Cong as I slid behind the mound with the two men.

"Private," I yelled, knocking on his helmet to grab his attention. "Call in an artillery strike here and prepare to hightail it out of here!"

"Yes, sir!" he said with a nod and grabbed the mic for the radio.

"Come on!" I rose from behind the mound and fired a short burst at an enemy soldier who was knocked onto the ground from the impact of my bullets. "Get on that horn and call in some more firepower!"

The other private ducked down behind the mound of dirt, ejecting his empty magazine from his rifle and took out a fresh one, knocking it against his helmet to make sure it was full before trying to jam it in.

"Hurry up, mate, I'm running low here!" I shouted over the noise, peeking over the mound.

"I could if it wasn't for this piece of crap standard issue M16!" he yelled back, still trying to work the magazine into his rifle.

"You're doing it wrong!" I said.

"Shut up, I am not!" he shot back.

"You're just having a panic attack," I said. "Here, gimme that!"

I ripped his rifle out of his grip and took his magazine, putting it in, and cocking the action to load the chamber.

"There!" I handed it to him and we traded positions; I began reloading my rifle while he returned fire.

"Where's the artillery support?" the private yelled as he fired short bursts at the Viet Cong.

"I can't reach them!" the radioman replied.

"Well, call them in!"

"Don't get your panties in a wad, I'm trying!"

The two privates were busy bickering with each other as I finished reloading my rifle, poked over the mound, and started firing at the oncoming VC.

2

"At this rate, we'll be surrounded," the young private observed amid the arguing. "They're trying to flank us! We gotta get back to the chopper, but how?"

"Yeah," the radioman said, putting the mic to his side and speaking in a much calmer voice than that of the young private. "For once I'm with this little piss-ant. There are just too many hostiles. We'll have more holes than a sponge before we make it within a hundred feet of the helicopter."

I sat in a stupor of thought about how we would get back to the helicopter without getting killed as the radioman played with the frequency dial on his radio and stopped with a look of relief.

"I've got them!" he said. He called for artillery support and began to relay the coordinates when he took a bullet between the chest and shoulder.

"Gah!" he exclaimed as he fell back into the dirt. Now bullets were flying everywhere and explosions from grenades rocked the ground.

"Damn!" I yelled, grabbing the radio and handing it to the young private, whom the radioman had been arguing with.

"You call it in!" I ordered. "I would, but I'm a bit preoccupied at the moment!"

A VC soldier was just feet from us before I noticed him. I then aimed my rifle at him and filled him with lead.

"We need artillery support; we're at . . ." he began to brokenly relay the coordinates as I tried my best to help the wounded radioman. I worked at his wound as he cried out in pain.

"Ah, cripes," I muttered.

"What?" the man yelled in a panicky tone. "What is it?"

"The bullet's too far in there," I said. "We need to get you back on that bird!"

I pointed to the landed helicopter that Kay and his squad were defending.

The radioman then cried out in panic as he lay in the dirt.

"Calm down," I said reassuringly. "No need to panic, you'll be fine."

"We've gotta get out of here!" The private yelled after finishing with the radio and putting the mic back in its slot on the radio itself. "The artillery will be firing in just a few minutes!"

"All right," I said. "Get to the chopper, now! Move or you're dead!"

The private grabbed his rifle and took off running, leaving the radio behind and me to take the wounded radioman to the helicopter. I got up, taking the radioman with me and wrapping his arm over my shoulder to support him and we began moving to the helicopter as fast as we could.

We were at a distance to where the run could've only taken a couple minutes, but with the pressure and tension from bullets flying all around us, one having grazed my right arm, and the grenades exploding everywhere, from which I took some shrapnel in my left leg, it felt like hours. When we finally arrived at the chopper, I helped the radioman into it.

"Where's the other private?" Kay asked over the sound of the helicopter's engine.

"I thought he made it here!" I responded, scanning the battlefield for any sign of him. Then, to my horror, I saw him lying on the ground roughly fifty feet away, bleeding from his upper side.

"Over there, cover me!" I ran out to him without thinking to fetch him.

The gunfire was pervasively thick now, coming from the remaining enemy troops, who still significantly outnumbered us, to the point where I could feel the bullets miss me as I sprinted over to the young private. The wound in my leg ached, as did the one in my arm; however, I wasn't abandoning that boy.

My first instinct was to get down and check his pulse, which was a mistake since I took a bullet through my left shoulder. I grunted as I fell back and landed on my tail. I quickly got back on my feet and began to return fire to wherever I could see any movement. I took two steps forward, still firing my weapon when the private spoke up.

"Ugh, don't stand over me like that!" I looked down, noticing that his head was between my feet, and being a fox, I didn't wear pants regardless of the fact that I was anthropomorphized, so his line of sight went right up to my exposed crotch.

"Privates to privates, mate," I said as I stepped aside, grabbing his hand and helping him up.

He leaned on me and limped alongside me as we made our way to the helicopter, for he had taken a round in his leg as well. The helicopter was now taking off. I tried to call for the pilot's attention to no avail and the chopper lifted off with its machine guns firing and left Kay and about nine other guys standing in the heat of the now less intense firefight. I walked over to Kay with the private leaning on my shoulder.

"Crap!" Kay muttered as a grenade went off nearby.

"What is it?" I asked. "Why'd they just leave us?"

"They said the chopper's full," Kay replied. "We have to go about a mile south of here for them to get us."

"This guy's bleeding out." I told him.

"Then we better get moving now," Kay said, suddenly aiming his rifle at a VC soldier who made his presence unnoticed behind me and firing a three-round burst at him.

"Damn gooks," said one of the soldiers as they began to run to a tree line South of our position.

I stood by and patted each soldier on the back as they ran by me, doing a headcount to make sure they were all accounted for. We still had all ten, not including Kay and me. Bullets from the enemy whizzed and snapped by us as we ran. When the bullets whizzed by, it meant they were passing us at low velocity, losing power. The bullets that snapped were the real killers, being fired from a closer range, hence, having more power and velocity.

I ran at the end of the line, slowing myself down as I noticed a Cobra attack helicopter flying low nearby. The helicopter took a few rounds in the cockpit, and the tail boom was cracked off from too much damage from the ubiquitous enemy firing at it. As soon as the tail boom flew apart, the helicopter began spiraling downward, toward me.

I began to run away and was only a couple of yards from where the helicopter plummeted to the earth and landed with a sizeable explosion that launched debris in all directions. A large piece of metal landed on my tail and I fell to the ground, my helmet getting knocked off my head.

"Ah!" I exclaimed as a sharp pain shot up my spine. "Dammit!"

Almost instantly, Kay came running over to me. When he reached me, he strained as he lifted the piece of metal, allowing me to free my tail and crawl away. Kay dropped the piece of metal and helped me onto my feet.

"You just can't stay out of trouble, can you?" he said, putting my helmet back on my head.

We began running after the rest of the group until we found ourselves in the jungle. The deeper we went, the more the gunfire seemed to fade away until there was nothing but silence. We slowed our pace to a walk.

It was hot and humid, typical of a place such as Vietnam, and the air was filled with the scent of the flowers and rotting leaves around us instead of gunpowder.

"Where the hell are we?" one of the men asked.

"I don't know," Kay replied, "but the chopper pilot said there's a clearing just south of where we were. Just keep moving."

6

It was now dead silent. The enemy had either fallen too far behind us or had just given up, but either way, we were alone. Something just felt so strange as we made our way through the dense foliage.

"Something ain't right," one of the men said, suddenly breaking the silence after a few minutes of walking in complete silence.

"Yeah, you're right," Kay said. "It's not really like the Viet Cong to just retreat."

We came to a halt and sat in awkward silence, listening. It was way too quiet.

Suddenly, the thought came to me that it could have something to do with artillery.

"Private," I said, approaching the guy I had call in the artillery strike when the radioman was wounded, "what coordinates did you give the artillery?"

The private swallowed and looked at me, holding his bleeding side and opened his mouth to speak when the silence was broken by the whistle of a shell, which grew louder and louder until an explosion knocked two guys off their feet, killing them both.

"Dammit!" Kay exclaimed, ducking away from the explosion.

None of the remaining eight soldiers needed an order to run, and they all fled. Kay and I ran after them. Shells began to explode pervasively around us, uprooting trees, disintegrating lush green plants, and creating craters on the "path" we followed that wound through the trees.

"I must've made a mistake on giving them the coordinates!" the young private said, panting as he limped.

"You think?" I replied as I caught up to him and gave him a push. "Just shut up and keep moving!"

Suddenly, a shell landed right behind us, and the explosion sent us flying a few feet to a clearing met by a large body of water.

I landed on the ground next to the young private, and my vision began to blur. I felt faint and dizzy. I could see the blurred outline of Kay as he ran toward me. His voice, along with all the other sounds were muffled to the point where I couldn't make out what he was saying, with the exception of when he called my name.

"Chance!" I heard him shout. "Stay with me, Chance!"

The explosions came to a stop, and I just couldn't keep my eyes open much longer as the feeling of faintness and dizziness began to overtake me.

In the distance, I could see a dark blur moving across the sky, which I made out to be a helicopter.

One of the privates fired his rifle in the air to grab their attention, but at this point, I couldn't even hear the gunfire.

The soldier who got blown up with me slowly got onto his hands and knees. He was covered in blood and dirt. He looked at me and said something, but his voice was inaudible to me, then all of a sudden, I was out.

"He's waking up, give him some room!" I heard a familiar voice say when I regained consciousness.

I was in the medical tent. I knew because I could smell the metallic scent of blood on the medical equipment and the stale odor of the tent fabric. I could also feel bandages wrapped tightly over the wounds on my arms and legs.

I slowly began to open my eyes when I felt a sudden impact on my cheek that resulted in a lingering, stinging pain. I had just been slapped.

I regained focus, and my eyes met with my girlfriend Katie's; she was an anthropomorphic fox like me. She had her arms crossed and wore a concerned expression.

"Have you forgotten what you promised me?" Katie scolded. The other nurses and medics hastily left the tent to give us some privacy.

"No, I haven't," I answered, cringing as I put a paw on my sore cheek.

"You promised you wouldn't die!" Katie scolded again. "And this is the second time *this week!* You had me worried sick!"

American women are always worried sick, I thought with a sigh.

"What day is it?" I asked.

"What?" Katie said.

"You know, the day?" I asked, in a bit of a sarcastic manner. "Like, November eleventh."

"It's November twelfth, 1973." Katie replied.

My jaw dropped, and I looked at her as she leaned against a table with her arms still folded and looked at me bitterly.

"So I was out for an entire day?" I asked.

She nodded and got up from the table and sat on the cot, looking into my eyes.

"I'm sorry, honey," she said. "I was just worried because I love you. You know that, right?"

"Of course I do," I replied.

"You're lucky we're leaving soon," she said, leaning in and giving me a kiss on my lips, then pressing her nose to mine. "At this rate, you'd probably be dead within the month."

"I know." I sighed. "I'm a bit reckless."

Katie just chuckled softly and gave me another kiss.

"So do you have any plans for when we leave?" Katie asked.

"I'm not sure," I answered. "I do have some things to square away with the CIA."

"Have you ever considered marriage?" Katie asked.

"Marriage?" I asked, confused.

"Yeah," Katie said, sitting up. "You know, finding your soul mate, your other half, settling down, having kids . . ."

"I don't know," I said with a shrug. "Why?"

"Well," Katie said, looking downward. "I was thinking you could maybe come with me when this is all over."

"Well, I don't know," I repeated, feeling like she was moving just a little too fast.

She suddenly had a disappointed expression. I felt my heart sink a little seeing her that way. She then looked at me, forced a smile, then got up and walked out of the tent, leaving me all by myself. I lay back in the cot and took in lungful of fresh, moist jungle air and let it out with a deep sigh.

Many were probably wondering, what are Katie and I, a couple of anthropomorphic foxes, and Kay, an anthropomorphic cougar, doing in Vietnam, fighting in a human's war? Better yet, where did we come from?

I was born on October 1, 1951, in London, England. Not in a hospital, though, but in a laboratory run by England's Secret Intelligence Service, most commonly known as MI6 (Military Intelligence, section 6).

I was created for a new program known as Project Anthro, a program that anthropomorphized nonhuman species and turned them into soldiers or operatives for the secret service.

I was an anthro developed in the project, so I was a fox that stood at five foot ten, not including the ears, and I have the ability to speak, think, and act like a human, or for short, I was anthropomorphic.

I spoke in a strong English accent, having been born in England and raised in Australia.

Australia was where I was transferred to begin my training for ASIS (Australian Secret Intelligence Service) in their facility in Canberra, which not many anthros ever got to do, but since I was a fox, someone in ASIS reserved a spot for me there just because of my species. Of course, being so young then I had no understanding of why I was there and what it even was.

The first few years of my life were spent being educated. I was at high school senior level by the time I was twelve, and ready to move on to combat training.

Since I was eight years old, I had been taught basic self-defense as part of my physical education, but by the time I was sixteen, I could take on several armed men at once. I was taught how to escape certain situations with limited gadgets and supplies, how to disarm and arm explosives ranging from C-4 to nuclear weapons, and how to be an expert shot with any weapon I was given.

When I was eighteen, I was pronounced ready to serve and got transferred to the United States Central Intelligence Agency, where I then began doing my first black ops missions to help their cause in the conflict with the Union of Soviet Socialist Republics, better known as the ruthless Soviet Union. Each of my missions increased in difficulty, until my last one in 1968, where the government had me sent to Ukraine to assassinate some Soviets, whose identity was classified even to me, and leave a package containing a deadly weapon for some undercover CIA operatives to take into the Kremlin.

After I had finished the mission, I remember looking back at the house I had infiltrated, wondering what exactly was in the box; it was highly classified, so if anything went wrong and the Soviets discovered it, then I couldn't take the blame for it.

When I arrived back at the States, I was temporarily discharged from the CIA and put into a classified unit in the US Army. It was the first day when I met Kasey, or Kay. He would be the leading sergeant of the unit, and the guy I had to share sleeping quarters with.

Kay wasn't the only one upon my arrival whom I met in Vietnam. There was one nurse in particular whom I had my eye on. Her name was Katie. She was a fox like me, standing at five foot six, and the most beautiful anthro I had ever seen. She had bright-blue eyes, her fur was a brighter orange than mine, and the white fur that ran from her chin to between her legs was clean and silky.

After getting finished with the daily routines, if there were any, I would head to the nurses' tent and try flirting with Katie, who didn't seem to be interested in me in the least. My whole life I was told that I was the only one of my kind, so her disinterest in me concerned me quite a bit.

Kay was married, so he took it upon himself to educate me on how to "pick up chicks."

"She's just shy," Kay told me after I had told him about how Katie didn't seem interested in me at all. "Females always seem disinterested simply because they don't know what to say when they encounter an attractive male."

I wasn't so sure, though; sometimes it was like she was deliberately ignoring my presence. But I wasn't going to let her get away from me. I became increasingly more persistent, and I would see her every day and continually flirt with her as she cleaned up my gashes and bandaged my lacerations.

One day in the heat of a firefight, I had taken a bullet in the upper thigh and had fallen into shock. I was quickly rushed back to camp by a helicopter and taken to the medical tent, where Katie showed up and instantly started working on my wound. By then, I was shaking violently because almost no one can shake off a 7.62x39mm bullet from an AK-47. Finally, Katie couldn't work with me shaking so violently, and she held me by the cheeks and told me to look at her.

I looked into her eyes, which were bright sapphire blue and shone brightly in the light. I was so awestruck by the beauty that I didn't even know she had pulled the bullet out, cleaned, and dressed the wound until she told me she had finished. I was no longer shaking; in fact, I lay perfectly still as if I were about to go to sleep.

Katie then waited for everyone to clear the tent before bending down and giving me a passionate kiss on the lips. I was stunned by this; I felt as if I had just been struck by lightning. When she finally broke the kiss, she began to exit the tent.

"I'll be seeing you later," she said with a smile. And that was the first night we spent together.

I finally had her like a fish on a hook, and I was reeling her in. She was about to be mine, but I had just one problem; I was an inexperienced fisher.

Later on, I asked Kay about what to do to make my relationship with Katie stronger.

"Take her out on a starry night," Kay said. "Chicks dig that mushy, romantic stuff. There's almost nothing more romantic than looking up at the heavens with your girl, and when a shooting star passes over, you two make a wish. Hell, what better place to do it than in an exotic place like Vietnam?"

That night, I took Katie away from the camp, and we lay alone in the field of waist-high grass, listening to the nocturnal creatures and watching the stars above as we cuddled.

"Hey, Chance," Katie said, after we had talked for a little bit. "There's something I want to ask you."

"Yes?" I replied.

"Will you stay alive for me," Katie asked, "until the war is over?"

"Indubitably," I answered, shifting over and giving her a big kiss.

2

As I lay on the cot, the tent flap door opened again, and Lieutenant Alvin Moore, a kind of heavyset guy with a bushy mustache styled like Stalin's and a southern accent entered with Kay, both in full uniform.

"Is this Mr. Logan?" Alvin asked.

"Yes, sir," Kay answered.

"Private Logan," he started. "I heard about what you did on the battlefield, and I've come to offer my gratitude for being a good soldier and saving those young men's lives."

"Thank you, sir," I said.

"I've also come to offer you a promotion," he said. "A promotion to sergeant."

"Thanks again, sir," I replied hesitantly, "but I can't accept."

"Why's that?" Alvin asked.

"Because when we pull out of here, I'd like to just get away from all the violence, settle down, and live a peaceful life."

"Suit yourself," Alvin said with a sigh. "I sure can respect your decision, but if there's anything you need, you know where to find me, right?"

"Yes, sir," I said.

"All right," Alvin straightened out his uniform then looked at Kay then me. "It's been an honor serving with you guys."

He nodded at us and began toward the tent door and then turned and faced us.

"By the way," he said, "you guys may want to try on some pants when we get back to the States. Just try it."

"Nah," Kay said as he swiped the air with his paw. "We've got fur to cover our junk, right Chance?"

"Yeah, right," I agreed with a forced chuckle.

All of us anthros never wore pants; it was a lot more comfortable to go without them. Even Katie wouldn't wear them.

Alvin exited the tent, leaving Kay and me alone.

"C'mon, let's get some chow, I'm starving," Kay said, lightly hitting me on the shoulder.

"I guess that sounds good right now," I said.

I sat up and swung my legs over the side of the cot. My left leg landed on my tail, and I felt a sharp pain shoot up my spine.

"Ouch!" I exclaimed, lifting my leg and pulling my tail from under it.

"What's wrong?" Kay asked. "Did a spider bite you or something?"

"No," I said, standing and searching through the bushy fur of my tail to find the source of the pain. "Something's wrong with my tail."

"Here, let me have a look," Kay said.

He came over, knelt on the ground, and looked it over as I stood there waiting.

"Ah," he said finally, "it's dislocated here." Without any warning, he twisted and pulled, and it hurt like hell.

"Ow, god!" I exclaimed, slightly jumping.

"There, all better," Kay said. We walked to the door of the tent, and Kay held the flap open for me. "Must've been that piece of metal that landed on your tail."

"Funny," I said, "it wasn't even that big."

We were all outside, having dinner, as the loudspeakers played Norman Greenbaum's "Spirit in the Sky," which was a song I never quite understood. It seemed to make death sound like such a good thing. Death was the most horrible thing I could think of, whether I were to die or take someone else's life, regardless of the fact that we're going to go up to the spirit in the sky.

The others talked and joked as a young man named Tyson got his hair trimmed by a private who was one of the few African Americans there named Thomas, who was the designated barber of the unit since he used to work with his dad in a barber shop in downtown Seattle.

"Want me to get the bangs, man?" Thomas asked.

"Eh, trim them just enough to get them out of the way of my eyes," Tyson said.

"I tell you," a young man named Brendan said, "when I get home, I'm going to slap my brother in the face for protesting against this war."

"Right," said Tyson. "We had the commies in a headlock, and our own just yanked our arm back and broke it. Now we get to leave the South Vietnamese to their certain demise."

"I was starting to like this place," Brendan said. "Now I'm being forced to leave."

"Well, you could come visit when the war is done," Kay said as he lounged in a chair with his arms folded, an empty bowl next to him.

"I don't think we'll be allowed in a communist country," Thomas spoke up. "Not that I'd ever want to visit one, but take North Korea for example—"

16

"Thomas has got a point," Brendan said setting his bowl down and standing. "North Korea allows nobody from the outside world into their country."

"God dang communists," Tyson said. "They claim to be helping the people by making a classless society, but they just want power over all of them."

"Yeah," Kay said, arms still folded. "It's a sad thing. I think it's all because of the Revolution of 1918, when the Reds wanted to turn Russia into that country we know and love, the USSR."

"Ugh," Tyson said, "don't even remind me."

"So what are you guys going to do?" Brendan said, looking at Kay then me. "The citizens in the US don't even know about you. Are you going back to the lab or something?"

"Nope," I said, shaking my head. "I've got a device where if I'm in the middle of a bunch of people, all I have to do is flash it in their eyes, and they'll remember me, but they'll just remember me as a human."

"That's cool!" Tyson said. "How does it work?"

"I'm not the scientist," I said. "But I've been instructed to use it on you guys when we're done here."

I glanced at Thomas who gave me a worried look.

"What?" Tyson questioned.

"I'm just kidding," I said with a laugh. "The government trusts that you won't tell anyone. And even if you do, who's going to believe a guy when he tells them about a five foot ten fox who can speak?"

"Yeah," Brendan said. "Now people would think that Vietnam was nothing but a mass acid trip."

There was some silence.

"So you're from Australia?" Thomas asked. "Because your accent . . ."

"Well, yeah," I said. "I mean, I was born in England, but I grew up in Australia."

17

"You going back there?"

"Nah." I shook my head. "I'm going to stay in the States. I've got some stuff to square away with the CIA before I do anything else."

"Which state will you live in?" Tyson asked. "You better choose wisely."

He put his fist to his mouth.

"California." He coughed.

"California?" Brendan said.

"Yeah, there's the beaches in San Diego, Los Angeles, Oakland," Tyson said. "Why, you could get a job at Disneyland as the Robin Hood costume."

"Who the hell is Robin Hood?" Brendan asked.

"Just a show for kids," Tyson said. "My brother told me about it in a letter. Sounds like a pretty freaking awesome idea, to be honest."

"Well," I said, "I'm not going to wear tights and a feathered cap at some hoity-toity theme park."

"Well, Robin Hood doesn't wear pants, so you still wouldn't have to either," Tyson said.

"Well, I'm not working there," I said. "Period!"

"Okay then." Tyson put his hands up in surrender.

"Speaking of which, why don't you guys wear pants?" Brendan asked.

"Oh my god, here we go again," Kay muttered.

"It's indecent," Brendan said.

"Like hell it is," I said. "Foxes or cougars or any other furred animal in the world don't wear them, so why should we?"

"Well, I ain't never seen a fox stand on two legs at six feet tall and speak either," Thomas said

"And you wear shirts, so . . ." Brendan said.

"That's different," Kay said.

18

"All done," Thomas said, handing Tyson a mirror. "What do you think?"

"Looks good," Tyson said. Thomas had gotten it to look exactly how he wanted it, as far as I could tell. "Thank you, Thomas."

He took a ten-dollar bill out of his breast pocket and handed it to him.

"Now I'm going to take a shower," I said.

As I walked to the shower tent, the music switched to "The Wanderer" by Dion, and Tyson started walking toward the music tent.

"Who the hell picks the music?" he asked. "How about some Judas Priest for a change?"

The cool water felt so good as it ran down my body. After sweating for many long hours in the hot and humid weather of Vietnam, nothing felt better than a cold shower. I scrubbed myself with a strong-smelling men's shampoo that made my nose tingle whenever I smelled it.

As I showered and minded my own business, I heard the swing door to my shower open. I looked with one eye at a squint to keep the soap on my face from running into it and saw Katie step in.

"Hey, babe," I said, rinsing the soap off my face. "I think you're in the wrong shower tent."

"There's only a men's one here," she said. She lightly shoved me to the side with a giggle. "Excuse me."

I watched her rinse herself off. I could smell the strong lavender perfume on her fur as it mixed with the water.

"Is there any girl's shampoo, Chance?" she asked.

I looked up and saw cheap children's shampoo that was scented mango next to my shampoo bottle on the top of the wooden wall that divided us from the next shower.

"No, but there's this," I said, grabbing the child's stuff that had a picture of a cute little toucan on the front.

19

"Thanks," she said, grabbing it, putting some on her paws and lathering it up, then scrubbing herself with it.

I watched as she scrubbed from her arms to her legs then her tail, which at this point looked skinny and bony rather than big and fluffy. She rinsed off.

"Do you need to rinse anymore?" she asked.

I came over to her and reached around her to turn off the water. I don't know what came over me, but I just suddenly felt so passionate toward her. My heart pounded in my chest as I felt this passion grow from within me.

I wrapped my arms around her, hugging her tightly, and we kissed. We spent a good long while passionately kissing in that shower tent.

I was back in my tent with Kay that evening. He had all his shirts neatly laid out on his hammock, and he put them all into his worn out brown suitcase.

"I'm telling you," he said, folding a brown undershirt and placing it in the suitcase, "why don't you just marry the girl?"

"I don't know," I said, sitting in my hammock. "It's difficult. I mean, she's CIA, I'm CIA and about to retire. It's just . . . and she seems to be going too fast for me."

I had told him what she asked once I had regained consciousness.

"I understand," Kay said, "but I've personally never met anyone who was married who said they didn't like it. I mean, what's better than being with the girl you love for eternity and having children of your own to look up to you and play with you? And the best part is making them."

He chuckled obnoxiously at his suggestive remark.

I just sighed.

"What should I do?" I asked.

"Well, from where I'm standing," Kay said, putting the last of his shirts into the suitcase, "you can either marry her or just live a lonely life and rot in England."

It seemed to make sense, but it was still so hard for me to decide. We were the only ones of our kind, and this could be a chance to populate and pass on our genes and stuff, but still.

"Listen," Kay said, "just think about it. It doesn't need to happen right away, just before you miss the boat. She may be the only chance you got."

I nodded.

"All right, you better get some shut-eye," Kay said as he reached up and pulled the cord to turn off the light. "It's going to be a long ride home."

I let my eyes adjust to the darkness and lay down in my hammock.

"See you in the morning," I said. I thought for a long time about what I was going to do with Katie. Kay was right; she was the only chance I had. I couldn't think of anyone else because there was no one else. I just pulled the covers up to my chin and shut my eyes then fell into a deep sleep.

3

The next morning, we were woken up at around 0500 hours. We loaded everything onto the trucks and took down the camp. As we drove away, I remember looking back and thinking about all the memories I would be leaving there, the good ones, the bad ones and somewhere in between. I would always remember that place for as long as I live. We drove a couple hours until our asses hurt from the hard wooden bench seats in the truck to a large airstrip in the middle of nowhere where a plane waited for us. We all loaded our cargo and piled ourselves into the plane. After a half hour, we were in the air.

Good bye Vietnam, I thought. *Good bye forever.*

I would never return there again.

I was woken up after dozing off to a big bump that shook the plane. I heard a skid, then another, and looked out the window to see that we had landed in London for a refueling stop.

As the plane got to the terminal, we were told that we would be able to go out and explore some, but we had to be back at the plane in two hours unless we wanted to pay for another plane home.

I went with Kay, Tyson, Brendan, and Thomas, and we all went for places to buy souvenirs. Kay bought a shot cup with an illustration of Big Ben on it just for the hell of it.

I made sure to use the flashing device on all the people we came across. Like I said earlier, that thing, when shined into someone's eyes, they'd remember me, just not as a fox but as a human. Those people will probably think they'd never seen me before.

After a half hour or so, we came across Katie and the lieutenant. I left the others and went with Katie to spend some time with her alone. We exchanged plans and told stories for a while.

"This is where I was born, Katie," I said as we walked along the English Channel. "London, England. It hasn't changed much."

"I thought you were born in Australia," Katie said.

"Nope," I said. "I was born in a special place run by MI6, just over there somewhere."

I pointed to the northwest.

We walked in awkward silence. The only sounds to be heard were the light waves splashing onto the gravel beach, the calls and squawks of seagulls, and the sounds of the everyday traffic. The air, softly blowing in from the channel, was fresh and cool and carried the scent of seawater.

"Chance," Katie said, breaking the silence between us. "I really want to know; do you love me?"

I smiled, put my arm around her, and gave her a kiss on the cheek.

"Yes, I do," I replied.

"Then why don't you come with me?" Katie asked.

I looked down at the sidewalk and kicked a small rock. I opened my mouth to say something when I heard a loud engine rev, and a black Aston Martin V8 pulled up alongside us. I tried to look through the tinted glass, and the window rolled down to reveal a man in his forties or so in the driver's seat. He wore a black suit, and his gray hair was cut short, in a military-style cut.

"Hello, Chance," he said, "Katie."

He had an accent, obviously Australian; I could tell through his dialect, but I'd never seen him before in my life.

"Who the hell are you?" I asked.

"No questions, just get into the car."

"How are we supposed to know if—"

"Chance, it's okay," Katie said, holding me back. "I know this guy."

We're obviously going to miss our flight home, I thought as we cruised through the streets to the large MI6 building.

Upon arriving at the gate, we each showed our IDs, and they let us through.

"Trouble is brewing," Jack O'Reilly said. Katie had told me his name. "The Soviets located a nuclear bomb in Ukraine and blamed the US for it. A few days later, it was unaccounted for."

"What does that have to do with us?" I asked.

"We can't talk here," Jack said, parking the Aston Martin. "Wait until we get into the office."

We got out of the car and made our way through the building. I tried to use my flash device on someone, but Jack said I didn't need to do that here. As soon as we got to the office and shut the door behind us, Jack answered my question.

"The CIA is coming after you," Jack said, sitting in his chair.

"Why are they after us?" I asked.

"Not after Katie," Jack said, "just you."

"Why?"

"Kiev, 1968," Jack said, pulling a file out of his drawer. "You were on a top-secret mission that was supposed to bring an end to the Soviets for good."

"I remember that," I said, grabbing the file. I opened it and flipped through the pages. Everything had been blacked out, with the exception of a few words. There was a picture in the lower corner, though, a picture of the box I made way for.

"I remember that," I said, placing the file onto the table and pointing at the picture, "but I have no idea what was in it, so why would the CIA be coming after me?"

"With the Soviets blaming the US for the bomb they discovered and lost, the CIA is trying to cover their tracks, taking out many operatives. Starting with ones who went to the Soviet Union."

He pulled another file.

I looked at this next file and flipped through it. There were pictures of different operatives, human and anthro, lined throughout every page, each with a description next to them. All had a big red *terminated* stamp over them. I looked at their descriptions. Each of them had served their last missions in anywhere from East Berlin to Moscow.

On one page, I found a guy who was just like me, a fox. His name was Aaron Richards. He had served in Berlin and was terminated about a month ago.

So Katie and I weren't the only ones. I turned to the back and they had pictures of Kay, me, and a cheetah by the name of Erich, all with no *terminated* stamp on them.

"I don't understand," I said, setting the folder down.

"We need to get this squared away," Jack said putting both files back into the drawer, "that package you placed in Kiev to be delivered to the Kremlin . . ." he paused. "Was the bomb."

"What?" I couldn't believe what I was hearing. "So I just helped deliver a weapon of mass destruction?"

"We need to find out where it is" —Jack leaned on the table— "or a nuclear war is going to break out between the two countries. The CIA already has operatives after you."

25

He glared at Katie as he said this.

I looked at her and she looked back at me with regret in her eyes. I felt my heart sink, and I figured out why she was being so pushy in our relationship.

"Why, Katie?" I questioned.

"The CIA assigned me to go after you in Vietnam," she admitted. "But—"

"I don't want to hear it." I got up from the chair and stormed out of the office.

"Chance!" Katie called, running after me.

"No, Katie," I said, "I don't want any trouble, just go back to the States."

I left her crying, standing in the hallway.

I couldn't go back to the States, so I got a hotel room and stayed there for the night. I wasn't able to sleep, so I sat on the bed, reading a newspaper article about the US in Vietnam. They would be pulling out their troops soon.

No matter what, I couldn't stop thinking about why Katie would betray me. I couldn't believe I fell for an operative sent to take me in. I looked out at the night sky. Somewhere inside, I still felt love for her and hoped she was going to make it safely. My broken heart ached as I thought about her.

As I read the article, I heard a clatter outside my door, then a knock. I dropped the paper and went to the door. I opened it, and there was a man dressed in room service clothes.

"What?" I said, a bit pissed at his arrival when I wanted to be alone.

"Just room service, Mr. Logan, excuse me," he said.

Something wasn't right. How did he know my name? Why didn't he have an English accent? And room service usually passed by if the room was occupied.

"I'm sorry, you can't come in right now," I told him.

"No, its fine," he said. "I'll be quick."

"You can't come in!" I said, blocking his way. That was when he pulled a pistol on me.

I quickly and vigorously slammed the door on his hand and he dropped it, then I kicked him against the wall. He hit his head on the wall and was knocked unconscious.

I began to walk out when someone with a pistol came out of the room across from me. I grabbed his arm with my left paw as he fired a wild shot, punched him in the gut with my left, and kneed him in the head as he bent down from the impact on his stomach.

Another guy came from behind me. He hit me in the back of the head and kicked my leg out from under me. I fell to the floor, turned over, and grabbed his leg as he attempted to stomp on me. I twisted his leg as hard as I could, breaking his shin. He screamed in pain as he fell, and I pushed him down and pinned him on the ground with my legs.

I then got up and kicked him to make sure he would stay down when another man came out of the nearest room with a Galil rifle. He was at point-blank range so he tried to hit me with the buttstock of his gun, and I hit him on his arm joint, kneed him in the gut, put my arm around his back, and slammed him into the wall.

Another came out of a room with a sharp object in his hand, and he swung at me with it, but I ducked just in time and hit him in the chest. He fell to his knees, and I punched his face as hard and as quickly as possible.

I had to get out of there, so I made my way around the corner of the hall, where yet another guy was waiting. He fired at me with his Galil, and I quickly bent down, grabbed a knife, from the belt of one of the guys on the floor, and threw it at him. He dodged it and turned to me just as I came at him.

I managed to knock the rifle from his hands, but he was fast, and punched me on the cheek as soon as I did, hit me again in the stomach, then swung me around and kicked me back, and I sprawled out on the floor.

He drew his pistol and I grabbed the knife I threw at him earlier and scrambled on my feet as he took aim. I quickly grasped his arm by the wrist, turned around and stabbed him in the chest, then jumped up and round house kicked him in the face.

Another guy came from behind me and put me in a headlock, and I threw him over my back and onto the floor, still gripping his hand, and stomped him unconscious. Yet another guy came out of a door.

Jeez, how many were there?

The first guy was followed by a second, so I had to deal with two guys this time. I still held onto the knife I took from one of the others.

I started with the closest one, blocking two of his hits, then hitting him in the face then facing my next attacker, who made attempts to hit me twice.

I blocked his fists as he strenuously swung them at me, blocked his knee with a kick as he tried to knee me in the gut, then hit him in the face with the hilt of the knife, and went back to the first attacker.

He missed a punch, and I grabbed his outstretched arm and brought him to his knees. I kneed him in the face twice, and he was out.

I turned on my other attacker, who round-housed me in the chest, and I fell against the wall. I quickly got back up, and he swung at me. I put my right arm around him through the arm pit, put my left paw on his head, and slammed him against the wall hard enough to leave a hole in the plaster.

I began to run down the hall, and a guy with a pistol came out of the next room. I ducked out of the aim of his pistol as he fired two shots, rolled toward him, and turned around to grab his arm. I hit his arm at the joint, pointed the pistol in his hand at his chest, and pulled the trigger.

He fell limply onto the ground. The bullet didn't hit any vitals, and the guy just lay on the ground, panting. I grabbed him by the collar of his black uniform and pinned him against the wall; a silver syringe fell from his sleeve. I recognized it as a heavy tranquilizer.

"Who the hell sent you?" I asked.

He didn't reply; he just sat there, breathing heavily and looking into my eyes.

"For god's sake, who the hell sent you?" I slammed him against the wall.

"The C . . ." he took a deep breath. "The CIA."

"*Who?*" I asked with emphasis.

"John Lance," he said, wiping sweat from his forehead. "His name is John Lance."

I remembered John Lance. He was the guy who carried out the mission in 1968. Operation Special Delivery, it was called, and John was the one blindly put in charge of the mission.

"Why the hell is Lance after me?" I asked.

"Kiev," the man whispered. "He's silencing everyone who— uh!" He put his hand over the bullet wound as he groaned in pain.

I looked at the wound, carefully examining it. "It missed the heart," I said, "you'll be fine."

I started to walk away, but the guy tugged on my tail. I turned around, and he motioned for me to come close.

"The Soviets are after you," he said. "They sent someone named Nikolai. He has an eye patch and a black coat with a red star. Watch out for him."

"I'll keep that in mind," I said and made my way down the hall. As soon as I opened the door to the staircase there was another man with a Galil standing there. I knocked him unconscious as soon as he turned around.

Another man started firing at me from the next level down, having evidently seen it, and I picked up the rifle from the unconscious man on the floor. I ducked as bullets ripped through the banister, and I fired blindly back, keeping my head low to avoid getting shot.

I tried to move, but there was no safe way out. I fired a few more rounds at the man and the action clicked. It was empty.

I heard a loud roar and a man scream as he was thrown against the wall next to the guy who was firing at me. I saw a tiger, wearing a black leather coat jump up to the man, knock the rifle from his hands, and kick him against the wall.

He then swung around the banister pole at the bottom and launched himself up to my level, where he landed on all fours, digging his claws in the wooden floor. He kept his head down and panted from exhaustion.

Finally, some help.

"Oh, thank god," I said. "Hey listen thanks for—"

He looked up at me. He wore an eye patch on his left eye. I noticed he had a big red star on each shoulder.

"Oh sh—"

He then grabbed me and tossed me through the banister, which shattered to pieces on impact. I grabbed the edge of the floor with one paw and swung down into the hallway toward the lobby. I tumbled to the ground, and he swung down after me.

I began to run, but he was faster, and he was catching up quickly, so I turned and went through the swiveling doors to the kitchen and he followed me. I headed toward the fridge, then stopped, swung the door open, and he hit it hard.

He vigorously pushed the door back, and I backed out of the way as it closed, but then he pinned me against the sink. He reached to his side and grabbed a knife, and I grabbed a plate and smashed it over his head. He backed off, holding his head, and groaning.

Something told me I should run, but I disobeyed the instinct and attempted to kick him. He grabbed my leg, picked me up, and threw me onto the ground.

"*Do svidaniya,* American," he said as he pinned me to the ground and made an attempt to stab me with the knife he still gripped in his massive paw. I blocked his arm and held the knife just inches away from my face.

I noticed that he moved his finger over a button. It was a ballistic knife. I quickly moved my head to the side as the blade was launched and stuck in the tile floor.

I then hit him on the side of his head and kicked him in the gut. I grabbed one of his pistols and, pushing my feet against his shins, launched myself away from him, sliding on the floor.

I fired a few shots as I slid away, but he dodged both shots and ran around the corner into the next area of the kitchen. I got up and went after him, the pistol up and ready for the next encounter. As soon as I turned the corner, he shot at me twice. One of the bullets was so close I could feel it brush against my cheek fur as it went by.

I grabbed his arm and slammed it into the corner of the wall, and he let go of the pistol, then he grabbed me by the arm and punched me with his free right. I fired a wild shot as he tightened his grip, then he swiped the pistol out of my paw.

He then picked me up, threw me over his back, and I landed on my back on the counter. He punched me twice in the forehead, and I reached my legs up and kicked him right in the nose. He fell on the floor, doing a backward somersault to get back on his feet quickly.

I got off the counter, came at him, and swung both arms. He dodged the first then blocked the next.

I blocked two of his blows, and he kicked my leg out from under me. I fell onto my knees. He proceeded to kick me in the face, but I leaned backwards to dodge it and brought my fist up to his crotch, which he kept uncovered like I did.

He groaned as he put his right paw over his crotch and leaned on the counter with the other. I got back onto my feet.

"Had enough?" I taunted in Russian, which was just one of the languages I was taught during my training years.

"I've been trained to overcome pain," he answered in his native tongue, "but when I'm done with you, you'll be begging for something as sweet and merciful as pain."

He stood straight and turned his head, popping his vertebrae. He towered over me, seven feet tall at least, and I was only five foot ten. He was a giant to me. Not only that, but his fighting skills were far superior to mine, obviously Spetsnaz trained.

He lunged at me, and I moved out of the way. He hit the counter and turned around to block my hits before I could land them. I managed to hit him in the gut, though, but then he grabbed my arm as I tried to hit him in the face. He pinned me against the counter, and I kicked his leg. He stumbled back, and I swung at him with both arms again.

He dodged both then grabbed my arm by the wrist as I went for a third hit. I twisted around, elbowed him in the chest, then lifted my fist to his face and turned around, then kicked him in the gut with so much force that I stumbled back against the wall.

He was mad now. He unsheathed his claws and swung at me. I dodged it, but the power cords on the wall I leaned against were severed turning off all the lights in the kitchen.

I looked over at where light shone into the darkness from the porthole windows of the door to the dining room and ran over to them. I tried to go through the swiveling doors, but they stopped me dead in my tracks. They were locked.

That's when Nikolai tackled me from behind, and we burst through the doors and sprawled out on the floor of the dining area of the lobby, separate from each other. The few people in the room panicked and ran out screaming. I got up, but Nikolai was on his feet well before me. He had a kitchen knife in his paw, and he swung at me with it. I dodged it, but fell back into an armchair against the section of wall that came out and divided the dining room from the lobby itself, through which there was a decorative square hole placed symmetrically to the doorway.

He flipped the knife and held it upside down then went to stab me, but I rolled out of the chair and the blade stuck in it.

I turned around as he pulled it out and came at me again. I ran to a table, jumped on it and leaped to the chandelier. I swung on it and kicked him in the face as I passed over and let go. I fell to the floor, jumped and rolled through the decorative square hole in the wall, and landed on a chair, identical to the one on the other side, where I front flipped off and onto the floor by a glass coffee table.

He came after me around the wall with the hole, still holding the kitchen knife, and thrust it toward me.

I grabbed his arm, wrapped my right leg around it, and kicked him in the face twice, then put my left foot on his chest, allowing me to let my weight throw him off balance and drag him down.

We both fell over, and as soon as I hit the floor, I launched him over me with all my might, and he flew to the other end of the coffee table.

We both got back up at the same time.

I grabbed the edges of the coffee table and lifted, turning it on its side height-wise, then kicked as hard as I could, and my foot broke through the glass and hit him in the stomach.

I then quickly grabbed a flower pot with a spider plant in it as he tried to get up, and I smashed it over his head, shattering it to pieces.

He fell to the floor and tried weakly to get up, but his arms gave out from under his weight, and he fell on the floor. He was out cold.

33

The first thing I did was gather the stuff I needed. The police would be showing up soon, and I needed to get out of there as soon as possible, but I was distracted when I caught my reflection in the mirror. I stood there, looking at myself.

It had been some time since I had seen my own reflection, and I hadn't changed much since I last saw myself in a mirror.

My brown eyes sat on either side of my long snout, which had two small black marks on either side ending with a black nose. White fur ran from my chin to the base of my neck and continued from chest to crotch and a bit of white fur on the end of my bushy tail. The fur that covered the rest of my body was bright red orange.

Some of my white fur had visible blood stains on it, which was most likely my own.

That was when I realized I was wearing absolutely nothing the whole time, except for the dog tags hanging around my neck, so I put on my black T-shirt and a brown leather jacket so I could have pockets to put my valuables, namely, my wallet and my flashing device, which looked like a tiny little pocket flashlight.

As soon as I did all this I heard the sirens and made my way towards the fire exit. When I got there, it was locked, so I kicked the door open and went out. I slid down the ladder and landed on the ground then ran away from the place through the alleyway.

I was walking across the London Bridge when I happened to look behind me and see the black Aston Martin coming. I kept myself ready, just in case as the car slowed, and Jack rolled down the window.

"Chance," he said, driving alongside me, "get in."

"Why should I?" I asked.

"Because you need my help," he said, "and I need yours."

"What do you need me for?"

"You're the only one who's alive who went to Kiev in 1968," he said, "and I know where the bomb is."

"Drop dead," I said, shaking my head. "Where is it then?"

"It was tracked down by the ASIS getting shipped to Brazil three hours ago," he said.

"So," I said, "it's not my problem."

"It is if stopping it will pardon you from the CIA," he said. "You're already pardoned by MI6 and ASIS."

I stopped and pondered whether I should go with him or not.

I was convinced to go with Jack and sat in the passenger seat as we drove to his apartment. We drove by the hotel I was in a half hour ago, which was surrounded by a vast assortment of emergency vehicles, their bright lights flashing. Jack's apartment was only a few miles from there.

When we arrived, he parallel parked the Aston Martin out front, and we went inside.

The desk clerk looked at me strangely once we entered the lobby, so I took out my device and gave her a flash. We went into the elevator, and Jack pressed the button for the third floor.

"I have some stuff for you as soon as we get up there," he said, "stuff you'll need."

"Why are you helping me," I asked, "if I'm just a fugitive?"

"I work for the ASIS," he answered, "and like I said, they, along with MI6, have pardoned you. They know you weren't responsible for all these recent mishaps."

"That's nice," I commented.

We arrived on the third floor and went to his room. He unlocked it and we went in. It was perfectly clean and organized, as if it had never been used. We went into the bedroom, and he got down and pulled a couple of black briefcases from under the bed, then placed them atop the covers. He then turned the combination dials, and opened them.

"This," he said, pulling out a pistol, "is a Colt 1911, .45 caliber, eight rounds."

He handed it to me.

"You familiar with that?" he asked.

"Of course," I answered. "I'm familiar with just about any weapon."

"You have two of them," he said, "four mags for each."

He pulled out a banana-shaped object.

"You know what this is?" He asked.

I shook my head.

He then pressed a button, and two pieces flipped out, each with the end of a bowstring tied on them.

"Folding bow," he said. "Handy for tight places. It can also be used as a baton when cornered or out of arrows."

He pulled out a large cylindrical object.

"This is the quiver," he said. "Each arrow has a notch where you can connect a zip line, which the bow can also be used for to slide down."

"What else is there?" I asked.

"Well, you have three fragmentation grenades, two flash-bangs, five smoke grenades . . ." he turned to the other suitcase. "There's passports, five thousand dollars in US bills, keys—"

"What are the keys for?" I asked as he handed them to me.

"A car and storage facilities in ten states." He said as he handed me a small card with a bunch of addresses on them. "The top one is for the car."

He handed me another card.

"Just show them this and they'll give it to you." He added.

I looked at the car key, which had *Oldsmobile* pressed on it.

"Anything else?" he asked me?

"How about some weed to help me calm down?" I joked.

"These suitcases can be taken on a plane," Jack said, reviving the subject at hand. "When they go through the x-ray, they show up as office supplies on the screen."

"That's neat," I commented.

"Here's a plane ticket to DC," he said, handing me the ticket. "First-class. The plane departs tomorrow morning at ten."

"All right, thanks," I said, closing the suitcases and taking them off the bed.

"The combination to both suitcases are one, two, three, three, two, one," he said.

"What a dumb-ass combo," I commented.

"I didn't make it," he said. "By the way, you're going to need this."

He went to the closet and pulled out a black uniform with an Australian flag on the right shoulder.

"This was mine, but it's too big for me," he said. "It'll probably fit you, though."

I was just slightly taller than he, probably by about two to three inches. I took off my brown leather jacket, took the uniform out of the plastic, took it off the hanger, and tried it on.

"Wow," Jack said, looking at me. "Looks great on you. I never thought I'd live to see this day."

"Hmm," I responded, straightening out the jacket.

There was something in the inside pocket. I took it out, and it was a bag full of crack cocaine.

"What the hell?" I said.

Jack swiped it out of my hand.

"That was confiscated from drug dealers a few months ago," he said, clutching the bag to his chest, avoiding eye contact.

"Uh-huh," I said skeptically.

"Oh, and you're forgetting these," he said, pulling a pair of slacks off the hanger. I took them, unfolded them, and gave them a big tear.

"I don't wear them," I said. "The shirt's enough."

He put his hands up.

"Okay," he said.

He then tossed the bag of crack aside onto the bed.

"Well," he said, "good luck Chance. It's been great to finally see you. We should meet again."

We shook hands and I started to walk out.

"Be careful with Katie," he said in a manner that told me she was my undoing.

I knew she was after me with the CIA, but I still felt a special love for her, and I didn't want to harm her. In fact, I couldn't. Jack probably knew it too, which was why he warned me.

I spent the night on the street, until I watched the sun rise from the Tower Bridge the next morning then took a taxi to the airport. Of course, I made sure to use my flashing device on the taxi driver and all the people who walked by and looked at me funny.

I went to the security, where I walked through the metal detector and my cases went through the x-ray. I gave all of them a flash. I made it to the terminal where my flight waited, handed my ticket to the ticket collector, and gave her a flash as well.

Someone's going to get brain cancer from this thing, I thought.

I went into the plane, which was one of those newfangled, at that time, Boeing 747's. As soon as I got on I took out my flashing device.

"Everyone," I said, grabbing their attention, "I'm going to need you to look here!"

I pointed at the light bulbs and pressed the button. Now all those people would just remember me as some weirdie who pulled out a light and flashed it in their faces.

"Thank you," I said and went through the club world seating, giving everyone a flash there, then continued into the first-class seating.

My strong sense of smell caught the scent of air freshener, which smelled a bit like the fresh, clean interior of a new car. I checked my seat number, and it was by the window and the closest to the very front of the plane. It was nice and spacious. Each seat had a good five-foot space between the one next to it.

My seat was right behind a little kid's, who apparently was the son of the rich-looking businessman next to him. This kid had been looking at me since I put my cases by my seat.

I sat in my seat and let out a sigh of relief as I relaxed and sprawled out in the soft chair, stretching out my aching legs. That's when I noticed the kid looking at me from over the back of his seat.

"What?" I asked, a little harshly.

The kid turned around and sat in his seat immediately. I thought about giving him a flash, but decided not to.

The plane departed at about ten o'clock, and an hour later we were over the Atlantic. Regardless of the fact that the seat was comfortable, I began to grow restless. I was never a big fan of sitting in one spot for long periods of time.

I was just staring at the clouds passing by when I noticed the slight aching pressure in my groin that told me my bladder was full. I went over to the bathroom, taking notice that everyone was staring. Some held their stare like I was some kind of alien or something. Others looked at me in a marveling manner as if I were a god. Others looked away as soon as I returned a look. But it didn't matter; I would give them all a flash once we landed anyway.

As I went to the bathroom I looked at the macaroni-shaped dial under the handle; it was red, with *occupied* in white letters, so I just waited. Finally, it opened, and a young blonde woman came out.

"Oh," she said, upon seeing me. "Well you're cute."

She left.

"Thanks," I said, puzzled.

That was awkward.

I went into the bathroom and looked at the mirror. I unbuttoned my uniform and hung it up, then turned my side to the mirror, rubbing my gut up and down. I was pretty slim, typical for an adult fox.

The door opened behind me, and a brunette woman came in.

"Oh, sorry," she said upon seeing me, "I thought the bathroom was unoccupied."

"Well, I can leave, and you can . . . I can wait," I said.

"No, it's fine," She said. She turned and shut the door, then pulled up a thin black briefcase. "I'm on an assignment, anyway. I'm sure a guy by the likes of you is familiar with this sort of work."

She opened it and pulled out a syringe, similar to the one I had seen earlier, which was dropped onto the floor by that guy at the hotel whom I, a little harshly, interrogated.

"Uh . . ." I said as I watched the silver needle in her hand. "What kind of assignment?"

"Don't worry," she said, flicking it softly then squirting just a light amount. "This will only hurt for a while, then it'll be over before you know it."

She came at me with the needle, and I swiped at her hand, but she was obviously trained, given by the way she grabbed my wrist, twisted me around, and bent me over, locking my elbow behind my back. My face was inches from the toilet, and I could smell the bittersweet scent of the little blue toilet bowl cleanser.

I felt a sharp pain as she stuck the needle into my thigh. I instantly struggled away from her grip, turned around, and grabbed her arm.

She pushed with all her might, trying to stick the syringe in me, so I stepped behind her, locking her arm in place, and forced the needle into her neck then emptied the contents of it into her. She fell on the floor, fast asleep.

I couldn't just leave her there, so despite my failing strength and sudden dizziness, I carried her out of the bathroom to an empty seat, then stumbled back to my own and flopped back into it. I felt as if the plane was spinning out of control, and I could barely sit up straight or keep my eyes open.

The kid peered around the back of his seat and looked at me.

"Help," I said, just before blacking out.

4

I awoke with a start, and it was nighttime. I could see the plane's landing lights illuminating the clouds as we began to slowly descend.

I was slumped so far down in my seat that my back was on the cushion, and my arms rested on the armrests on either side of my head. I blinked a couple of times, regaining my focus and clarity of vision when I saw the little kid looking at me from around the back of his seat.

"Put your seat belt on," he said. "We're landing."

I quickly snapped out of my dizziness, sat upright in my seat, and put my seatbelt on and tightened it around my waist. The plane began to descend more rapidly; I could feel my stomach get pushed up into my chest along with most of my other organs. The plane then slowly touched down onto the runway, and there was a small jolt as the landing gear made contact with the pavement, and the plane skidded to a long, slow halt.

The plane then taxied to the terminal and stopped there. The captain told us to get off in an orderly fashion, and as everyone stood up and began gathering their stuff, I looked over at the seat where I had set the woman from the bathroom, and much to my expectation, she was still sound asleep from the heavy dose of tranquilizer I had injected into her with her own needle.

I picked up my cases and began to leave the plane when I noticed the little kid and his dad both looking at me. The dad looked down and resumed tying his son's shoe, and I gestured to the kid to cover his eyes. As soon as he did, I pulled out the flasher.

"Excuse me," I said, grabbing the dad's attention.

As soon as he looked at me, I hit the button and gave him a flash then left the plane.

I walked through the airport, feeling surprisingly full of energy. It may've been from my body finally overcoming the pain from whatever I was injected with. I suddenly remembered that I had to piss really bad, and my prostate had started aching, like I had sat on a thumbtack and punctured the worst place possible, so I went to the bathroom and relieved myself then headed out.

When I got out the door, I waved down a taxi and asked the driver to take me to Langley.

It was another twenty-minute drive until we finally arrived. I looked out the window at the building's eminent composite glass structure, paid the driver, gave him a flash, and got out of the car.

Since it was November, snow covered the ground as far as the eye could see. The cold Virginia winter air froze the moisture on my nose as I walked over to the building entrance. Upon entering, I immediately began giving each of the staff a flash then headed straight into the bathroom. As soon as I got in, I set my cases on the sink counter, opened the one containing my Colt 1911s, and put a full magazine into one of them, cocking the action to put a bullet into the chamber.

I made sure the safety was on then opened my uniform jacket, sliding the weapon into a concealed pocket on the inside then zipping it back up. I closed the cases and hid them in an access panel then left the bathroom and went straight to the front desk.

"Excuse me," I asked, approaching the lady at the desk, "can you direct me to John Lance's office?"

43

"Oh," said the desk lady, startled upon seeing me then telling me the office number.

"Thank you," I said, giving her a flash.

Lance was walking through his office with a handful of documents and a cup of coffee. His reflection came clear on the window, since it was rather dark in there. He went to his desk and sat in the chair, looking over the documents while sipping his coffee, and that was when I came into the picture.

I stepped out from behind the opened door and quietly closed it, then walked over to his desk, sitting in the chair across from him while pointing my pistol at him and grabbing his attention by pulling the hammer back.

"Well," John Lance said. "If it isn't Chance Logan."

He looked up at me; he hadn't aged a day since I saw him last.

"Somehow I knew you'd be coming."

"Let's just say a little birdie told me what you were up to," I said with a sneer.

"What I'm up to?" John asked.

"Don't play dumb," I said. "You've sent wet teams and hitmen after every operative who took part in Operation Special Delivery, including me. Now, they're all terminated."

"We can't have the Reds know about Operation Special Delivery," John said.

"Right," I responded sarcastically. "If that were the case, then I should definitely be dead now, but here I am. There's a reason I was to be taken alive, otherwise, you wouldn't have sent someone with heavy tranquilizer after me and now you're going to tell me."

"Listen, I—" Lance started to get up, but I jumped up and grabbed him by the collar of his suit, with my pistol muzzle just inches from his forehead.

He didn't even flinch. He just stared back at me with a low brow.

"Secret security button cliché," I said. "Hand. Off. *Now*."

He slowly took his hand off the panel on his desk that had a secret button to call for security under it, and I let go of him as he sat back in his chair.

"Now, I'm not leaving until you tell me," I said, sitting back in my chair.

"All of this is your fault, though," John said. "What happened in 1968 was kept secret from me, and I was forced against my will to conduct it. The reason you're still alive is because I have questions of my own."

"What are you talking about?" I asked.

"The assassination," John said, leaning forward in his seat. "You were ordered to kill three targets, but were you aware that they were a civilian family?"

I sat in a stupor of thought as I tried to recollect what happened that night. I was never given the identity of the targets, and I couldn't see whom I was shooting at, due to the severe lack of light.

"Were you aware that it was *my* family you killed?" John asked.

My jaw dropped. I couldn't believe what I had just heard. I rested the pistol on my lap.

"Go on," I said.

"The authorities arrived just minutes after it happened," John said. "When they got there, they identified three guards, my wife, my daughter, and my young son who only came into the world six years ago. They were being held for ransom."

"Why would they hold your family for ransom?" I asked.

"Clearly, you don't know me as well as you think," John said. "I was a Soviet, dedicated to my country until I was betrayed. I took part in the KGB, but I was framed on my first mission and sent to the gulag for ten years, only to escape and flee to the US, where I changed my name and joined the CIA and their cause. But when the Soviets found out that a

45

former KGB operative had gone missing, they captured my family and threatened to kill them unless I was returned to the Soviet Union. This was kept secret from me and I never knew, and I was forced into blindly sending you to kill my family."

He sighed and looked at the floor.

"All I wanted was to bring down the Soviet Union for betraying me, and be reunited with my family, whom I cherished above all," Lance continued. "But I've been betrayed again for the lust of becoming a world power. That's all this race for power is going to provoke, just more blood-shed, and it will never stop as long as world superpowers exist."

He looked back up at me with rage in his eyes.

"And they'll keep on senselessly creating more experiments, like you, to do all their killing as much as they please." he added.

"I didn't mean to—" I started.

"Oh, don't give me that crap!" Lance said. "You slaughtered them without even thinking!"

I suddenly felt the immense weight of regret drop in the pit of my stomach.

"Do you even know why they decided to make anthros like you, Kay . . . and Katie?" he asked.

I just sat in silence, looking down at the floor.

"Because you're all animals," John said. "Killing is your instinct. You don't care what lives you take, just as long as you're still alive."

"That's not true," I quietly choked.

"Oh really?" John said. "If I recall correctly, you said that this is 'not your problem' in London."

How the hell did he know I said that to Jack? I thought as I glared at him.

"So I'm sure you won't mind if I conduct my mission," John said, standing up again. "Given that it's 'not your problem.'"

"What mission?" I asked.

46

"Operation Special Delivery is still in commencement," John said, "and with it, I'm going to obliterate the world superpowers, save one to keep the whole world under control."

"You can't do this," I said. "This is tyranny! And mutiny! You're betraying your own country!"

"Not any more tyrannical than the existing superpowers." Lance said, resting his hands on the surface of his desk. "With only one superpower, there will be nobody to stand against it. No governments creating secret combinations to senselessly kill, no constant threat of weapons of mass destruction—"

"How could you possibly destroy the whole US and Soviet Union?" I asked.

"Once all the bombs from Special Delivery are placed," John started, "then they'll all go off, and both powers will have no one to blame except each other, spiking a mass-scale nuclear war that will blow them from existence, leaving the world ripe for the taking, since I have all these weapons and men at my disposal," He pulled a small remote with a large red button on the top from his drawer.

"What's that?" I asked, staring at it.

"This," John said, rubbing the button with his thumb, "is what I call war at the touch of a button. That's how it all works today. It's linked to all the bombs here in the US and in the Soviet Union." He smiled fiendishly. "Isn't technology these days amazing?"

He pushed the button.

"No!" I said, jumping out of my seat.

"Don't worry," John said. "They'll only go off once they are all activated in their set position. You're safe for now."

"The bomb lost in Ukraine," I said in realization. Jack told me it was headed to Brazil. I grabbed Lance by the arm and held my pistol to his head.

Where is it going?" I asked

47

"You think I'm just going to tell you?" Lance asked.

I heard a click from the desk and looked down. Lance had pushed the security button on his desk.

"Oops," John said sarcastically. I turned around to run, but he reached over the desk and grabbed me by the tail, which still ached from the dislocation.

"Where do you think you're going?" Lance said. "You have some amends to pay. Just simply suffer as long as I have from losing something you love and you'll be free to go. And after I kill Katie, it'll be all down-hill."

Suddenly filled with rage, I chopped at John's elbow and punched him in the face, forcing him to let go and fall back into his chair. I made a break for the door and opened it as Lance pulled his pistol from his desk drawer. He fired through the glass that separated us as I ran through the hallway as the glass was shattered to pieces.

I heard guards coming from the other end of the hall, and I rounded the corner into a perpendicular hallway. I heard the guards right behind me. I got to the stairwell, where more guards, dressed in black and carrying M16s were coming up. I kicked the nearest one in the face and he fell back onto all the others, falling like dominoes down the stairs.

I then descended the stairs to the lower platform, grabbed a rope with a grappling hook on the end from one of the downed guards, shot the window out with his M16, then hooked the grappling hook on the window frame, tossing the rope out the window, and quickly climbing out the window and down the rope as the guards behind me arrived. I figured they would look out the window, so I immediately began looking for more options and saw the window to what I was sure was the bathroom I was in earlier. I quickly launched off the wall and slid down the rope, swinging to the side slightly and crashing through the window. As I fell to the floor amid the glass shards, I heard a scream, but it was not a man screaming.

I quickly got onto my feet and looked around. I was in the girl's bathroom. One of the women had shrunk against the sink counter, staring in cowardice at me. I felt my stomach get weighed down by the feeling of embarrassment.

"Sorry, miss," I said as I fumbled my flashing device out of my pocket and gave her a quick flash before bolting out of the girl's room and into the men's.

I quickly slid on the floor to the access panel where I had left my cases then, after grabbing my stuff, instantaneously fled, not even bothering to close the access panel I had left open.

Instead of heading to the main entrance, I headed for the garage. I needed a set of wheels to get me out of there quickly; for I now had the whole building's security team after me, and there was no way in hell I was going to get out alive, on foot at least.

Upon arriving in the garage, I grabbed a set of keys and "politely borrowed" one of the GMC Suburbans from a guy who was just getting out of it. I gunned the engine and sped to the exit, just before the garage doors closed on lockdown.

As soon as I got onto the freeway, I heard the police sirens behind me and saw the police lights in my rearview mirror. There were multiple police interceptors on my tail.

I shifted up, stepped on the gas and took the truck to full speed, which was about one 136 kilometers an hour. A Suburban definitely wasn't the best idea for an escape vehicle.

I merged left and right, avoiding two cars. The cops followed my lead. I came upon some thick traffic, and merged into the shoulder and drove past them. Once again, the cops did the same.

I grabbed my case and pulled my gun from it. I wanted to avoid killing anyone, but I hoped to lower their confidence by firing back at them. I turned around in my seat with my left paw on the wheel and leaned out the window. I fired a few shots at them to no avail, for the cops weren't so easily intimidated by a few wild shots.

An exit was coming up, but it was blocked off with big orange road work signs. I turned to that exit, regardless, and plowed through the signs. The truck bumped over some humps on the ground, tossing me left and right in my seat until it reached the pavement. I ran a red light and swerved into the traffic, sideswiping a civilian car.

The passenger windows of the Suburban shattered and flung thousands of glass shards in my direction.

I managed to regain control and headed toward the next intersection, where more police cars came out and blocked my path. I braced for impact, pushed the pedal against the floor, accelerating to near full speed, and was nearly thrown against the dashboard as I plowed through two of them.

I immediately heard bullets ping off the back of the truck as cops fired at me and more police cruisers came after me, lights flashing and sirens wailing.

I looked at the streets as I passed the intersections; East Capitol Street NE, Constitution Avenue NE. I was on Second Street NE, headed toward the train station. I figured that was my best ticket out of here.

A police car suddenly came up alongside me, so close that the cop in the passenger seat reached his arm out of his window and grabbed onto the Suburban. He took his stun gun out and pointed it directly at me. Just as he pulled the trigger, I swerved away from the cop car, dragging the young officer out of his seat and out the window.

I slammed his hand against the window frame and he dropped the stun gun out of the window.

I then saw a second police car pull up on my right and the driver started shooting at me. Bullets whizzed right through open passenger window and right past my head.

"Sorry," I said to the cop grabbing onto the truck, then punching him in the face.

He let go and tumbled out of his car onto the road. I hit the brake and screeched to a halt at the next intersection, and the police cars zoomed past, only to have one of them get hit by a transit bus and flip onto its top. The other one skidded and made a quick U-turn on the opposite side of the intersection.

I hit the gas and cursed as I realized that was Massachusetts Avenue NE, which would take me to the train station. I knew that H Street passed right over the train tracks, so I figured that was where I would go.

The cop was on my tail again, so I opened my other case and pulled out a smoke grenade. I pulled the pin and stuck it out the window. The smoke obscured my sight of the cruiser; hence, his sight of me was probably obscured as well.

I then noticed bright lights to my left, where the vehicle appeared again, so I threw the smoke grenade out of my passenger window and it went right through the police car's open window.

Smoke filled the interior and the car lost control, swerved and crashed into the foundation of a building.

I made it to H Street, turned there, and screeched to a stop on the sidewalk. I grabbed my cases and opened them, taking only my pistols, along with the magazines and frag grenades, which I all clipped onto my double holster belt.

I then grabbed the folding bow and my quiver, which I slung over my back. I grabbed all my USD cash, stuffed it in my pocket with my wallet, ran to the side of the bridge and leaned on the side railing, waiting for a train to come. Yes, I was going to jump onto it.

I heard the cops coming and a train horn blare. The cops skidded to a halt right behind me, and I turned around, nearly blinded by the bright lights shining in my eyes as they all got out and pointed their guns at me.

"Freeze!" one of them shouted. Out of my peripheral vision I saw the train pass under the bridge, so I jumped over the side and landed with a big thud on the roof of a passenger car close to the rear.

I immediately saw a metal structure that was barely taller than the train coming, I got on my feet and hopped over it to see some signs come up.

"Oh, for god's sake," I said to myself.

I ducked out of the way of the first sign, then moved to the side to avoid the next. A third came, and I spun to the side to dodge it. Some more of those structures came up, and I quickly stepped through each gap like a speed agility ladder, then bent over backward to avoid another sign. I spun around like a ballerina, barely missing some side signs that were close together, then I sat on the roof to miss another sign and swung my legs around me, moving my arms out of the way for them as some low signs mixed with high signs came up. I lay backward on the roof as an extra low sign came. I felt it barely brush the end of my nose; I was that close.

I got up, and there were more signs, so thick that I was literally break-dancing to avoid them. I saw some large signs approach, ones I wouldn't be able to dodge, so I somersaulted backward toward the rear engine of the train and jumped down to the door. The signs passed over not a second after I got there.

I sighed with relief, opened the door, and went in. I found out that this train, in my favor, happened to be headed to Los Angeles, where the address Jack gave to me for my car and one of the storage facilities was located. I figured I would hang out on the train until we got there.

5

The train ride was a grueling two-day ride without food, hardly any water, and a measly amount of sleep. I was tired and hungry near the point of insanity. I could hardly keep my eyes open but my body just would not let me sleep. I had a massive headache and felt nauseous. My tail still ached, and my back, legs, and gut did as well.

When the train had finally reached Los Angeles, I bailed out of the rear car before the train got anywhere within the train station boundaries.

I got on my feet and brushed off my ASIS uniform. I began to brush off my uncovered thighs when I noticed my fur was very oily instead of the usual soft and silky. I felt disgusting and filthy. To add to the list of adversities of the current situation, the hot California sun shone directly onto me from its peak position in the afternoon sky. I really had to find my storage unit and a place to stay quickly.

After walking for some time, keeping my eyes, ears, and nose open for anything to aid me, I eventually found an old map dropped in a gutter. I immediately began to scan the map for the street that was on the card Jack had given me.

Eventually, I found it then looked for the street I was on, which ended up being not too far away. The road the storage unit was on was also fairly short, so it wouldn't take too long to find it.

Regardless of the fact that the storage unit wasn't so far away, I spent roughly an hour walking through the blistering heat of the day through the noisy, polluted, more run-down part of the city until I arrived at my destination.

The storage facility was a fairly worn-out old place with faded, peeling paint, cracked up concrete, and complete with a rusty old gate across the entranceway. I saw the gate guard through the relatively translucent windows of the security booth by the entrance.

People still store stuff here? I thought as I walked toward the booth.

"Afternoon!" I greeted the gate guard.

"Afternoon, sir," the gate guard said, stepping out of the booth. "I was told someone by the likes of you would be coming."

He took out his keys, unlocked the gate, and opened it.

"What, did they tell you that you'd be met by a six-foot-tall fox?" I asked as I walked through the gateway.

"For the most part," the guard responded. "Right this way."

I followed him to a storage unit near the middle of the facility, where he unlocked the door and pushed it up to the ceiling. I eagerly look inside and my jaw nearly dropped. The unit was full of weapons. Tons of different kinds of weapons. Some of which of, I had never seen or any of the likes of them.

"All this is mine?" I asked a bit excitedly.

"Yes, sir," the gate guard nodded.

"Wouldn't this be considered illegal, though?" I asked.

"Only if you were civilian," the guard answered. "But since you're obviously not a civilian, you can have this stuff here just as long as you're CIA, MI6, or ASIS."

"Well, I am all of the above, technically," I said.

The guard just nodded. I stepped into the unit and picked up a CAR-15 rifle and examined it. As I was testing out the holographic sight mounted on the top, my ear flicked toward the sound of the door of the unit next to me open, and I stepped out to see what was going on.

"This is yours too," the guard said, pointing at the next unit. I stepped out farther to see what was inside the other unit. Parked inside was a black 1971 Oldsmobile Cutlass with a white double racing stripe painted down the middle. I reached in my pocket and took out the keys Jack had given me as I walked toward the car.

As I grabbed the door handle, I noticed there was something fairly peculiar about the way it felt. I knocked on the door of the car, but instead of hearing the hollow sound of a regular, thin-steel body chassis, it sounded completely solid, like a rock.

"What the hell?" I said.

"It's reinforced steel," the guard said, "able to withstand any bullets smaller than fifty calibers. The windows are also fully bulletproof."

"Wow," I said, impressed as I stroked the window with my paw.

I grabbed the door handle again, opened it, and was greeted by the fresh smell of new car. I took a deep breath, savoring the scent as I sat down inside the car on the well-padded light-gray leather seat.

I then put the key into the ignition and started the engine, which loudly roared to life with the sweet sound of more than 300 horsepower. The radio played "Mississippi Queen" without any interference whatsoever.

"I imagine this gets horrid gas mileage," I commented.

"Actually, it's pretty standard," the guard said. "About nine to fourteen."

"Hmm," I said, cocking my head and shrugging one shoulder. That was almost average for the cars at the time.

"You should probably get it out of there before too much exhaust gets trapped in," he said. "I'm already going to have to air it out."

I could smell the exhaust overtaking the oxygen in the storage unit.

"Right," I said, putting the car into gear.

I drove out of the unit and backed up to the one with my weapons arsenal. I opened the trunk and began to load some stuff in, starting with the CAR-15. Next I put two Skorpion VS61 machine pistols in, then a bag of explosives, including the grenades I already had with me, and some ammo for each one of my guns.

"I take it you're keeping this unit," the guy said.

"Yeah," I said, "but you can give away the one that the car was in." We shook hands and paws.

"Well, thank you . . . uh . . ." I said, circulating my paw trying to get his name.

"Stan," He said.

"Stan," I repeated. "It was nice meeting you."

I went to the rear of the car, closed the trunk, went to the right side door of the car, and sat down. I put my paws on the invisible steering wheel, which I realized wasn't there, and got out of the car.

"Dammit, America!" I muttered.

I was more used to the fact that in both England and Australia, they have their driver's seats on the right. But everywhere else, except for Africa and Asia, they have their driver's seats on the left side. I walked to the other side of the car where I got in and put my paws on the actual steering wheel. I opened the windows to get some air circulating through.

"Got work to do?" Stan asked.

"My work is never done," I said, pushing on the clutch pedal and shifting the car into gear. "Have a good one."

"You too," he said as I slowly drove the car out of the facility.

I couldn't believe I had that whole weapons arsenal, and to think, that wasn't the only one either, unless the others had more awesome muscle cars in them.

I suddenly felt exhausted. My stomach roared. Now that I found the storage unit, I needed to find a place to stay.

I drove out of the facility and onto the road, where I met a car heading straight for me. I remembered that I was in America, where driving was different, and swerved into the right lane. I began thinking of America's vacuous driving scheme when I remembered that I was in California. Tyson lived in California, and he and I were close friends in Vietnam.

I figured I would stop at a pay phone before I got horribly lost. Hell, I was lost the second I arrived, LA is a chaotically large city. I put the car in a parallel parking space next to a group of run down thrift stores, cafés, and other small businesses. I looked around for a pay telephone and found one in an old phone booth by a pizza parlor.

I looked around to see if anyone was within my proximity, and there were some people, not that many, but I didn't know exactly what range my flashing device was effective up to, so I just opened the door and rushed to the phone booth.

Upon getting in the phone booth, I grabbed the phone book and began looking for Tyson Stone. Luckily, he was the only Stone named Tyson in the area. I dug into my wallet for loose change, found a couple quarters, and inserted them into the slot, then dialed the number.

I put the phone to my ear and waited. The phone rang five times or so before he answered.

"Stone's residence," his voice said through the earpiece.

"Hey, Tyson," I said, "it's Chance."

"Chance," he asked, "from Vietnam?"

"The one and only," I said.

He guffawed.

"I knew you'd fall for Cali! What's up man?"

"I'm having some trouble," I said.

"Trouble," he asked, "with what?"

"Well . . . I . . ."

"Rough night?"

57

"More like a rough few nights."

"Hey, that's all right," he said. "We all have those hard times. I guess that cute vixen just wasn't for you, huh?"

"No," I nearly scolded, "it's not about her. I just need a place to stay overnight. Do you know of a good place?"

"You can stay at my place," he answered right away.

He lived in an apartment with his older brother and his six-year-old brother. I didn't want to impose. I assumed the apartment might be small.

"No, I couldn't," I said.

"No, it's totally fine," he insisted.

I heard loud knocking on the door behind me and turned to see a large man wearing worn-out clothes and a beanie.

"Hey, man, hurry up," he said.

"Just a sec," I told him.

"What?" Tyson asked. "What was that?"

"Nothing," I said.

"Man, what the hell are you, a furry?" the guy asked.

"Uh . . . yeah," I fibbed just to get him off my back.

"Man, you be taking this anthropomorphic animal stuff too far," the guy commented. "What did that suit cost, like three thousand?"

"Will you shut up?" I scolded.

"Who are you telling to shut up?" Tyson asked.

"Not you," I said. "This asshat here thinks I'm a furry or something."

"What did you call me?" the guy said.

"Can you give me the address?" I asked.

"Certainly," he said and gave me the address of the apartment building and the unit number, which I kept in my head.

"Man, I ought to bust a cap in yo' ass," the man said.

58

"Thank you," I said to Tyson and hung up. I then turned to the man standing at the door of the phone booth.

"You aren't busting any caps in any asses," I said to him.

"Oh yeah?" he said, pulling a Glock from inside his coat. I shoved the door open and it folded on his hand. He yelled and was forced to drop his weapon. I wrapped my arm around the back of his neck and pulled his head into the glass, which shattered to pieces. I then turned him around and put him on the ground, locking his arm at the elbow.

"Oh my god," I heard someone say. I looked around, and I had attracted the attention of everyone there.

"Help!" the guy said as he struggled. "These furries are damned crazy!"

I quickly let him go and hopped back into the car. I put my paws on the steering wheel, which wasn't there.

"Dammit, America!" I said as I moved to the left seat and started the car.

"Okay . . ." I said then recited the address to myself.

That was when a small panel on the dash opened, and a screen slid out. It recited the address back to me. The screen had all the roads displayed in yellow. The route it was taking me was highlighted in pink. My car was displayed as a little blue triangle.

"Whoa" was all I could say.

"You have arrived," the guide device said as I parallel parked the Cutlass outside the large apartment complex.

"Whoa," I commented, as if Tyson were sitting in the passenger seat, "your brother must make bank."

I got out of the car and straightened out my uniform, then put the keys in the pocket. I went to the front door of the complex and let myself in.

No one was at the desk, so I just passed by it. Tyson had given me a room number on the second floor, so I headed to the elevator, pressed the up button, and waited. I looked around, nobody in sight. The place was quiet. The elevator door opened, and a forty to fifty-year-old woman was in there.

"Oh, uh," she said, and quickly walked past me.

As soon as she turned around, I gave her a flash. I then got into the elevator and pressed the two button. I felt my innards sink to my stomach as the elevator ascended to the next floor. When the doors opened, I looked for the room. I found it at the very end of the hall, where there was a window facing the metro area with its tall buildings, chaotic traffic, and smog-filled atmosphere.

There was no snow, typical for that area of California, and the sun rode high in the sky. I knocked on the door and admired the view as I waited. I heard a clutter in the room and some chatter then heard footsteps approach, and the door opened. There was a man there with his hair spiked up at the front and combed down at the back; he was wearing shorts and a bright-blue polo shirt. I guessed this was Tyson's older brother.

"What the hell?" he said upon seeing me.

"Yeah, I'm Chance." I said.

"Who are you?" he asked.

"A friend of Tyson," I answered, "from Vietnam."

"Hey, Chance," Tyson eagerly greeted, putting a hand on his brother's shoulder, and shoving him aside. "Don't mind my brother. I haven't quite told him everything."

"I understand," I said. "It's a lot to take in."

"Why don't you come in?" Tyson stepped aside and motioned with his right hand to come in as he held the door open with his left.

"Thanks for letting me crash here," I said, as I entered the large room. By the main entrance were three couches, two sitting across from

60

each other with one more sitting perpendicular. All their sides touched a side table acting as the corners. The couches sat in front of a large TV that sat in a hole cut into the wall. There was a large clear space between the couches and a flight of stairs that ascended to the second floor, where the bedrooms and bathroom were located.

Tyson led me to the kitchen, which was around the corner where the stairs began. The kitchen wasn't very spacious. It consisted of a double sink, a fridge, rows of cupboards, and a counter set in the middle of the room with four stools around it. The apartment continued.

Past the kitchen was a living room that had a smaller TV in the left corner set on a small table with shelves, a couple of recliners, and a couch, with a fireplace in the wall to the right of the TV.

"Nice place," I said. "What does your brother do?"

"He's a stockbroker," Tyson said, "and boy I'll tell you, those guys make bank."

Kind of coincidental that he would say that.

"What's his name?" I asked.

"Jeremy," Tyson answered.

"Hmm," I nodded. "So how have things been since Nam?"

"Good, good," Tyson said. "Though I've been searching pretty fruitlessly for a job."

"Fruitlessly?" I asked, not quite understanding what he meant.

"Yeah, I've been turned down a few times. Some won't even look at my applications. Lot of folks aren't all too fond of us Vietnam vets," Tyson said.

"Huh," I said.

"So how are things with you?" Tyson asked.

"Well," I said, rethinking my whole dilemma, "not so good. I found out that the CIA has been after me for a while and that Katie is one of them. We met this guy in London, and he was telling me all about a mission, which I learned resulted in a plot to start a war between the

61

United States and the Soviets, and now the CIA is killing off all the operatives who were part of that mission. Now I'm on the run. I *barely* escaped from DC."

"Sounds . . . tough," Tyson said.

"No kidding," I said. "I haven't slept in two days."

Tyson raised his brow in a look of concern.

"You should probably get some rest before dinner," he said. "The guest room is upstairs at the way end of the hall."

"Hey, Tyson," Jeremy said, coming into the kitchen where Tyson and I were conversing, "I'm going to pick up Ethan from school."

He talked with strong *S*'s, and I was pretty sure he was homosexual. Not that I had anything against that; homophobia was a characteristic I didn't possess.

"Hey, Jeremy," Tyson said, getting a pot from the cupboard. "You haven't formally met Chance yet."

"Oh yeah," Jeremy said, coming back over and shaking my paw. "Hi, I'm Jeremy. Tyson told me all about you except that you were a talking wolf."

"Fox," I corrected him.

"Fox," he repeated, and he dropped his keys which clattered on the floor. I noticed a Porsche badge on the car key.

"Oh damn, I'm so clumsy," he said, bending over and picking them up. "Sorry, I'm . . . I'm just going to go now."

He turned around, left the kitchen, then stumbled on the corner of the stairs. He turned around, gave us a wide grin, and waved his fingers as he disappeared around the corner. We were quiet until we heard the door shut.

"What a comic, eh?" Tyson said.

"He seems so frantic," I commented.

"Yeah, he doesn't do too well around strangers," Tyson said. "He's pretty shy, and has a phobia of saying something stupid or offensive."

"That's a real thing?" I asked.

"You should've seen him when he met Derek," Tyson said as he widened his eyes and shook his head.

"Who's that?" I asked.

"His boyfriend," Tyson said. "Jeremy's gay."

"I realized," I shrugged. "Doesn't bother me."

"Okay, just making sure," Tyson said. He took out a few packages of Ramen noodles and began opening them and emptying the contents into the pot. Tyson chuckled as he did so.

"Funny how for a guy who makes a lot, he's sure one helluva cheapskate."

After adding some water to the noodles and setting it on the stove to boil, Tyson showed me to the guest room.

"Get some rest," he said, opening the door and turning on the light. The room wasn't all that big, but it was big enough for a one-person bed and a dresser with a TV sitting on the top. There was a radiator under the window and a small closet on the opposite side by the entrance of the room. There was a photo of birch trees juxtaposed with a light-gray sky hanging on the left side of the bed. On the right was a small side table drawer with a bedside lamp perched next to an alarm clock on top.

"You must be feeling weak," Tyson said, "having gone two days without sleeping or eating."

"I can go longer without food," I said, "but I need my sleep."

As a fox, I can go for quite a long time without food, which is just another survival characteristic. I need sleep, though, because who can go days without sleeping and be able to maintain their sanity?

I took my uniform off, leaving on my black T-shirt, and hung it on the bed post. I remembered that my pistols were in the interior pocket and took them out.

"Oh," Tyson said, seeing the weapons, "um, why don't you just . . . put those in the drawer of the side table or something."

"Okay," I said, pulling back the action on each, locking them and taking the magazines out.

I set them in the side table drawer and flopped on my stomach onto the bed.

"Guess I'll see you later then," Tyson said, rubbing my head then leaving the room, shutting the door behind him. The room was completely silent, perfect sleeping conditions. I closed my eyes and was asleep within a few minutes. I didn't even have the covers pulled over me.

I woke up about two hours later. The sun had gone down, and the room was dark. I had my arms wrapped around the pillow, and I had some saliva leaking out of the corner of my mouth. I was dreaming of Katie and the times we had and what may have happened if it all worked out. I still held a strong love for her, but her betrayal had basically put me in a state of mild depression.

I was thinking about her all the time, brooding over the fact that I may never see her again, and my heart broken over the fact that we may never be together.

I'm sure maybe a lot of guys who've broken up with the love of their life know what that's like, but for them, there's plenty of fish in the sea, but for me at this given point in time that wasn't the case.

Katie was the only fish in the sea that I could get. I hooked her once, but I cut the line. Mostly because she was the kind that drags you down to the bottom of the lake upon where she resides and leaves you for dead on the lake floor. But that wasn't going to be me. It was every genetically altered fox for themselves, and I wasn't going to let her lead me into the clutches of a currently corrupt CIA.

I tried not to bust my balls over it, though, and forgot the whole thing as I left the bedroom and descended the flight of stairs. I came into the kitchen, where Tyson and Jeremy were talking about investments.

"What about this one?" Tyson said, pulling up a piece of paper with the descriptions of some company that had a multicolored apple as its logo. "Seems to be doing well."

"What do they do?" Jeremy asked.

"I don't know," Tyson said, shrugging and shaking his head. "Looks like a fruit company, you know, with the rainbow apple and all."

"Fruit company?" Jeremy asked, lowering his pen from his chin.

"Yeah," Tyson said, using his pen to point on the different colors of the apple. "The green is green apples, the yellow is bananas, the orange is oranges, the red is . . . red apples, the purple is grapes, and the blue is . . . blue raspberry."

"Well," Jeremy said, "they must be one helluva fruit company for only selling six fruits. Look at their stocks."

"Damn," Tyson said. He noticed me leaning against the wall with my arms folded across my chest, eavesdropping on their conversation.

"Oh, hey, Chance," he said. "We're just looking at the stocks."

Jeremy looked up from the paper.

I walked around the counter and stood behind them, studying the piece of paper that Jeremy held up a little so I could see better.

"Apple Incorporated, huh?" I said.

"I don't know," Tyson said. "Do you think it's worth it?"

"Well, have you looked at their stocks?" I asked.

"Yeah, they're doing pretty well," Jeremy answered.

"But I don't know what they do," Tyson said.

"That's why you read the description here," I said, pointing at the paragraph that explained what the company did.

"Oh," Jeremy said, "it's a technology company."

"Do you still think it's worth it?" Tyson asked.

"Well, from where I'm sitting," I said, "that company is probably going to change the world."

"Well, there's some Ramen left in the pot if you want some," Jeremy said, pointing his thumb over his shoulder at the stove where the pot sat.

"Don't mind if I do," I said, grabbing a bowl and dishing up some of the brown-colored noodles. I grabbed a fork and sat down across from the two brothers.

"So what's it like being a six-foot-tall, talking fox?" Jeremy asked, either trying to keep a conversation going to avoid awkward silence or just out of curiosity.

"Well, it has its ups and downs," I said. "Like there are only two of my kind that I know of, one being me and the other, she works for the corrupt CIA, who's after me."

"So you can't repopulate?" Jeremy asked.

"Trust me, we were getting close," I said.

"You mean she was your girlfriend for a while?"

"Yeah."

"You should have given it to her," Jeremy said. "God didn't give you those balls for nothing."

"Okay, can we move on?" I said. The conversation was taking a wrong turn.

Tyson backhanded Jeremy on the shoulder.

"What, I was just trying to—" Jeremy started. Tyson just shook his head.

"Okay, so what else?" Jeremy asked.

"Well," I said, "I get a lot of looks . . ."

"I imagine," Jeremy commented. "Probably because you don't wear pants. Speaking of which, why don't you?"

66

"Don't ask him that," Tyson said, evidently remembering the last time he asked me that.

"Well, I'm just trying to get a conversation going!" Jeremy scolded.

"Well, you don't have to ask those awkward questions!" Tyson shot back.

I looked back and forth from one to the other as they argued and called each other names. I shoved some Ramen noodles into my mouth and chewed slowly.

So that's what it's like to have siblings, I thought, as the argument got louder and more awkward.

"Quiet!" I heard a young voice shout.

That was number 3, Ethan. He was standing at the living room entrance.

"For God's sake, I'm watching TV!"

"Dammit, you don't say that!" Jeremy said, looking over his shoulder and pointing at him with his pen.

"Why the hell not?" Ethan asked snottily.

"You're too young," Tyson said, "that's why!"

"What the?" Ethan said, looking at me. I just raised my brow and waved to him silently.

"Oh," Jeremy said, "Ethan, this is . . ."

"Chance," I said quietly.

"Chance," Jeremy repeated. Humans have cruddy memory.

"Is he in a costume?" Ethan asked.

"No, he's a genetically altered wolf—"

"Fox!" I corrected. "My God." I then muttered.

Humans couldn't remember diddly-squat to save their own asses.

"Fox," Jeremy said, putting his fingers to his forehead and thrusting his arm forward toward Ethan.

"But foxes are supposed to be small," Ethan said, "and he's taller than both of you."

That was true. I was taller than Jeremy by roughly an inch and a half to two inches. Jeremy was taller than Tyson by about five inches. Ethan was a little over four feet, about to my belly.

"Well, not Chance," Tyson said.

"There's also his girlfriend," Jeremy added.

"And Katie," Tyson said, pointing in acknowledgment to Jeremy.

"Well, anyway, I'm trying to watch TV," Ethan reiterated, "so shut the—"

"Don't you dare!" Jeremy interrupted, pointing his pen at Ethan as a threat.

Ethan just turned around and went back into the living room.

"Did you do your homework?" Tyson shouted.

"No!" Ethan answered.

"Get it done!" Tyson said.

"Later," Ethan said.

"Oh my god," Jeremy said, running his fingers through his hair. "What are we going to do with him?"

It was very late, around 10:00 p.m. When I finished the noodles, I washed my bowl and fork and went to my room while Jeremy and Tyson conversed about the stocks more. I kept all articles of clothing off, including my T-shirt, to keep cool in the warm room.

At about nine, Jeremy came upstairs and went into his room. I heard Tyson tell Ethan to do his homework, and Ethan stormed up the stairs and into his room. Tyson was the last one up. He turned off the hall light and went to his room.

The Andy Griffith Show played quietly on the TV on the dresser. I loved that show. All of it was just uplifting comedy with no negativity, sexuality, drugs, or any of that crap you find in modern TV shows. I especially loved Don Knotts's character, Barney Fife. I just loved how he always made himself look stupid and half the time not even knowing about it.

To be honest, it broke my heart when they stopped running in 1968, but that was a year of all kinds of troubles for me, so that didn't even compare.

As I sat on the bed and chuckled at the comic masterpiece playing on the TV, my ear flicked over to the sound of my door opening. I turned in that direction and saw Ethan standing in the doorway, holding a book, a piece of paper, and a pencil.

"What are you doing up so late?" I asked. I looked at the clock. "It's almost ten thirty, son."

"Tomorrow is Saturday," Ethan said. "Plus, I'm having trouble with my homework."

"Really?" I asked. "Why didn't you ask your brothers?"

"They're asleep," Ethan answered. "Plus, Jeremy is always busy."

"Hmm," I said.

"Plus, I heard somewhere that foxes are really smart," Ethan said.

"Yeah, that's true," I boasted, chuckling at his statement. "So what's the problem?"

I scooted over to the side a bit and patted on the space next to me, telling him to sit, then grabbed the remote and turned off the TV.

"I don't get this," he said, as he sat down next to me.

He showed me what he was working on. Dividing fractions; this was a little challenging for me at his age, but now it was nothing.

"Dividing fractions, huh?" I said. "Now here all you have to do—" I drew on his paper, some indication of my instructions— "is flip the second fraction, then you multiply by the reciprocal. So this equals six-twelfths. But what do we do next?"

Ethan sat there, silently thinking, then answered, "Simplify?"

"Yup," I said, "so what is half of twelve?"

"Six?"

"Uh-huh, and so if the six is on top and a twelve on the bottom, that makes it one-half." I gave the paper and pencil to him. "You try the next one."

He took a little while, and I had to correct him once, but he did all right.

"Good," I said when he finished. "Can you simplify that?"

Ethan thought a little more.

"No?" he answered.

"Why not?" I asked.

"Because those numbers don't multiply or divide to each other."

"Yeah." I nodded. "So you got it now?"

"I think so." Ethan said, looking up at me.

"One of the best ways to remember it is . . ." on his paper, I wrote one-half divided by one-third. Under the one-half, I wrote *leave me,* then under the division symbol I put *change me,* and for the one-third I put *turn me over.* I handed the paper to Ethan.

"Thanks, Mr. Chance," he said.

"Mm-hmm," I said and turned on the TV.

Ethan stayed in his spot next to me. He finished up his work as I monitored him every now and then, and when he was done, he opened the front cover of his textbook and slid the paper in.

The episode I was watching in the first place had finished, then another followed. It wasn't until the end of the next episode that I turned off the TV and realized that Ethan was leaning on my shoulder, sound asleep. I didn't want to wake him, so I just let him be. Eventually I dozed off.

6

The next morning, I woke up to Jeremy dropping his Porsche keys on the floor and muttering curses to himself. I proceeded to get up when I felt some weight on my lap. I looked down and saw that Ethan, still sound asleep, had his head resting there. He must have slipped from my shoulder and down to my soft lap in his almost boneless state of slumber.

I carefully lifted his head off my lap and moved out from under it, then laid his head on the pillow and tucked him in.

I looked at the alarm clock. It was 0600 hours, the time I usually got up no matter where I was. I exited the room and descended the flight of stairs, then went into the kitchen where I found Jeremy getting a quick breakfast from the fridge that he could eat on the go. He looked over and saw me.

"Morning," he said upon noticing me.

"Morning," I replied.

"I saw that Ethan paid you a visit last night," Jeremy said.

"Yeah," I said, "he needed help with his homework."

Jeremy just nodded as two pieces of bread popped out of the toaster. He grabbed them and took a butter knife out of the drawer. He then went to a cupboard, grabbed a bowl with butter in it, and scraped a piece off with the knife, then spread it on the bread.

"Where's Tyson?" I asked.

I knew him to be an early riser, and sleeping in wasn't like him.

"He went for a run," Jeremy answered. "Ever since Vietnam he's been kind of a fitness nut."

"Really?" I asked, a bit surprised.

"Yeah." Jeremy put the butter back in the cupboard and got some jelly out of the fridge. "He lifts weights, runs five miles every morning. Hell, he used to be thin as a fish bone, now he's like the Incredible Hulk."

"Huh." Honestly, I was a little surprised at that. I didn't know that Tyson was into physical fitness at all; regardless of the fact that he was pretty built, he was always one of the smaller guys in the battalion.

"Well," Jeremy said, putting one piece of toast on top of the other, "how long you planning on staying?"

"Not long," I answered. "I have to get to Brazil."

"Spy work?" Jeremy asked, putting the jelly in the fridge.

"Mm-hmm." I nodded.

"Well, you gotta do what you gotta do," he said. "See ya later, I gotta go."

"All right, take care," I said.

"Have fun with Tyson and Ethan!" he shouted from the door. I heard it open, and close and he was gone. The apartment was silent. I could hear the kitchen clock ticking. The fridge hummed as it cooled its contents.

I sighed and went back upstairs and into my room. Ethan was still on the bed, sound asleep. I softly scooted him over and sat on the bed next to him. I turned on the TV. They were playing *I Love Lucy,* which I watched for about fifteen minutes. Ethan began to stir, and I thought it might have been me chuckling at the show, so I turned it off and decided I would take a shower.

I got up from the bed, opened the door, and went across the hall to the bathroom. The bathroom was a little chilly, not as chilly as the rest of the apartment, though. California usually got cold on winter nights, but warmed up a little during the day.

I made sure there was a towel hanging on the rack and stepped into the shower. I turned on the water, and as soon as it warmed up, it felt so good. It reminded me of when I was in Vietnam and how I looked forward to a nice, cool shower at the end of the day and how good it felt when I finally did. I thought of how funny it was that now it felt good to take a warm shower.

As soon as I began to scrub with the shampoo, I began thinking of Katie again. That one day when we were both in the same shower, passionately kissing. I felt my heart sink, and I sighed sadly as soon as that thought popped into my head. I missed her so much it hurt, and I wondered if she missed me too, feeling a constant heartbreak, dreaming about the one she thought she loved.

I turned off the water as these thoughts ran through my head. I got out, stepping on the floor mat. I got down on all fours and shook myself off. I then stood back up, grabbed the towel, and began to dry myself off, rubbing the towel on my body until my fur was dry enough. I didn't bother to hang the towel back up, but took it down the hall, toward the stairs where a washer and dryer sat in a wide closet. I folded the doors open and opened the washer, then threw the towel in, poured in some detergent, and shut the washer, pressing the start button.

I heard the washer begin to fill with water, then start chugging when I closed the closet doors. That was when I heard the door open. I looked over the side of the top of the staircase, and Tyson was there, panting in his gym shorts as he shut the door behind him. He looked up and saw me.

"Morning, Chance," he said.

"Morning," I said back.

When Ethan finally woke up, Tyson and I prepared breakfast. I wore a bandage on one of my fingers, having gotten a burn on the griddle. It wasn't too bad, though I could smell the fur of my paw being singed as it happened. When we finished breakfast, we cleaned up the kitchen and wrapped the leftovers in Saran Wrap and stored them in the fridge.

Tyson figured that he'd show me around LA. While he took a shower, I went to my room and put on my black T-shirt and uniform, making sure I had my wallet, car key, and my flashing device. When Tyson finished up in the shower, he got dressed, and we headed out. We passed by the front desk in the lobby, and I gave the desk clerk a flash.

"That's the flasher you were telling me about?" Tyson asked.

"Yup," I answered, tucking it into my pocket.

We went out front, where there were a few cars parallel parked, my Cutlass at the back of the line.

"Whoa," Tyson said when I opened the driver's side door. I got it right this time. "Nice ride."

"Thanks," I said.

"Where in the hell did you get it?" Tyson asked

"A guy from ASIS gave it to me," I answered.

"Must be a generous as hell guy." He grabbed the door handle.

"And it's armored too," he added. He opened the door and folded down the seat to let Ethan into the back then put the seat back into its spot and sat down.

"You all got your seat belts on?" I asked, starting the car.

"Damn," Tyson said, "listen to that engine roar."

"I got mine on," Ethan said.

"All right," I said, "where should we go?"

"Hmm," Tyson said, resting his chin on his fist. "Ever been to the beach?"

"Yeah," I said, "in Australia."

"Well, trust me," Tyson said, "you've never been to one like this."

"All right," I said, putting the car into gear. "Let's go."

"To the beach!" Ethan said.

The screen suddenly popped up and a woman's voice said, "Request not acknowledged, voice key incorrect."

"What the hell?" Tyson said, looking at the screen.

"Oh yeah," I said, remembering the map thing that led me to their place.

"Watch this," I looked at the screen and said, "Find the quickest route to the beach that takes us through the metro."

"Request acknowledged," the guidance system said. Within seconds, the route was highlighted in pink.

"That is awesome," Tyson said.

I just smiled satisfyingly and pulled out onto the road.

Waves crashed on the shoreline, growing bigger and bigger as the tide rose, releasing its scent into the wind which carried it to us. Ethan ran about as Tyson and I conversed. We walked along the vast expansion of sand as I was telling him everything about the whole Operation Special Delivery because he was curious and wanted to know what was going on.

"I wish I could help," Tyson said. "Really, I do."

"It's far too dangerous," I said, "And way over your head. You've got your whole life ahead of you."

"So do you," Tyson said, "I mean, you're what, like, twenty, twenty-one."

"I'm twenty-two," I said, "going on twenty-three."

"Yeah, you've got your whole life to think about. Hell, I'm older than you," Tyson said.

"Really?" I said. "How old?"

"I'm twenty-six."

"Oh." I nodded.

"How old is Katie?" he asked.

"She's nineteen," I said.

"My, she's a young'un," Tyson said.

"She's about my age."

"Do you miss her?"

"Well . . ."

"I mean, not to sound weird or anything, but even I thought she was pretty."

I just chuckled softly at his comment.

"I'm serious," he said. "She has a way with guys. I took a bullet in the gut once, and she had me look into her sapphire blue eyes. It took my mind off the wound, and I began thinking of my girl I left behind."

"You had a girlfriend?" I asked.

"*Had,* but she sent me a letter saying we just couldn't go on." He picked up a rock and tossed it into the water. "I was gone for so long that she didn't feel like I loved her. My point is, don't make the same mistake I did. If you're gone too long, she will all-out think you don't care anymore. You still have time to make amends."

"But where would I find her?" I asked, not expecting an answer. "Last time I saw her was when I left her at the MI6 facility."

"You got a phone number or something?" he asked.

"No."

"Could you ask the CIA for her."

"They're after me, remember?"

"Oh, yeah." He kicked a broken sand dollar.

"She'll probably find me, though." I said. "She's still loyal to the agency, as far as I know, but Lance is going to do away with her once she completes her task."

"Hmm," Tyson said, "the CIA is pretty corrupt right now."

"I need to find her and tell her," I said. "If she doesn't accomplish her task, they'll kill her anyway."

"You've got a lot to think about," Tyson said. We walked along the beach in silence for a few seconds.

"So when are you going to Brazil?" Tyson asked.

"As soon as possible," I said. "It's being smuggled here, I'm not sure exactly where, but I need to find it before we find out the hard way."

"Right," Tyson said with a nod, "and before the rest of the US and the USSR find out, too."

I sighed.

"Why is Lance doing this?" he asked.

"Because of me," I said.

"What?"

"In 1967, they recruited me to the CIA," I said, kicking another sand dollar. "In 1968, they had me carry out the mission I told you about earlier."

"Yeah, Special Delivery?" Tyson clarified.

"Mm-hmm, and we reached the drop zone, a small apartment building in Kiev. My director said, 'Take out anything that moves.' Since I was supposed to make an assassination and I didn't know who the targets were exactly, I killed everyone in there."

"But you're no killer," Tyson said, "I know you. You seem to spare more lives than take them."

"Yeah, now I do," I said. "Then it was all about orders, and I was submissive to any command no matter how cruel. But it turns out that the targets were Lance's family, and the government had me make the assassination to avoid a hostage situation and losing Lance."

"You're kidding!" Tyson said with a disturbed look.

"I only wish I was," I said. "I found out only a few days ago. But he's been bent on getting back at me and the rest of the US because the government supported using guys like me, Kay, and Katie to carry out the dirty work."

"Why would they do that?" Tyson asked.

"Because," I said, "Lance said that 'animals don't feel emotion and kill without remorse.'"

"Do you believe that?" Tyson asked.

"No, but sometimes it's hard not to," I said, kicking yet another sand dollar and, seeing that it was a full one, bent over and picked it up.

I brushed the sand off with my paw. I could smell the foul remnants of a creature that once lived inside the now uninhabited shell.

"What do you say we go get lunch," Tyson said, "take our minds off all this."

"I guess that sounds good," I said. Ethan came running to us, and I tossed the sand dollar to him. I told him it was for luck.

We got back to the car and piled in.

"Where to?" I asked.

"Well, I don't know about you," Tyson said, "but Ethan and I usually go to Kentucky Fried Chicken when we eat out, don't we, Ethan?"

"Yup!" Ethan said from the back.

"You're cool with that, right?" Tyson asked.

"Please," I said, starting the car, "I'm a fox. I could eat chicken by the sleeve."

I put the car in reverse and backed out.

"Map Thing," I said, calling the strange navigational system by its new nickname I gave it, "take us to the nearest Kentucky Fried Chicken."

"Request acknowledged," it said, highlighting the road in pink. I put the car in drive and drove away from the beach.

When we got to the KFC, I stopped the car and asked Tyson to take the driver's seat.

"I've got a better idea," Tyson said. "Scoot your seat back." I pulled the lever under the seat and scooted it back a little.

"Now, Ethan, get up here," Tyson said. "Sit on Chance's lap."

"What are you up to?" I asked.

"Shh," Tyson shushed. "It'll be funny."

I found out where he was going with this once Ethan sat on my lap and chuckled, remembering the pranks we pulled in Vietnam. I could only imagine the look on the faces of the cashiers at the drive-through window when they saw a little kid at the steering wheel of a '71 Cutlass. When we reached the speaker with the menu, I whispered into Ethan's ear to get the forty-piece bucket and handed him one of my hundred dollar bills. Ethan placed the order.

"Will that be all?" the cashier asked.

"Is that all?" Ethan looked back at me and whispered.

"Yeah," I said with a nod.

"Yeah," Ethan relayed to the cashier.

"Okay," the cashier said and told us to go to the window. I chuckled lightly at the thought of the cashier seeing Ethan.

"Ready?" I asked.

"Yeah," Ethan answered.

I pushed on the gas lightly, and Ethan steered around the corner. Not gonna lie, but Ethan was pretty good for a kid his age. He steered perfectly around the corner and kept the car straight until we got to the window. I peered through the back window and saw the cashier's face. Her expression was priceless, jaw gaping open eyes wide. It was hysterical. Tyson had a hard time keeping a straight face.

"Did you just order?" the cashier asked.

"Yeah," Ethan answered, acting and looking like one of the typical "pissed off, get what I want, me, me, me, mine, mine, mine, now, now, now," fast-food customers.

I began to laugh, covering my mouth and making a snorting sound as I tried to squelch it.

"The forty-piece bucket?" the cashier asked.

"Yeah," Ethan raised his voice some and handed her the hundred-dollar bill. Her eyes widened even more when she saw it. She grabbed it and held it up, studying it to make sure it was real.

"Can I have my chicken now?" Ethan asked.

Tyson was losing it, covering his mouth and his face turning red.

We hadn't pulled such a prank since the spider in the colonel's tent back in Vietnam. Tyson and I would always be pulling pranks, but we never got caught, at least as far as I know. Katie may have known that I put the giant frog in the nurses' quarters.

The cashier got the change and handed it to him along with the bucket of chicken.

"How old are you?" she asked.

"I'm seven," Ethan said.

"You shouldn't be driving." The cashier said, looking disappointed.

I whispered in Ethan's ear, telling him what to say.

"What are you going to do," Ethan asked snottily, "call the police?"

My guts were going to bust. I couldn't suppress the laughter being forced through my diaphragm and building up in my mouth and lungs.

"Put shifter on the one," I whispered, chuckling to Ethan.

He gave Tyson the bucket and the change and I pressed the clutch with my foot as he shifted to gear one. I stepped on the gas softly, and we began to move forward.

"Have a good one," Ethan said to the cashier, resting one arm on the window frame and steering with the other. I rolled up the window, and Tyson and I broke out laughing. Ethan steered around the corner to the other side of the building where I stopped to let him get back to his seat. As soon as he did, I exited the parking lot onto the road and stepped on the gas, hastily driving away.

We got back to the apartment where we devoured most of the chicken and left the rest in the fridge. It was afternoon then; we didn't actually arrive until about 1530 hours.

By the time Jeremy arrived we were in the front room watching the UCLA American football game on the big screen.

"Hey, Jeremy," Tyson greeted.

"What's going on here?" Jeremy asked, grinning.

"Just watching the UCLA game," Tyson answered.

"Who's winning?"

"We are."

"Hey, Chance, who are you going for?" Jeremy asked.

"Honestly, I don't have a team here," I said.

"Why not?"

"Because I watch football."

"This is football," Tyson said, looking at me as if I were stupid or something.

"No." I shook my head. "Football is a thirty-two paneled ball that can only be touched with your feet, legs, and head, and you try to get it into the goal."

"That's soccer," Ethan said.

"Well," I said, "where I come from, it's called football."

"So you like team England?" Jeremy asked.

"No, Australia," I said.

"Oh," Jeremy said. "I assumed you were British because of your accent."

"Don't assume that," I heard Tyson quietly tell Jeremy. "He hates that."

"All Australians hate that," I commented. Tyson and Jeremy looked at me accusingly for eavesdropping on them.

"What?" I said. "My ears catch anything."

7

Later in the evening, we had the rest of the chicken for dinner and, when Ethan got tired, Tyson sent him to bed. We figured that just us guys would hang out.

"Where do you wanna go?" Tyson asked.

"Anywhere except for a strip club sounds good to me," I said.

"Why not?" Tyson said, smiling almost fiendishly.

"Because I'm not having any human girls lap dancing on me," I said.

"Besides, Jeremy probably wouldn't prefer it either," I whispered.

"True," Tyson said, straightening out his smile.

"Hey, Chance," Jeremy said from the top of the stairs, "I'm washing your uniform, so why don't you put this on?" He tossed me a blue and black flannel shirt.

"All right," I said, taking off my black T-shirt and putting on the flannel. I buttoned it up, except for the top two buttons, which revealed my dog tags.

"How do I look?" I asked.

"If only you could come across Katie tonight," Jeremy said, motioning for me to toss the T-shirt up to him, which I did. He set it on the washer, and there was a knock on the door. "Oh, my date's here."

"You invited Derek?" Tyson asked.

"Yup," Jeremy said, rushing down the stairs and flying around the corner to the door. He opened it, and there was a guy about his age wearing a black collared shirt and jeans with glasses and a clean-cut beard.

"Hey, Derek," Jeremy said.

"Jeremy!" Derek said. They hugged and kissed. Tyson covered his eyes with one hand.

The kiss was brief, and they began to comment on each other's clothes. Jeremy was wearing a red-and-black flannel, similar to the blue one he let me wear.

Derek looked at me and fell silent.

"Oh," Jeremy said, "this is the guy I told you about."

He then leaned to his ear.

"Remember what I told you," he whispered. "He's all right."

I heard it, but chose not to say anything.

"So," Derek said, walking over to me with an outstretched hand, which I took and shook. "You must be Chance."

"The one and only," I said.

"Well I'm honored to meet you," Derek said.

He seemed frantic, like Jeremy when I first met him, but if I walked up to you and shook your hand and said hi, you would probably be acting the same way.

"Thanks," I said. "I don't think Jeremy told me about you—"

"Hey," Jeremy loudly interrupted me, "why don't we get going? We're burning . . . moonlight."

"Yeah, he's right," Tyson said. "Let's go."

Jeremy led the way to the back parking lot, where all the people living in the apartments kept their cars. There weren't that many, regardless of how big the building was, but I guess people preferred to live in houses or cheaper apartments.

He led us over to his bright red Porsche 911 and opened the door, then pulled the lever on the side of the seat and pushed it forward, allowing Tyson and me to get into the claustrophobic backseat.

As soon as we did, Jeremy put the seat back, which crushed my legs, not painfully, but to the extent to where I couldn't move them. I couldn't even move myself to move my tail to a comfortable position.

"So," I said as Jeremy and Derek buckled their seat belts, "where are we going?"

"I figured we would just go to the bar or something," Jeremy said.

"Are you sure?" I asked. "Because we would have to wait a while before going home."

"True," Jeremy said starting the car. "But I guess that gives us more time to hang out."

He put the car into gear and drove out of the parking lot and onto the road.

We were sitting at the counter at the bar, and I kept getting funny looks from some people. Honestly, everyone acted as if they had never seen a fox before. I mean, seriously, if I were to lose the shirt and get down on all fours, I would look like a normal, everyday fox that grew as big as a mountain lion, but other than that . . .

We ordered some beers and drank many gulps at a time. I could feel the ice-cold beverage rush down my esophagus and settle in my stomach, just to rush back up as a gas resulting in a burp.

The place was heavy with thick, foul-smelling cigarette smoke, with little to no oxygen, making it hard to breathe. A couple of heavy built guys played pool in the back, while others laughed and joked or played a game of cards.

"Well, have you figured out when you're going to head to Brazil?" Jeremy asked.

"Probably in a couple of days," I said.

"Honestly," Derek said, "I wish I was you."

"Why?"

"Because, spy work," he said. "You get to travel the world and do these dangerous missions. It's like an adventure."

"Well, how does this sound?" I asked. "I don't have anywhere to live, I'm constantly on the run, there's a mole in the agency who's doing everything he can to find me and start a nuclear war with the Soviets and the US, the Soviets are after me too, and so is my ex-girlfriend. Not very appealing, is it?"

"Hmm." Derek nodded, seemingly understanding the stress I was under.

We began talking about what I do, and sometime at the peak of a conversation, I tended to show my views of the subject and start to rant. I would always try not to, but it usually came with heavy stress.

"Sorry to rant," I apologized, "but it's difficult."

"I understand," Derek said.

"You need to quit worrying about your old girlfriend and find a new one," Jeremy said.

"Yeah," Tyson said. "There's plenty of other girls in the world."

"But they're all human," I said. "I mean, I don't know about you guys, but bestiality isn't my thing."

"Oh, c'mon," Tyson said. "I think you'll learn to love human girls."

"What's wrong with you guys?" I asked as Jeremy and Derek laughed.

"Speak of the devil," Tyson said, as the bell on the door rang. I looked over and saw a couple of attractive young human girls walk in, one blonde and one brunette.

"God, no," I muttered, turning around and covering my eyes. I didn't want to get forced into relations with these girls by my friends.

"Relax, it won't last long," Tyson said. I didn't know whether he was talking about a meet and greet or intercourse when he said that, which made my stomach churn.

Tyson got up and went over to them. The brunette saw him and squealed as she threw her arms around him. Apparently, Tyson knew these girls, and they knew him. Tyson began to lead them over to us and I heard a *psst*.

I looked over to Jeremy who gave me a thumbs up. I swallowed.

"Oh my god," the brunette girl said, upon arriving within my proximity. "You're so cute."

I took a deep breath, put my confident face on and turned around.

"Why, thank you," I said with a grin.

"Tyson said that you wanted to meet us," the blonde girl said.

"Well . . ." I was going to have to convince them to fall for Tyson, but I would have to choose my words carefully, as to not offend them or increase attraction to me. "After the way he described you, who wouldn't?"

They just giggled.

"Aw, thank you," the brunette said. "You're so sweet."

I just kept my confident smile on but almost sighed as it had become rather obvious these girls weren't about to leave anytime soon.

"So what's your name?" the blonde asked.

"Logan," I said. "Chance Logan."

"My name is Chanel," the brunette girl said, "and this is Clarice." She pointed to the blonde next to her.

"Well, um . . ." I was losing confidence, hence, losing my sense of wording. "Hi, it's nice to meet you."

I turned a little toward the counter and did my best to conceal a face-palm. The girls must have sensed my sudden shyness and giggled.

"Mind if I sit down?" Chanel asked.

"Not at all, honey," I said, laying my arm across the counter and forcing the smile back on my face. I turned back toward the counter, and suddenly, she came over and sat across my lap.

"Oh, um . . ." I stuttered. I felt my face get hot from a blush as she put her arm around my neck leaned on me.

"Your fur is so soft," she said with a voice like silk.

"Uh . . . thank you," I said almost questionably.

"Mm," she leaned her head on my shoulder and put her face to my neck. "You're like a big plush toy. I just wanna cuddle with you."

I swallowed, thinking this was going a little too far.

"You should've worn pants, Chance," Tyson whispered.

That did it. I could feel my temples pulsating with my heartbeat hard in my chest from my suppressed frustration and annoyance.

Shut up, I mouthed inaudibly at Tyson.

"Would you like to cuddle?" she asked, taking her head off my shoulder and looking into my eyes with her misty blue ones.

I was straining to make an answer, choking on my own words.

"I . . . err . . . uh . . ." I looked behind me at Jeremy, who just shrugged and put his arm around Derek. I then jerked my head around to look at Tyson, who gave me a thumbs-up and nodded his smiling face.

I looked at Chanel and grinned.

"Will you excuse me for a sec, dear?" I said.

I let her get off my lap, and I walked to Tyson, put my arm on his shoulder, and we walked a few feet from the girls, who were whispering and giggling to each other.

"I can't do this," I said. "It's just too messed up to me."

"Chance," Tyson said with a funny-looking expression as he shook his head, "What are you talking about?"

"You know what," I almost berated. "You're trying to get me to . . . you know?"

"What?"

87

"It's pretty obvious to me,"

"No." Tyson shook his head. "You should in no way take this suggestively. Chanel is a nice, sweet girl. She doesn't roll that way. She just really likes animals."

"Are you sure?" I asked. "Because she sounds pretty damn seductive to me."

"Chance," Tyson said, calling me by my name again, "she's nice, trust me. Just spend a little time with her, get to know her. Plus, she's had it pretty rough lately, and I think it would mean a lot to her. On top of that, what are your chances of coming across Katie again?"

I thought about it, and he did have a point. I didn't want to look stupid in front of my friends, old and new; plus, I didn't want to offend this pretty young girl, and I sympathized at the fact that she'd had it rough lately, so I gave in to the peer pressure. It was only a friendly cuddle, right?

"Okay." I nodded.

"All right," Tyson said, a little out loud. "That's the spirit."

I grumbled as we walked over, and thought about what to say, but when we got there, what came out was,

"Yes, I'd love to cuddle with you, sweetheart." I felt like my conscience face-palmed at my cheesy remark.

Clarice, however, seemed impressed as she put her hand over her mouth, and both of the girls started to giggle.

Clarice stayed in the bar with Tyson as Chanel showed me the way to her Cadillac Sedan deVille, which stood out like a boat among the other cars parked along the sidewalk. Literally, if you've ever seen a 1969 Sedan deVille, it was like a boat on wheels; it was a huge car.

Chanel unlocked it, and we got into the backseat. Once we got in, Chanel locked the doors and turned her attention to me. I sat a little pressed up against the door, creating some space between us. She smiled, and I smiled crookedly back. She scooted toward me, and when she reached me, she began unbuttoning my flannel. Once she exposed my entire front side, she wrapped her arms around me and pressed her head on my chest.

"Your fur is so soft and warm," she said.

I could feel my heart pounding, and I'm sure she heard it.

"Are you nervous?" She asked.

I couldn't think of what to say. I was indeed nervous, but I thought telling her might offend her, but I was definitely not confident at that time, so I put it in between.

"A little," I said weakly.

"Why's that?" Chanel asked.

"Uhh . . ." I couldn't think of how to word it right, but it slipped out without processing in my mind first. "I thought Tyson was trying to get me to . . . you know, make love to you."

"Oh," Chanel said in a puzzled tone. "Well, I'd never do that. Unless I were a fox like you, then I'd be all yours." She looked up at me and winked.

"I take it you like foxes," I almost stuttered.

"I like anything furry," she said. "They give me comfort in my turbulent life. Usually as a kid, I would cuddle with my stuffed bear, just wishing he could understand me and say something back. Now I only have my dog. He only understands 'Sit' and 'Come here.'"

"Yeah," I said.

"Tyson told me about you when he got back from Vietnam," she said. "I didn't believe him at first, but he just kept telling me more and more, and I started to believe it. I wanted to see you because talking animals was always a childhood dream of mine. So he called me and told me and Clarice to meet you guys here."

"Sorry," I said, kind of veering off the subject at hand, "but I'd prefer not to be called an animal."

"Why?" she asked.

"It makes me feel like a freak or a savage," I answered.

"Well, what do you prefer to be called?"

"Just a fox."

"Okay," she said. We just sat there, Chanel with her head pressed on my chest and I rubbing her shoulder with my paw, my arm wrapped around her back.

"So," I said, "Tyson tells me you've been having it kind of rough lately."

"Yeah," she said.

"Well," I said, "what's going on?"

"You really want to talk about it?" she asked.

"Well, if you wanna talk . . ." I said. "I wanna help. I was made to help people, apparently."

"Okay," Chanel sat up and straightened out her hair. "So just a few weeks ago, we received news that my mom had died. She was a nurse in Vietnam. My dad got so upset that he started drinking. Now he's not as dependable, and I had to quit my job to take care of my brother and sisters."

"What was your mother's name?" I asked, seeing if I would recognize the name.

"Erin," Chanel said. It didn't ring a bell. "Why?"

"I was in Vietnam," I said. "I was just seeing if she was someone I knew. You may continue."

"Well," Chanel continued, "I'm also studying law at UCLA. I already have it all paid for because of my mom and dad setting aside some money over the years, but it just makes it so hard because I've got no support from my dad."

Tears began to well in her eyes.

"It's all because mom died. I miss her so much." She began sobbing and pressed her head to my chest again. I wrapped both arms around her, rubbing her shoulder with one paw and running the other softly through her hair.

"There, there," I said, "it's okay, honey. It'll all turn out."

She collapsed, lying down on the seat and resting her head on my lap. I stuttered a bit, flustered by this.

"I know what it's like to lose ones close to you," I said, referring to the many friends I lost at war and Katie. I picked her up off my lap and held her in my arms, and she turned over and buried her face in the white fur of my belly. I gave her a kiss on the head, and we sat that way for a while until she calmed down. We were silent for a bit until Chanel spoke up again.

"So," she said, sitting up and wiping her eyes, "why don't we just get to know each other now?"

"Sounds good," I said, "take your mind off of all the trouble."

"So . . ." she wiped her eyes again. "Do you have someone in your life, girlfriend, wife . . ."

"I did," I said.

"Did?"

"Yeah," I said. "She was a nurse in Vietnam, and I was a soldier. We officially met when I took a bullet in the thigh. I still remember the way she told me to look into her eyes to take my mind off the pain. She had the most beautiful blue eyes, blue as the sky."

I smiled as I described her fairness, but that smile turned upside down as I explained what happened between us.

"But I've gotten into trouble with a corrupt director of the CIA," I continued, "and apparently, she works for him, and she was sent to Vietnam to come get me. But it wasn't her who left me. I left her."

"I'm sorry," Chanel said.

"It's not your fault," I said, putting my arm around her back and resuming my paw's position on her left shoulder, held her close, and she

91

leaned her head on my shoulder. She had grabbed my tail and stroked it with her hand as it rested on her lap.

"What was her name?" Chanel asked.

"Katie," I said. "Her name was Katie."

"She sounds lovely," Chanel said.

"She was the prettiest girl I ever met." I looked at Chanel. "Well, the prettiest vixen I ever met. You're very pretty too."

"Aw," Chanel's eyes lit up, and she smiled in amusement. "You're so sweet. I don't know why anyone would be trying to kill you."

"Well, I never said the CIA is trying to kill me," I said. "They want me alive."

"Why?"

"It's complicated," I answered. "But the director thinks I'm a killer, and that's why I was created."

"Well," Chanel said, "I think you're a big softy, as soft on the inside as on the outside."

She gently caressed my chest as she said that.

"I wish everyone saw me that way." I sighed, resting my head on hers.

"You're like a childhood dream," Chanel said. "Almost any kid would love to meet someone like you."

"There are others too," I said.

"Really?"

"Yup," I said, nodding. "There's Kay, a good friend of mine from Vietnam. He's a cougar. There's Erich. I've never met him in person, but he's a cheetah. Then, there's Aaron, he's also a fox . . ."

"I wish I could meet them all," Chanel said.

"Yeah," I said. "Kay is a fun guy."

"I don't get it," Chanel said randomly. "If you're a fox, why are you taller than I? Foxes are usually no bigger than my dog."

"I have no idea," I said. "It's some kind of height alteration, but I'm no biological engineer."

Chanel leaned in more and pressed her head to my chest again. She put her hand next to her head on my chest and looked up at me with those misty blues. I smiled at her.

"You remind me of Katie," I said, brushing a few strands of hair away from her face.

"How long has it been since you left her?" Chanel asked.

"A little over a week," I said.

"Then it's not too late to go back for her," she said. "As a woman, I know what I'm talking about."

"What do you mean?" I asked.

"When it comes to relationships, women think with their hearts," Chanel said. "Katie probably feels a massive empty space in hers now that you're gone." She sat up. "How did leaving her go down?"

"Well I was at the MI6 headquarters with her, and I was told that the CIA was after me. He kept eyeing Katie whenever he mentioned the CIA. And that's when she came clean and told me how she was sent to Vietnam on a mission. I began to leave, and she wanted to tell me something, but I didn't hear her out," I explained.

"Well, that's a simple fix," Chanel said. "If I were you I would go back to her, apologize, and hear what she has to say."

Chanel was right. All I had to do was hear her out, because Katie sounded pretty urgent when she tried to say something. But there was one major problem.

"What if I can't find her?" I asked. "What if she doesn't care anymore?"

"Just take your chances," Chanel said. "She's with the CIA, she'll probably find you." That was true. The CIA has tracked me to the most unlikely places lately.

"All right," I said. "I'll try."

93

"That's the spirit, Chance," she said.

We sat for a while longer.

"Can I have your number?" she asked. "I'd like to keep in contact."

"Oh, I don't have a phone," I said, "so you could give me yours."

"That's all right," Chanel said.

She got up and reached all the way to the glove compartment in the way front of the car, with her rear in my face. She then closed the glove compartment, sat back down, and handed me a card.

"I used to have a boring office job," she said. "But that's my house phone number."

I turned the card over and there was her full name, Chanel A. Parker, and a phone number on the front.

"Great," I said. "I'll give you a call if I need anything or if you need anything."

"Well, thanks for coming out here with me," she said. "It helps to have someone to talk to. And it was really lovely to cuddle with you."

"You're welcome," I said.

She threw her arms around me, and we exchanged a long, friendly hug. That's when I happened to look out the windshield to see a mysterious-looking black Lincoln across the street and ahead of Chanel's car. I looked hard into it and saw the unmistakable silhouette of Nikolai in the driver's seat.

Damn, they found me.

"We have to go," I said, frantically breaking up the hug. I threw open the door, grabbed Chanel's hand, and we ran into the bar, where I found the others.

"Guys, we have to go!" I said, putting my paw on Tyson's shoulder and turning him around.

"Why," he slurred.

"We just gotta move now!" I said.

94

"Well, why?" Tyson repeated, stumbling a bit as he stood. He was so damn drunk.

"Where's Derek and Jeremy?" I asked.

"Right here," Tyson said, pointing behind him at them, who had their heads resting on the bar counter.

I think they were either blacked out, or they just got tired and fell asleep; I couldn't actually tell.

"Why?" Tyson asked again.

"No time to explain," I said. I grabbed him and shoved him toward the door. Clarice followed him. She was drunk as well. I managed to get Jeremy and Derek to their feet and helped them along to the Porsche.

"I'll drive," I said. "You guys are drunker than all hell."

They all got into the car. Derek and Jeremy passed out in the back seat almost instantly. Before I got in the Porsche, I had some things to take care of. I went over to the Cadillac, and Chanel rolled down the window.

"I'm sorry to head out so quickly," I said, "but something's going on. Spy stuff, hope you understand."

"Yeah," She said starting the car. I wanted to thank her, for she reminded me of Katie and gave back the passion I held for her.

"Listen," I said, "thanks for the . . . cuddle. And the advice. It helped me decide what I need to do."

She looked at me and smiled.

"I also enjoyed getting to know you a bit," I said.

"You're welcome," Chanel said.

"Will we ever meet again?" I asked, feeling that it might be appropriate to start a long-lasting friendship after this night.

"I hope so," Chanel said.

"Well," I said, feeling myself blushing, "just in case . . ." I leaned in and kissed her on the lips, which she didn't seem to mind as she kissed back. I cut it short and broke the kiss.

"Seriously," I said, "I've been a real dick. You helped me realize what I should do."

"Just remember what I told you," she put the car in gear and let me move away before she drove away, leaving me standing there, thinking about my reunion with Katie. I was bent on finding her and being with her once again, but this time it was going to be forever. Never again would I leave her.

I then remembered the current predicament, and I ran into the bar. I called everyone's attention and pulled out my flashing device, giving everyone a flash at once, then left the bar and went to the Porsche, getting into the driver's seat and closing the door. I started the car and quickly put it into gear, casually driving off at normal speed. I looked at the rearview mirror and saw the Lincoln turn around and begin following us.

"Damn," I said.

"Chance," Tyson said, "what's going on?"

"The Soviets are here," I said. "They found me."

Tyson just widened his eyes and sucked in a mouthful of air at my response. I drove a couple of blocks, and the Lincoln still followed. I wasn't about to lose Nikolai anytime soon at this rate, so I stepped on the gas, and the Porsche flew down the street. The Lincoln accelerated after us.

"Oh, god," I said.

I passed a few blocks, flying down the almost empty streets of the urban area of Los Angeles. All of a sudden, a couple of cars followed by a Peterbilt with a trailer swerved around the corner of the next intersection. One of the cars swerved away from the Porsche and hit a light pole, which fell over until the wires caught it.

I saw the side door on the trailer of the truck open, and there was a man and a couple of others standing there. The Lincoln pulled up along-side it, and I saw the door open. Nikolai hopped out, and the man grabbed his paw as he jumped into the trailer. The Lincoln decelerated and fell

96

behind. Nikolai took an AK-47 from one of the men in the trailer and aimed it at us.

"Crap!" Tyson and I said in unison.

Nikolai fired at us. Bullets pinged off the car's body and broke the window.

"Ah!" I exclaimed, shielding my face from the bits of glass.

Jeremy quickly sat up.

"What in the hell?" he said.

"Hey, Jeremy," I said over the bullet impacts. "Sorry about the car."

"That's all right," he said. I couldn't tell whether he was highly intoxicated or just had money to burn. "Open the glove compartment."

Tyson reached down and pulled on the glove compartment, which slid out like a dresser drawer. There were two MP5's and a ton of magazines in there.

"I keep those in case of an emergency," Jeremy said.

"Well, now would be a good time to use them," I said.

Jeremy got up and squeezed his way between the seats and into the passenger seat.

"Get into the back," he told Tyson, which he did with no less effort than Jeremy.

"There's a car behind us," Jeremy said. "Slow down, and if I'm correct, he should go around us and end up in front."

I hit the brake, and the big Lincoln car swerved by us. He ended up right in front, just as Jeremy said, but they tried to take it to their advantage and slow us down so Nikolai could have a clear shot.

Jeremy rolled down his window and leaned out with the MP5 pointed forward and fired a few shots. One bullet found its way to the driver's head, and the Lincoln spun out of control and flipped after colliding with a fire hydrant. One down and two more to go. Three, including the truck, but I was surprised that Jeremy had managed a shot like that in his drunken state.

"Here," he said, handing me a loaded MP5. I took it in my left paw, aimed, and began firing at Nikolai. He ducked as the bullets left sparks as they ricocheted off the trailer hull; one of his men took a bullet and fell out of the truck and onto the road.

One of the Lincolns sped up and heeled to the trailer like a dog to his master. I handed the MP5 to Jeremy, and he handed me his other one, which he had just got done loading.

"Get the action, will you?" I said.

`The action was locked open. Jeremy hit the knob, and the action closed.

"Thank you," I said, pointing the MP5 at the Lincoln and started firing again. The first few shots ricocheted off the body of the car, but after about half of the magazine, a bullet went through the widow and killed the driver. His car swerved under the trailer, and Nikolai and the others on board braced themselves as the trailer ran over the car, bumping over it and nearly flattening it.

"Nice one, Chance," Jeremy said.

We just had one car and the truck left now. The car sped up to us and hit the Porsche on the side, attempting to run us off the road.

"Dammit, Dammit, Dammit!" I said, holding on to the steering wheel, keeping the car on the road with all it had. The Lincoln merged away from us and hit us again. This nearly knocked my paws off the wheel, but I held my grip.

"These guys are going to run us off the road!" Tyson shouted from the back.

I saw an electronic road sign coming up that said Road Work Ahead. Behind it was a class eight with a gasoline trailer hooked up to it. I thought fast as the Lincoln prepared to hit us again, and stepped on the brake as he maneuvered to hit us. He swerved to keep his car on the road, and I turned the tables on him.

I pulled up to his left just like he had done to me earlier, and I merged over, our cars side to side in contact, and I kept him in place. His car hit the sign, which fell over and stopped at about thirty degrees from the road. The went over it like a ramp and flew into the air, just to hit the gasoline trailer on the truck, and they exploded in a big ball of fire.

"Damn, Chance," Jeremy said, "quick thinking."

"Now all we have to do is get rid of that truck," I said as another hail-fire of bullets pinged off the Porsche's frame.

"I wish I had bigger weapons in this car," Jeremy slurred. That's when we got near an intersection by a bunch of run-down apartments and cafés and other small businesses, and a Volkswagen beetle drifted onto the main road right in front of us.

"What in god's name?" I exclaimed.

Then all of a sudden, a panel on the front side of the Beetle opened, and a rocket launcher came out. The driver of the Beetle angled the car toward the truck, and the rocket was fired. It flew all the way to the other lane and hit the truck right in the cabin. The truck went up in a ball of fire.

As for the trailer and everyone on board, they all held on as the trailer dislodged itself from the truck's hitch and scraped the pavement until it screeched to a halt. I hit the brake on the car and brought it to a stop as well.

"You good enough to drive?" I asked Jeremy.

"I think so," he said.

"All right," I said, handing Jeremy the MP5. "I'll get their attention. It's me they want, just get outta here and get home."

I got out of the car and left them behind.

"Good luck, Chance!" Jeremy shouted. The Porsche sped away and I watched its taillights fade in the distance.

I looked around, wondering whatever happened to the Volkswagen or its mysterious driver, but they were nowhere in sight. The truck lay on its side, with flames licking the frame through the now open windows and the fenders. The trailer was about twenty feet from it, and everyone was getting out, at least everyone who was still alive.

"Hey," I shouted, "over here!"

I caught their attention and turned around, then started sprinting to a nearby alley. I heard a couple shots and some bullets snap by me. I made it to the alley and turned the corner behind the café, then I came to a dead end blocked by a metal wire fence. I stopped at the fence and looked around for a way out.

I then heard the others sprinting over, and I turned around to face them as they came. I figured I would have to fight my way through, but as I hit the first guy, the second guy grabbed me from behind and locked my arms behind my back. He threw me against the fence, still holding my arms back, and that was when I heard Nikolai.

"Where do you think you're going, fox?" he asked in his native language.

"You're making a big mistake!" I said in Russian.

"*Niet*," he said. "I see no mistake in following my orders." I heard him cock his pistol and I could almost feel him aiming at my head.

"Say hello to Stalin for us," he said.

I then heard a shot; not the loud pop of a pistol, but the deafening bang of a rifle. It wasn't Nikolai, for my ears pointed forward toward the source of the noise, through the fence. The guy holding me fell down dead with a bullet wound in his head.

At that moment, I turned around, and Nikolai kept his pistol trained on me, looking around. The other guy held an AK and looked around as well. That was when there was another shot and a hole exploded in his chest. He was knocked backward onto the ground. I heard the distinctive click of a bolt action, and there was another shot. The bullet destroyed Nikolai's pistol as it was ripped from his paw.

"Damn," he said once again in Russian. He turned his tail and fled the alley.

I sighed and leaned on the fence, but I had to know who my mysterious savior was, and I began to look around and I spotted her. I could see her shadowy figure approaching. She came within the proximity of the light on the cafe. It was Katie.

"Oh my god," I said. "Katie!"

She climbed over the fence and jumped down to the ground. I hadn't seen her wear clothes most of the time, but some days she would wear her white nurse uniform when she was working. This time she was wearing a dark-brown leather jacket.

I went over to embrace her but, she held up her L96A1 sniper rifle, aiming it at my chest.

"All right, Chance," she said, "let's make this quick. No trouble."

"Whoa, Katie, what are you doing?" I asked, holding my paws in the air in surrender.

"I'm doing my job," she said. "What have you been up to?"

"Nothing," I said, "just hiding out at Tyson's place."

"Private Stone?" she asked.

"Yeah."

'Well, hope you said good-bye," she said, "because now you're going to be living at Lance's place for a while."

"Katie," I said, walking toward her, "you don't have to do this."

"Stay back," she said, her gun trained on me. "I will shoot."

"Go ahead," I said. "Who's stopping you?"

"Lance wants you alive," Katie said.

"It's not Lance that's stopping you," I said. "More like Cupid."

"Oh, nu-uh." She shook her head. "Don't even think for a second that—"

"What?" I said. "It hasn't been that long."

"No," she said, pushing me back with the gun. "But you left me. I loved you, and you left me without hearing me out. I was going to tell you something important, but you still left."

"Katie," I repeated, "you don't have to do this. We can start over."

"This is all I've got now," she said. "Now that you've left me on my own, Lance is the only one I have left. I do my job, and he pays, simple as that, but you're making it difficult. Now I'll just ask you to please come with me."

"What if I told you that I had a little visit with Lance?" I asked.

"Yeah, I know about that," she said. "You pissed him off pretty bad."

"And in that visit," I continued, "he told me about a plan to start a nuclear war, and that he would kill you later."

"Lance wouldn't kill me," she said.

"He told me himself," I argued.

"You're lying."

"Am I?"

"Yeah," she said. "Lance has always been loyal to his operatives."

"Well, what about all those operatives who were terminated?" I asked, scolding. "What about them, huh?"

"Well, I—" She stopped herself in a stupor of thought.

"And it just so happens," I said, "that Lance was the director of that mission in the Soviet Union. The one with the bombs?"

"And?" Katie asked.

"And," I continued, "all of those operatives placed bombs all throughout the Soviet Union. Coincidence? I don't think so."

"It can't be," Katie said.

"Well, who are you going to believe," I said, "the one who was sent to Kiev to place a bomb by Lance himself, or Lance himself who

102

hasn't told you why he's after me? Better yet, the guy you loved for over a year or the man you don't know jack about? It's my word against his."

She lowered her gun.

"He hasn't told you anything, am I right?" I asked.

"Yes," she said.

"There you go," I said. "Now if you'll excuse me, I have a nuclear war to stop."

"Chance," Katie said. I thought she was falling for me but instead she casually asked, "Where's Tyson's place?"

"Come on," I said, motioning for her to follow me with a sneer. "Do you have a car?"

"Yes," she said. We walked out of the alley, keeping our distance from each other and around the café, where I saw the Volkswagen Beetle sitting.

"Oh my god," I said. "You're kidding me."

"What?"

"While we get the cool cars, you get stupid little Volkenhagens?" I asked. "I thought the CIA treated female operatives equally."

"Hey," she said, "I chose this car."

"Why?"

"I thought it was cute."

"Okay," I said, "and I thought my Cutlass was adorable when it was issued to me."

"Quit mocking me," she said. She opened the trunk, located on the front, and slid her rifle in, then closed it. She then opened the driver's side door and sat in the driver's seat, closing the door behind her. I got into the passenger seat.

"Cute," I said with a snort.

"Shut up, Chance!" Katie said, starting the car.

"Does Hitler know you have his car?" I asked jokingly.

"Shut it!" Katie scolded.

And she's back, I thought. I couldn't help but stare out of the corner of my eye as she moved her tail to a comfortable position.

We made it to the Stones' place. I told Katie where to turn and stuff for she didn't have a positioning system in her car. We made it at about one o'clock in the morning, if not two o'clock. We entered the building and went to the elevator. We were both tired, and we needed sleep, bad. When we reached Jeremy's apartment, I knocked on the door. Jeremy answered.

"Thank god you made it," he said.

"Yeah," I said, "thank god."

"This must be Katie," he said as we walked in.

"Yup," Katie said.

"Hi, I'm Jeremy." He took her paw and shook it. "Chance has told me and Tyson so much about you."

"Well," she said, "I hope he told you we were no longer in a relationship."

Jeremy hesitated with an open mouth.

"Yes," he finally said, "he told us that."

"Good," Katie said. She looked at me coldly. Those blue eyes were more like ice than the sky, and I nearly shivered.

Jeremy showed us to our room after he got to know Katie a little.

"Why can't we have separate rooms?" Katie asked.

"This is the only guest room," Jeremy said. "Unless you would prefer to sleep with Tyson."

"I'm good," Katie said.

"Well, if you guys decide to have fun—"

"Jeremy!" I shouted.

"Okay," he put his hands up. "Jeez, I'm just trying to be funny."

"I'm sure you're a fun guy," Katie said, "but we're no longer in cahoots with each other."

"Whatever," Jeremy said, "sleep well."

I realized that I was still wearing the unbuttoned flannel.

"Hey, Jeremy," I said before he closed the door. I took off the flannel and threw it to him.

"Thanks," he said as he caught it. He left, shutting the door behind him. Katie and I were now alone.

"I get the side with the side table," I said.

"Why are we choosing sides?" Katie asked.

"Because that's where my guns are," I said, "and my wallet."

"Fair enough," Katie said, taking off her jacket, lying down in the bed, and pulling the covers over her.

I shut off the light and got on my side of the bed, pulling the covers over me. I couldn't believe it. I had always dreamed of lying in the same bed as Katie when I met her, but now that we were a bit sore with each other, we were.

"Good night," I said.

"Night," she said back with a sigh. We both turned away from each other, and I fell asleep almost instantly.

8

I awoke the next morning, noticing that I had a lot more room on the bed. Katie was gone. Upon noticing this, I looked around the room. She wasn't anywhere. I noticed the door was cracked open a bit and figured she went downstairs. I got out of bed and made my way to the staircase. That's when I heard her talking to someone. She was talking to Jeremy.

"Well, you shouldn't be so harsh," I heard Jeremy say.

"I know," Katie said, "but I feel he needs to . . . how do I put it? Pay, I guess, for his mistake."

"I feel you," Jeremy said.

"I mean, it's hard for me," Katie said. "He's a very sweet guy."

I assumed they were talking about me and eavesdropped some more at the bottom of the stairs.

"Well, he's been talking about you ever since he got here," Jeremy said. "That should be enough for you."

"It's going to be a while." Katie sighed. "He walked away from me without even listening to me."

"Understandable," Jeremy said. "I've left some people who wouldn't hear me out."

"Yeah," Katie said. "I love him, and I was willing to tell him I would quit the CIA just to be with him. In fact, that's what I was going to say when he left."

"But you're still in the CIA."

"Yeah," Katie said. "I figured since he was gone, that was all I had. The only reason I came back to him was to carry out my task at hand."

"To capture him?" Jeremy asked.

"Mm-hmm."

"Why is that?"

"Lance just told me to," Katie said. "It didn't seem all that odd that he never said why, until Chance brought it up last night."

"Well if you didn't know why, why didn't you ask?"

"I don't question his authority."

"Oh, well, that's a good spy characteristic," Jeremy said, "but it'll get you nowhere in life outside of the spy business."

Katie just sighed.

"Eventually you're going to have to go with him," Jeremy said. "You're the only ones of your kind, as far as I can tell."

"No," Katie said. "There's another guy. His name is Aaron."

Aaron Richards? He looked like he was at least thirty, if not forty, in that photo from the file Jack showed us. Plus, wasn't he terminated?

"Well, Chance has obviously been very heartbroken over you," Jeremy said. "I think it would be best to go with him."

I heard Katie let out a deep breath through her nose.

"I'm going to take a shower," she said.

I quickly scrambled to the top of the stairs and rounded the corner to the hallway just before she reached the staircase. I heard her walking up the stairs, and I messed up the fur on my head a little and walked toward the staircase, rubbing my eyes and acting like I just woke up. I rounded the corner and Katie was right in front of me. She was wearing a

T-shirt Jeremy gave her. A yellow shirt with a crimson 88 on the front. It was a kind of ugly shirt that didn't match Katie's light-orange fur.

"Oh," I exclaimed, startled. "Morning, Katie."

I tried to sound a bit cold but nice.

"Morning," Katie said almost questioningly. I walked past her and went back down the stairs and into the kitchen. Jeremy had the leftover pancakes out on a plate, and he had his own plate, eating away at two of them.

"Morning, Jeremy," I said.

"Morning," he said enthusiastically, as if getting up early in the morning was super exciting.

"Hey," I said, almost whispering and sitting across the counter from him, "you didn't tell us you liked guns."

"Well," Jeremy said, "I don't actually like guns, I just don't feel comfortable without them."

"Why's that?"

Jeremy sighed hesitantly before responding.

"To tell you the truth, I used to be an assassin for hire." he said.

"Really?" I asked, lifting an eyebrow.

Jeremy nodded a bit regrettably.

"You didn't think I got all this from being a stockbroker, did you?" he asked.

"I did actually," I said. "So why'd you leave?"

"It just wasn't for me anymore," Jeremy said. "Taking someone's life is a lousy excuse for a job, and it shouldn't be a high-paying job to kill a guy you know nothing about."

"Uh-huh," I said understandingly. The ASIS had had me do that a few times.

"I still feel the scars," Jeremy said, "and I still see the faces of those people I had to take down. It's no fun. It makes life suck, knowing what you've done."

"Who did you primarily work for?" I asked.

"Whoever paid highest," Jeremy said. "Just a few years ago, this CIA guy came to me and told me he would pay two million to take a guy who had joined the army and shipped out to Vietnam. He told me something about setting up an attack in which he would be captured and handed over to him. It sounded too much like betraying my own country, so I refused and quit the job. I haven't touched a weapon since."

What he just said made me a little suspicious. A guy in Vietnam who would be taken alive and handed over to this guy who just asked Jeremy to go to the Viet Cong and set up an attack with them. Sounded a bit like . . .

"What was his name?" I asked.

"I have no idea," Jeremy said. "He never told me, and he didn't have a name tag or anything."

I thought hard for a minute.

"I'm starting to think that guy," I said, "was John Lance."

"Lance?" Jeremy said. "I had a talk with Katie earlier, and she said she worked for Lance to get you."

He paused, obviously thinking.

"You don't suppose," Jeremy said, "the guy he wanted me to get was you?"

"My god," I said. "Jeremy, what have you heard about the war in Vietnam?"

"Well, the fighting has died down," Jeremy said, "and there was the POW release this March and the peace treaty, why?"

Lance was shedding American blood for his cause. So many young men's lives had been spent on that attack just to get me. This, however, wouldn't be the end, for Lance, being as heinous as he was, would have no problem taking more innocent lives just to get me and complete his mission.

"This is starting to make sense now!" I said.

109

I stood and proceeded to leave the kitchen.

"I need to stop Lance before he does anything else." I shouted as I ran up the stairs. "I need to get to Brazil ASAP!"

I ran to the hallway and into my room, where I found Katie. She had taken that ugly shirt off and had evidently been in my drawer. She sat on the side of the bed and was holding my Colt, marveling at it.

"What are you doing?" I asked.

"Where did you get these pretty guns?" Katie asked, turning the gun in her paws and studying the craftsmanship.

I still didn't quite trust her regardless of what I had heard her talking about with Jeremy.

"Give me the gun," I said, walking toward her and motioning with my outstretched paw for her to hand it over.

"Why?" She asked. "I'm just looking."

I noticed she had pointed it at me. Whether it was a careless mistake or on purpose, I didn't know, but I wasn't taking any chances. I lunged her and grabbed it.

Luckily, the gun was on safety so it couldn't be fired, but as I tried to yank it away, Katie maintained her grip and went up with it, being forced off the bed and onto her feet. She then came at me with such great velocity that when she hit me, we both fell on the bed, and she landed on top of me. I rolled to the side, and she slid off me. I got on my knees on the bed and tried again to yank the gun away, but she had one hell of a grip, and she didn't let go.

"Come on," she said. "I just want to look at it!"

I thought I heard her cover up forced laughter.

"Just let go!" I shouted.

She pulled back, and I fell on top of her. My hips were between her thighs, and our groins made contact. I didn't take that into account in the heat of the moment.

"Give it to me!" Katie nearly moaned.

"Hey, what's going on in there?" I heard Tyson say. He opened the door and saw us. His mouth dropped open.

Yeah, you'd be thinking the same thing if you saw us like that. Me on top of Katie and both of us not wearing a single article of clothing.

Tyson threw his hands over his eyes and screamed in utter disgust as he ran away from the room. Katie and I turned our attention from the door to each other. Both of us stared at our groins, then back at each other's faces, and realized what had happened.

"Oh, Katie!" I said seductively.

She scoffed and threw me off her, finally letting go of the gun. I fell onto my back on the side of the bed and watched her go. I thought I saw a smile on her face as she went through the door to take her shower like she said she was going to do earlier. The way her tail swished back and forth as she walked showed some excitement. And when I thought about it, in retrospect, I guessed she meant for that to happen.

Still lying down, I put the gun into my drawer and put my paw behind my head and put a pleasured smile on my face.

I finally decided I would be going to Rio that day. I told Jeremy and Tyson about it and, at the same time, telling Tyson what had taken place earlier and apologizing for the confusion.

Jeremy called the private jet service that served him as a contract killer. I even asked Katie to come with me, saying I'd appreciate the help. She agreed, not without time to ponder, though. We said our good-byes to everyone and I told Ethan I would be back sometime.

At noon, we took our cars to a storage area, where Katie left her Beetle, and we took my Cutlass to the airport. It took forever to get there for the traffic in Los Angeles was nightmarish.

"Sexy car," Katie said to me when we left it at the garage at the airport.

Jeremy told us the plane would be waiting on the runway at one o'clock; Katie and I made it almost a half hour early. Luckily, we didn't have to go through any terminals or anything, so our flashing devices stayed in our pockets. We found the plane sitting a good distance from the airport building. The pilot greeted us as soon as we got to the plane. He was a sort of chubby African American guy with a bald head and a deep voice.

"You Chance?" he asked.

112

"Yeah, that's me," I answered.

"Great," he walked up to us and shook my paw, "I'm Mike, I'll be your pilot for today."

"It's nice to meet you," I said with a friendly grin.

"And this must be Katie," he said, smiling at her, then taking her paw and kissing it. Katie laughed, flattered by his manners.

"Jeremy told me you were coming," Mike said. "He also told me what to expect, regarding your appearance."

"What else did he tell you?" I asked.

"He told me not to call you a wolf," he said. "And to also not ask why you and Katie don't wear pants."

"Good," I said.

"One thing he also told me was that you would be carrying weapons," Mike said. "Would you like to put them in the cargo bay, or would you rather have them up with you?"

"Um . . ." I thought about it. "I'll just keep them with me." I finally answered.

"All right," Mike said, "that's honestly a wise choice."

He let us into the plane and allowed us to sit. We sat in two seats facing each other on either side of a small table. I set the bag with my weapons on the floor next to my seat.

"You chose the right flight," Mike said.

"So how long have you been working with Jeremy?" I asked.

"A couple years," Mike said, "up until he quit." He shrugged, lifting his arms and bringing them back down at his sides. "But I guess the killing business just wasn't for him. He only did it his rookie year, but I understand entirely though. I hear he's doing well as a stockbroker."

"You got that right," I said, remembering the apartment, and the Porsche.

Mike just nodded. "Well, enough of that. Charlie!" He called toward the cockpit.

113

"Yeah," came a voice from up front.

"Come meet the passengers."

"All right, give me a sec."

Mike just looked at us and raised his brow as a paper-thin Caucasian man with glasses emerged from the cockpit. "Charlie," Mike said, slapping a hand on his shoulder, "I'm sure you remember their names; Jeremy told us about them."

"Yes," Charlie said, extending his hand to me, which I grabbed and shook. "You're Chance—"

"Uh-huh," I said with a nod.

He turned his attention to Katie. "And you're . . ." he raised his hand and paused, trying to reach the back of his mind and grab the memory of her name. "You're Kat."

"Actually, they're foxes," Mike said. "Very big species difference."

"It's Katie," Katie said, shaking his hand.

"You think I didn't know that?" Charlie said to Mike.

"Well, you just called her a cat," Mike said.

"No, I said Kat," Charlie said. "Kat, K-A-T, the name."

"Well, I just assumed that because they are bigger than normal foxes, that you didn't know."

"What the hell made you think that?" Charlie responded in question. "You think I don't know a fox when I see one?"

"It's just that they're bigger," Mike repeated. "Hell, Chance is taller than I."

"What do you think I am, stu—"

"Guys," I berated, "knock it off. Let's just get going and quit bickering like Laurel and Hardy, all right?"

"Got it," they said in unison, giving me a thumbs-up.

They both went to the cockpit, bickering quietly among themselves as if I couldn't hear them, but I could. Perfectly. I wasn't born with those large, pointed ears for nothing.

I just palmed my face and sighed, as if embarrassed. Katie got up from her seat and walked to the cockpit. I could hear her whisper to the pilots and close the cockpit door. She came back and sat in her seat.

"Thanks, Katie," I said.

"Mm-hmm," was her only response.

We took off after about a half hour. The sun was riding high in the sky, well, at least as high as it would get, since it was winter. As I stared at the spread-out clouds blowing by, the thought of when Katie and I were fighting over the gun popped back into my head. I thought I would inquire her as to what her intentions were at that time.

"So," I broke the silence, with the exception of the sound of the plane's engines. "I was just wondering . . ." I looked at her.

"About what?" she asked.

"Earlier today," I said, "when we were fighting over the gun."

"I just wanted to look at it," she said, not refusing eye contact.

"Really?" I said.

She seemed to sense the sarcasm in my voice.

"I did!" she said.

"I don't think it was an accident when you pulled me on top of you either," I added.

"Of course it was." She sounded a little more frantic. "Why would I do that intentionally?"

"Because you've still got the hots for me," I said. "Come on, admit it, you like me."

"Mm-mm." She shook her head and covered her eyes with her paw.

"Katie," I said, hunching over to see her face. "C'mon, Katie."

"Stop it, Chance," she nearly scolded.

"Oh, come on," I said, reaching over to pinch her cheek. "Don't be so square. I like your body curvy."

She slapped my paw as it was getting near her face. I chuckled playfully, then sighed. More silence. I figured I would push her and expose what she was hiding. I knew she was hiding something. I knew that deep inside she still liked me. I was going to get it out of her, verbally skinning her and disemboweling her.

"So," I started again, "was it true?" I paused. "What you said to Jeremy?"

"What did I say to Jeremy?" she asked with her paw still hiding her eyes from view.

"That you were going to tell me that you were quitting the CIA for me?"

"You were eavesdropping on us?" She slapped her paw on the table and shot me a cold glare.

"Wasn't dropping any eaves," I said, "just thought I would listen."

"Good lord," she whispered, putting her paw on her forehead and shaking her head. "Yes, it was true."

"Well, why didn't you tell me?" I asked.

"You walked away without hearing me out!" she scolded.

"Well, you never told me you were in the CIA to begin with," I said. "Jack had to tell me!"

"Well—" She stopped herself. *Touché.*

I thought I had accomplished something that was unfathomably impossible, and that was to win an argument with a woman.

"Would you still quit?" I asked, carrying the conversation further.

"Maybe," Katie said. "It depends."

"On what?" I asked.

"You," she said, "and me, I guess."

She looked out the window at the clouds rolling by. I just stared at her and sighed. *god, she's so hot.*

I dozed off after a while with my head resting on the table, and I awoke at Mike's voice coming over the radio.

"Good afternoon, passengers, this is your captain speaking, we've arrived at our destination and will be landing shortly. Please fasten your seat belts as we begin our descent." He began beatboxing into the microphone, and I heard a slap.

"Why you—" The last part was cut out. Those two. Laurel and Hardy; swear to god.

I sat up and wiped the drool off my mouth onto the sleeve of my uniform and looked out the window to see Rio below. Such a beautiful city. I reached across the table and shook Katie gently, who also had her head rested on the table in a state of slumber. She looked up at me, eyes almost half closed in fatigue.

"We're here," I said. "Better get your seat belt on.

We landed not long after. We said good-bye and thank you to the pilots, and Mike handed me his card and told me to call if I needed anything. I was getting benefits since I had befriended Jeremy. I was so glad I got to know that guy.

It was just Katie and me from that point on, and we needed to find a place to stay. I was limited on cash so I had to find a cheap place. We found one eventually, with only one room open. Katie suggested we combine our money to pay rent. I figured that was best since we were sharing the same room. When we got to our room, I dropped my weapons bag and looked around the room. It was hideous. The walls and ceiling were falling apart, rotten, chipped, and fading paint, holes in the wall, and the room reeked of the stale smell of rotten wood. I was utterly surprised I didn't see roaches crawling all over the floor and walls.

The one-person bed had a rusty frame and squeaky springs. The mattress was torn in multiple places, with some yellow stains here and there. The only nice things in the room were the radiator, which looked like it had just been replaced, and the blanket that lay folded at the foot of the bed. Katie began to unfold the blanket and spread it across the bed.

"I can sleep on the floor," I said. "It's all right."

"No," she said, "you can come sleep on the bed with me."

"It's only one person," I said.

"There's only one blanket," Katie replied.

I looked at her, and she had her brow raised, and she smiled slightly.

"So you do like me," I said.

"Cut it out or you'll sleep on the floor," Katie said.

"Okay," I said, putting my paws up in surrender.

"So where is this truck?" Katie said. "You better not have lied to me as another trick to save your ass."

"Lance said it would be here," I said, going over to the small window and looking out at the metro area. "He didn't say when."

"How will we recognize it?" Katie asked.

"It's being driven by Lance's men," I said. "They'll most likely be wearing CIA uniforms."

"But they would be going under cover, I'm sure," Katie added.

"Hmm," I tried to reach back into my memory of the truck that was used to deliver the bomb back in 1968. It was black. A military five-ton, painted black, with a metal canopy instead of a canvas one, but what made it stand out was an American flag on the side by the door that had an LD written in the blue rectangle rather than fifty stars. Lance Division.

Lance had his own division in the CIA, those who did the dirty work. The animals. The mutants, etc. Those trucks were specialized to carry those bombs, and the metal they were made of was thick, reinforced. It could resist an RPG straight on the broad side. The only nonreinforced parts of those trucks were the glass on either door, for the need of a quick escape.

But as I thought about this, I realized what we would need to look for. The LD American flag by the door. That would settle it. I gave Katie a detailed description of the trucks and told her about the LD flag.

"Rio's a big city," Katie said.

"So where should we start?" I asked.

10

We had spent a few days in Rio, for it was now December fifth. We bought a motorcycle and searched the whole city. Instead of using the flashing devices, we just convinced the locals that we were people in costumes and that it was for promoting a business that was opening soon. It seemed to work.

Another language I was taught was Portuguese, but Katie never learned the language. She spoke more Asian languages, including Arabic. The only Asian languages I knew were Chinese and Japanese. I was taught more European languages, including Russian and even Gaelic, since European languages such as French, Spanish, and Portuguese were spoken in more than one continent, such as South America and some of Africa, but anyway.

We searched the city for days with no luck. Katie and I thought we saw a black five-ton at one point, and before we could turn around, it was gone.

Now we were on the roof of a small building, searching with binoculars for the truck.

"Any luck?" I asked.

"No," Katie answered. She was wearing her brown leather jacket and looking through another pair of binoculars.

"Well, keep searching," I said, "it's got to be here somewhere."

"You know," Katie said, "at first I thought all this was kind of a trick. But now here we are, and I realize you're not screwing around."

"Why would I lie?" I asked.

"I don't know," Katie said, "maybe out of self-preserving selfishness or winning me over."

"Well," I said, "on the side, one of those could be right."

"Which one?" Katie asked.

"We'll find out," I responded.

Silence.

"Tell me, Chance," Katie said. "Do you love me?"

I remembered that question. London, right before Jack found us. When I smiled, put my arm around her and gave her a kiss on the cheek. "Yes, I do."

And then when she said, "Then why don't you come with me?" I remembered it so clearly.

"Yes, I do," I answered, just like that day in London. Except I was still looking through my binoculars.

"Seriously," Katie said, grabbing me by the shoulder and yanking my eyes from the binoculars so our eyes could meet. "Do you love me, Chance?"

She stared at me with those sapphire eyes, like that day in Vietnam when I took a bullet in the thigh, and she told me to look into them, then she gave me a kiss, a long, passionate kiss. When we realized for the first time that we were meant for each other. My heart started to beat faster, because that was just what passion did.

"You bet I do," I said

"Then maybe you should show it," she said.

She began to lean in for a kiss when out of the corner of my eye, I saw a glint.

"Wait!" I said, raising the binoculars back to my eyes, interrupting her.

It was a black truck. A military five-ton with a shiny metal canopy, which caught the sunlight and blindingly reflected it in my direction. It was pulling up to another truck just like it, parked in a heavily shaded area. Men in black directed the truck as more carried a box out of the stationary one.

They were cloning. A tactic used in the black ops fields of the CIA where a truck carrying classified cargo would trade off its load with an identical one, but to be sure it was the right one, I looked at the door of the truck. As a fox, I had fairly keen eyesight, and I spotted the flag and made out the LD in the blue rectangle where the stars would be.

"Hey, I found it," I said. It was as if by the grace of god.

"Where?" Katie asked.

"Right over there," I said, pointing and handing her the binoculars, "at that glint of sunlight."

She looked through the binoculars.

"Do you see it?" I asked.

"Yeah," she said, "I see it."

"They're cloning," I said. "There's two of them. We need to get there and stop them before they get away. See, that box those guys are carrying is the bomb."

I recognized the box because I had my paws on one exactly like it in 1968. I left it in that building in Kiev for the truck to clone.

"The problem is getting in there," Katie said. "There's armed men surrounding the place."

"I've got an idea," I said.

I stood by an alleyway across the street from one of the armed guards, having split up with Katie, and she was waiting in a car somewhere down the street. My job was to distract the guard to the point where he would approach me. Katie would know her cue.

Her original idea was for her to distract the guar. She would act all sexy and everything, then yell, "Don't you wanna take this costume off and see what's under?" However, I told her that wouldn't work. The guys of Lance Division couldn't be distracted no matter how sexy the person approaching them was, but they would immediately respond to hostility, which was why I was doing the job instead, and because Lance Division was after me, and they would most likely attack if they saw me anyway.

I could picture in my mind Lance giving a detailed description of me: "He stands at about six feet tall, has a long nose, orange fur all over his body, white fur on his front side that runs from his chin to his groin and brown fur on his feet and hands, doesn't wear pants, only a black ASIS uniform shirt, and you should probably know he's a fox."

He may have also mentioned Katie. "Six feet tall, long nose, lighter orange fur, white fur from chin to groin, light brown fur on feet and hands, doesn't wear pants, only a brown leather jacket with an American flag patch of the same material on her right shoulder, also a fox."

Katie gave me her pocket mirror to flash in their face, which I took out and opened. I looked up toward the sun then began moving the mirror so I could gain a visual of where the light was. As soon as I spotted it, I slowly tilted the mirror up towards the guard's face. As soon as the light hit his eyes, he casually turned his head away, most likely thinking it was because of a passerby of some kind.

I shined it into his eyes again. This time he looked in my direction and spotted me, and I just waved my paw at him.

I saw him say something in the radio, and he began walking toward me. Exactly what I wanted. He aimed the gun at me and ventured onto the road, and that was when I heard tires screech and a red car came speeding toward him. The car screeched to a halt, but not without clipping the guard. He flew back about a yard and landed on the pavement. He groaned in pain as he grabbed his side. Katie stepped out of the car.

"Oh my god," she said, running over to him, "are you all right?"

"Yeah I just—" He looked at her. "Hey!"

She used her flashing device, which was a little more modernized than mine, flashing it into his eyes then punching him hard in the face. He fell unconscious on the ground. I ran over to Katie.

"Nice one," I said, handing over her mirror, which she took and put in her pocket.

"So what now?" she asked.

"Now," I said, pulling a gas grenade off his belt, "we smoke them out."

She picked up the rifle and cocked the action.

I pulled the pin on the gas grenade and held down the safety lever. We made our way into the alleyways and stopped as soon as we caught sight of the trucks. It had been a while since we spotted them from on top of the building, and they had parked next to each other. Now we couldn't tell which one had the bomb and which one didn't, but as soon as we smoked them out we would have time to figure that part out.

There were some guys talking off to the side. I spotted Lance talking with them. He was probably there because he knew I would be there as well, and he wasn't wrong.

"Crap," Katie whispered, "which one is it?"

"We'll have time to find out once these guys clear out," I said.

I released my grip on the safety lever, held the grenade for about three seconds, and chucked it all the way to the trucks. The grenade went off, releasing the yellow gas into the air.

I heard one shout, and they all scattered, tripping over one other, bumping into one other, but they didn't leave. They just piled into the trucks, and some escort cars with the LD flag painted by their doors too.

"Dammit!" I yelled as I watched Lance get into one of the escort cars. They all drove out of there as if they knew exactly what was going on.

"C'mon, Katie," I said, grabbing her paw and running after the trucks that had just begun to leave.

We ran to a certain point where the trucks split up at a T-intersection.

"Katie," I said, "follow that truck!" I pointed to the one that went left. "I'll take care of this one!"

"I'm on it," Katie said. She ran over to a rack with parked motorcycles, and she picked out a red dirt bike. She pulled open a panel, messed with the wires, then started it, driving off as soon as it did.

I did the same with a blue motorcycle, and I took off after the truck that went right. I had the bike at full throttle by the time I reached the truck. My guess was that the bomb was on that one because both escort cars drove along with it. They were all hauling ass, way above the speed limit, about fifty miles per hour.

One of the guys in the car saw me coming, leaned out the window with his rifle, and opened up on me.

I maneuvered the bike to a safer spot in front of the car and behind the truck. By this time, we reached the Favela, a large shantytown at the outskirts of Rio's metro area. I hoped the people were aware of the cars, the truck, and the motorcycle barreling down the narrow streets.

Due to the narrowness of the road, the cars positioned themselves at the front and rear of the truck, and I was stuck at the rear with one of the cars a few hundred feet behind me. I could hear the lead car smashing through fragile structures, selling canopies, other stuff. Not much I could do about it, though.

Bullets pinged off the backside of the truck as the guy in the passenger's seat of the car behind me fired. I had to stay with the truck; it most likely had the bomb on board, and I couldn't risk losing it. I moved over to the right side of it. The passenger of the truck leaned out and began firing at me with his pistol.

"Jeez," I muttered as I hit the brake, slowing down behind the truck and maneuvered to the other side. The guy in the escort car was still firing at me, and I had no cover, so I jumped from the motorcycle which lost control and rolled along the road and eventually stopped.

I grabbed onto the truck and climbed to the top of the canopy and lay there. Now I could stay with the truck and maintain cover. I was confident in my newfound spot until I caught the guy from the passenger seat climbing on the top to greet me. I didn't even think to grab one of my pistols, which I had on the belt I put around my waist. My first instinct was to hop onto my feet, for some reason.

As soon as the guy got on top of the truck, he pulled a knife, holding it upside down, and came at me with it. The first move he made was a stab, but I grabbed his hand with my left paw and his elbow with my right and shoved it away. He swung his arm back, and I ducked out of the way of the knife. My turn.

I kicked his leg and attempted a punch, but he moved his arm in the way, and I hit his forearm.

He began swinging his arm carrying the knife around wildly, and I blocked and dodged the best I could. I accidently stepped back and stumbled over the side. I almost lost balance, but I somehow stepped back onto the truck and regained my balance. Only to have the guy swing his knife at me again, shaving off some of the fur on my cheek.

"Whoa!" I exclaimed.

He grabbed me by the neck, threw me down on my back, and pinned me on the canopy.

"End of the line!" he said. Such a common, overused phrase for one about to take someone out.

"I don't think so!" I said.

I kicked him in the nuts and used my legs to throw him over me. He went over the back of the truck and tumbled onto the road.

"Ta-ta!" I shouted as I stood on the canopy.

Another guy climbed onto the truck from the ladder on the side that I had climbed up. He most likely jumped on from one of the escort cars. He was bigger than the last guy, yet I still didn't think to pull one of my guns on him.

He swept his arm at my legs as he climbed, and I fell onto my back again. He then got on top of the canopy, grabbed me by the ankles, and threw me off the back of the truck.

"Ah!" I exclaimed in panic as I saw the pavement below.

I shielded my face, ready for impact when something broke my fall. I looked up and saw the driver and the passenger of the escort car right in front of me through the windshield.

The passenger aimed his rifle at me, and this time I pulled out both of my pistols. I stood on the hood and fired three shots through the windshield into the passenger then moved sideways along the hood of the car and fired four more shots through the windshield into the driver.

The driver was knocked back in his seat, and his foot hit the accelerator, then the car veered off toward a large cement roadblock on the side of the road, which the truck had circumvented. I hopped over the roof and ran to the rear of the car and put the guns back into their holsters.

As soon as the car crashed, I was launched in the air at about ninety miles an hour toward the truck, and the car flew through the air, over the cement block, and landed on the ground, crumbling on impact.

I drew one of my pistols and emptied the clip on the guy on top of the truck, and he tumbled over the side, hitting the wall of a small building right next to the narrow street on his way.

I tried to grab the back of the truck, but the edge of the canopy was too smooth and too rounded, and the fur and pads on my paws didn't help any, and I slipped and fell over the back of the truck. I rolled on the pavement. Pain gripped my whole body when I finally came to a stop.

I struggled onto my feet. I was dizzy, my uniform had a big tear on my right shoulder, where blood leaked out from a deep cut. One of my guns was still intact and strapped in its holster but gave me a Charlie-horse in the process of tumbling along the pavement. The other lay on the ground in front of me, scratched and slightly chipped from the impact with the pavement. I picked it up and began to run after the truck, regardless of how hopeless it was to catch up with it on foot.

Suddenly, my ear flicked toward the sound of an approaching motor vehicle. I turned around to see Katie on the red dirt bike coming at me. She hit the brake and skidded to a halt, and I quickly jumped on the bike behind her.

"Hold on!" she said. I moved her tail out of the way then wrapped my arms around her slim waist, and she gunned the engine.

"Whoa!" I exclaimed as she nearly popped a wheelie in the process.

"I take it you had no luck with the other truck!" I shouted over the loud buzz of the dirt bike engine.

"It didn't even have the bomb on it!" Katie shouted back. "That leaves us with this one!"

She sped through the streets. People moved out of the way of the bike, and looked at us funny as we passed them.

"Where's the truck?" Katie asked.

"I don't know," I said. "I couldn't have been that far behind!"

"You know, it sure is nice to be held by you like this again!" Katie commented, taking notice that I had my arms around her waist with my whole front side pressed to her backside. I just chuckled.

"Let's just focus on the task at hand, honey," I replied.

We drove for a few minutes with no visual on the truck until we spotted it, down the hill from where we were. Katie drifted the bike and jumped over a ledge, a risky move, and she didn't even warn me. I yelled as we fell until we landed with such great force that I hit my nuts on the seat.

"Ah," I yelled, "my balls!"

"Sorry," was all Katie said. Something was strange about the truck. Well, really not with the truck, but the escort car. It followed the truck, when it was in front before.

Katie pulled out her stolen rifle.

"You drive," she said, letting go of the handle bars, which I grabbed, reaching around her body. "Get me to the driver's side window!"

I twisted the accelerator, and we flew toward the truck at full speed. We passed the car, and I slowed the bike as we reached the driver's window.

Katie fired a few bursts into the window, and I heard the driver let out a death scream. I was unaware that a man with an RPG was aiming at us from over the roof of the truck until the vehicle lost control and plowed through one of the sheet metal houses and flipped onto its side.

We lost the escort car, it seemed, and Katie brought the bike to a stop. I was the first one to hop off, and Katie set the bike on the ground. We both approached the truck slowly.

"Time to finish this," I said. I went to the rear of the truck and got to the number pad that unlocked the door. I knew the code, for like I said before, I've worked with these trucks.

I typed in the six-digit code, and the door opened slowly. I grabbed it, hastened the opening, and looked inside. Nothing.

"Dammit!" I yelled, hitting the metal canopy. "They cloned again," I said.

"What do you mean?" Katie asked.

"Before, the car was in front of the truck," I said, "I knew there was something wrong with the car being behind the truck."

"So where's the bomb?" Katie asked.

"You're too late," I heard someone say. I walked over to the cab, and the driver was looking at me straight in the eyes. "It's already at the airport being loaded onto a plane. I just got confirmation."

"Katie," I said as we walked to the road where the stolen dirt bike was, "go back to the hotel. I'll be there in a bit, and we'll go to the airport."

"You should probably take this," Katie said as she unzipped her jacket and pulled out a hand-held radio.

I took it and put it in my pocket.

"All right, now go. I'll be there in a bit, got it?"

"Got it." Katie gave me a hug.

I put my arms around her, surprised at that gesture. I looked around and saw the escort car coming. I let go of Katie and ran over to the cab of the truck, grabbing the RPG that the now dead passenger had. I made sure the grenade was locked in place on the launcher as I walked back to the street. The car was speeding toward us.

"Go!" I told Katie, who was already on the bike.

She looked at me and gave the bike a start then hit the throttle and was off. I looked back at the car speeding toward me, and I aimed the RPG right at it. I locked the car in the sights, and as soon as it was in range, I pulled the trigger. The grenade rocketed from the launcher and flew the whole thirty feet to the very front end of the car.

The whole front end exploded on impact and the car spun out of control, but it was headed straight for me, and I stepped aside and moved out of the way as the burning vehicle barely missed me. It hit a cement block on the side of the road and was stopped instantly. I figured that was the car Lance got into, and I walked over to it, dropping the launcher and pulling out one of my pistols. I went to the driver's side window and thrust my elbow through it, and it shattered to pieces, and there was a fairly young man sitting in the driver's seat.

"Chance," I heard Katie say over the radio, "I'm at the hotel."

I took the radio out of my pocket and pressed the speak button.

"All right," I said, "be there in a few."

Where I was wasn't very far from the hotel, roughly less than a mile or so.

I turned my attention back to the car and leaned down to peer into the passenger seat. I found John Lance in the passenger seat, with a little blood trickling down his forehead.

"You know why I pulled you over?" I asked almost jokingly.

"So," John said, "we meet again, and you're killing. Just like I said."

"Where's the bomb?" I asked.

"What are you going to do," John asked, "kill me? Then you'll definitely never find out."

"Death is the easy way out," I said. "It's not about the destination. It's the journey."

I cocked the hammer back on the pistol.

"You've already tortured me," he said, referring to when I *accidentally* killed his family.

"And it won't be the last time," I said, with a bit of unintentional sadism, "unless you tell me where the damn plane is."

He swallowed, then sighed.

"I already told you before," he said, "it's headed to Los Angeles."

"Where?" I asked.

"In the most unlikely place," John said, facing forward in his seat. "That's all I'll tell you."

I was getting mad at this guy. I fired three shots right by Lance's head.

"And by the way," I said, "stop sending guys after me. It's just wasting my time and yours."

"No problem," John said, "the Soviets already have that part cut out for me."

"What?" I questioned his statement.

"They're here right now," John said. "Thanks for attracting attention."

I caught him looking in the rearview mirror. I looked in the driver's side one and saw men in the black uniforms of the Soviet Counter Intelligence coming.

I cursed and stepped away from the car. The Soviets indeed were closer than they appeared in the mirror. One of them grabbed me by the shoulder.

"You're coming with me," he said.

I elbowed his nose instantaneously then his stomach. I spun around and punched another guy trying to grab me from behind. Another came at me, and I grabbed his gun and hit him in the face with it, knocking him to the ground. I still held the gun and pointed it at the four remaining guys. I began to step backward, but they followed my every move, keeping their guns trained on me, then I heard the radio crackle.

"Chance!" Katie yelled in agony. "Help me! The Soviets are—" She was cut off.

I fired some wild shots at the guys and they all ducked, giving me a chance to run to a nearby alley, climb up the side and onto the roof of one of the sheet metal shacks. I strapped the gun over my shoulder and took off running toward the hotel.

I had had a little instruction on parkour, and I used what training I had to run and jump on the rooftops of these structures. It really helped to get to the apartment fast.

I jumped up, grabbed onto the edge of the roof on the second floor of one structure, and quickly hoisted myself up, then I jumped down and somersaulted on landing. I spotted the hotel not much farther away, and I broke out to a full sprint, because the room Katie and I were staying in overlooked a pretty wide road, and if I even dreamed of making it, I would have to give it all I got.

I hurdled over a block and maintained my sprint. As I reached the edge across from the hotel, I put all the strength I had into my legs. I reached the edge and jumped, then crashed through the window and sprawled out on the floor.

"Well hello, Chance!" Nikolai said. He had his claws against Katie's neck and she breathed hard, panicking. I sat up, unstrapped the gun I had over my shoulder, and aimed it at his head.

"Let her go!" I said.

He didn't comply to my request. I fired, and he ducked, letting go of Katie. She fell onto the floor. I fired a few more shots at Nikolai, and the gun clicked. Empty.

I got up and approached Nikolai, who swiped at me and knocked the gun out of my paws. He then kicked me in the back of the leg, and I fell onto my back on the floor. He hit me in the chest twice and prepared for another blow to the face when I swept my legs at his, knocking him to the floor. I rolled on top of him and tried to pin him down like a wrestler, but of course, any human-sized creature isn't going to do much with the world's biggest cat.

He got up and wrapped his arm around my neck. I gagged as he did so. He stood up, and my feet weren't even touching the floor.

I brought my leg up all the way to my shoulder and kneed him in the face then elbowed him, and he dropped me. I then turned around upon hitting the floor and blocked a strike with my left paw and another with my right. I made a strike at him, and he blocked it with his forearm. I made another strike, and he blocked that one too. He then kicked me, and I flew back, landing on my back on the floor.

I got up as he approached me and ducked under his arm, which he swung at me and I grabbed it by the wrist and elbow, then kicked him in the back of the leg. He was forced onto one knee. I struck his face hard, and he fell to the floor. I tried to stomp his head in, but he rolled out of the way, rapidly getting back up onto his feet.

I swung my arms at him and he managed to block or dodge every blow. He returned, and I managed to block and dodge all his blows, until he hit me in the mouth. He tried to kick me but I blocked that with my leg. I then swung both arms at him. The first blow hit him on the jaw, but he blocked the second with his paw. I was backed into the small bathroom, and he made a swing at me. I ducked then got back up, grabbing his arm and hitting it against the doorframe.

He exclaimed loudly and made a strike toward me, and I locked his arm in mine. I pushed him away from the door and was out of the bathroom and back in the bedroom. He managed to pick me up with his locked arm and throw me onto the old bed. As soon as I landed on the mattress, he took out his claws with an angry scowl. He was pissed now.

"Dodge this," he said. Then all of a sudden, Katie grabbed him from behind. She hit him hard in the back and pulled him by the shoulder. He elbowed her in the stomach hard, and she fell to the floor with a groan of pain.

I was up and out of the bed by this time, ready to face Nikolai again. We were both on opposite sides of the bed. I moved to one side, and he followed. I moved to the other. He followed again.

I quickly bent down, picked up the bed by the frame, and flipped it on its side at him. He tried to shield his face from it as it hit him. He shoved the bed back, and it fell back to its regular position, and I quickly jumped onto the mattress and bounced off it, flipping over Nikolai's head. As soon as I landed, I turned around to block another blow with my arm.

This was hopeless if I didn't have a weapon. He was so much bigger than I and stronger. I blocked another blow with my arm then spun around and blocked another. He then kicked me, and I fell back onto my ass on the floor. I began frantically looking around the room for something I could use as a weapon.

A bed knob? No, sure it could screw off the bed frame, but how would I use it to my advantage? Pipe from the radiator? How would I get it off? Pen?

I decided to make a grab for the pen on the dresser, which I was right next to. I grabbed it, took the cap off, and made a jab at Nikolai's paw as he reached for me. He barely pulled his paw away from it, and I got onto my feet.

"Let's end this," I said.

"End it for you!" Nikolai said.

I attempted multiple stabs at Nikolai, but he blocked and dodged every one. He grabbed my arm by the wrist and elbowed me between the eyes. I fell backward onto the floor, my forehead throbbing in pain.

He made an attempt to hit me with his fist, but I swung both of my legs at him. One swiped his arm away and the other hit him in the cheek as he was knocked forward from the first blow. I used my legs to throw my weight and did a kip-up onto my feet. Nikolai then made another swipe at me but I knocked his paw onto the dresser, then stabbed it deep with the pen.

He roared and hit me so hard that I flew to the wall on the opposite side of the room.

"That's it," he said, ripping the bloody pen out of his paw and tossing it aside. "No more games."

He drew his pistol and fired. The bullet went into my right shoulder, near the chest.

I yelled as I felt the pain of the bullet tearing through the flesh of my shoulder and almost lodging itself in the bone. Nikolai kept his gun trained on me, ready to fire another round.

All of a sudden, Katie came out of nowhere and kicked him in the face. He fell back toward the window, and Katie roundhouse kicked him in the gut, and he fell backward, shattering the glass and tumbling out. I heard a crash and a car alarm, so I got onto my feet, and went to the window next to Katie and looked down.

Nikolai was lying on a car, which he had flattened the whole top half of as he landed on it. He moaned and groaned in pain.

"We should probably find a new place to stay," Katie said.

"No," I said, "we've gotta get out of here. That bomb is already on the plane."

"Chance," Katie said, "you've been shot. We'll just spend the night and get there tomorrow."

"All right," I sighed.

We found another hotel in the metro, a little fancier and cleaner than the other one. Katie had turned the TV on to keep me distracted from the pain while she searched for some first aid stuff. The wound was aching up a storm, and I was losing it. I began shaking violently, breathing hard. I tried to keep my attention on the Portuguese-translated comedy show on the TV, but the bullet wound was too much. The bone in my shoulder ached so badly, for that was where the bullet stopped. Katie came out of the bathroom.

"Nothing in there," she said. "I'm going to have to ask the lady in the lobby."

"Okay." I winced.

Katie looked at me and left the room. Lucky for her the lady in the lobby spoke some English. Pretty damn good English. That was how Katie managed to get us a room in the first place.

I sat there, shaking from the pain in my shoulder. I tended to lose it under extreme amounts of pain, just like that time when I took a bullet in the thigh in Vietnam. I all of a sudden started laughing deliriously at the thought that in the multiple times I got injured in Vietnam, I never got one purple heart. It helped me calm down a little; it took my mind off the aching, stinging pain, and I stopped shaking. I took some deep breaths, filling my lungs with the fresh tropical air coming in through the open window.

"Keep your cool, Chance," I said to myself. "Stay calm, mate."

I must have waited a good five minutes before Katie came back in with some first aid equipment, and judging by the size of the box, I'd say she was all set. She turned off the TV and set the box down on the side table next to the bed, then opened it.

"All right, Chance," she said as she took of her jacket rummaged through the first aid kit. "I know it's going to hurt, but I'm going to need you to take off the uniform."

"All right," I groaned. I reached for the zipper, but my arm was restricted by the pain. My arm dropped to my side, and I groaned again. "Gah!"

Katie came over to the bed and sat at my left side.

"Here," she said. She grabbed the zipper and pulled it down. She held my left sleeve as I pulled my arm through then she pulled the whole uniform down to get my right arm through the sleeve without me having to move it. I didn't have my black T-shirt on because I didn't want to add any extra clothing with South America's extreme heat and humidity.

Blood had stained the white fur on my chest and made a dark spot on the uniform, which Katie took and tossed aside, then unstrapped my belt with the pistols and set that aside as well. She then grabbed a tool that was something like a pair of large tweezers.

"All right, just try not to move," she said. "This is going to hurt. Just hang tight, like you did when I pulled that bullet out of your leg."

My jaw dropped, and I looked at her, surprised.

"You still remember that?" I asked.

"How could I forget?" Katie asked as she dug into my wound with the tool. "That's when we first fell for each other."

"Oh, Katie—Ow!" I exclaimed as she yanked the bullet out. Pretty sizable, but not too big. It had made my wound so large because it had mushroomed for lethal effectiveness.

"Sorry," she said.

"I remember," I said as she put the tool away and quickly pressed some gauze on my shoulder so blood wouldn't get everywhere. "When I was shaking, in shock, and you told me to look into your eyes."

She gave me a light smile.

"I remember looking into those beautiful, phenomenal sapphire-blue eyes. I was hypnotized," I continued.

She got an anti-bacterial wipe, pulled the gauze off my wound, and began to clean it.

"I remember thinking about your eyes," she said, "and I've gotta say, I like that shade of brown. It reminds me of agate, sort of."

"The rock?" I asked.

"Mm-hmm." Katie finished disinfecting the wound and grabbed a roll of gauze.

"Lift your arm," she said.

I complied, and she wrapped the gauze around my arm, under my armpit, and over my shoulder.

"Katie," I asked for her attention, "do you still love me?"

"Why do you ask?" Katie asked.

"I just wanna know," I said, "because since I left you, I've been kicking myself in the ass over it. I couldn't let go of the burden of regret that kept me down because . . . I love you."

She looked at me, surprised.

"Really?" she asked.

"More than anything," I said, "even life itself. But tell me, do you love me?"

She put on some medical tape and put the roll away, closing the box on the side table.

"Yes," she said, "I do."

"Then say it," I said.

"No," Katie said. I was almost disappointed until Katie continued, "I'll show it."

She grabbed me by the chain of my dog tags, pulled me to her, and our lips made contact. She had her eyes closed, but mine were wide open. I couldn't believe it; it was like being in heaven. I was shocked just as much as the first time we ever kissed. My heart felt so warm as it beat with passion inside my chest. I wrapped my arms around her and fell on my back onto the bed. We were still kissing. She then broke the kiss.

"And you know something else?" she said. "What happened at Tyson's place, with the gun and everything?"

"Yeah?" I said, remembering when we fought over the pistol, and she pulled me on top of her into a position where Tyson thought we were having intercourse in the guest room.

"That was sort of intentional," she said. "I knew I could break you."

"Oh, Katie," I said, pulling her down and resuming our long, passionate kiss session. I rolled over with her on top of me, and we then lay on our sides, facing each other and still kissing. I pulled the covers over our bodies and reached over to turn off the light.

I awoke the next morning with my arms wrapped around Katie's waist, her backside pressed against me. We cuddled the rest of the night after our moment of making out for a long time, and that was how we fell asleep. I was lying on my shot arm, which I didn't take into account because I couldn't feel any pain anymore. I turned and rested on my back, which woke Katie.

"You okay?" she asked sleepily.

"Of course, babe." I gave her a kiss on the neck. "Just getting comfortable."

She turned over and looked at me.

"Weren't you already comfortable?" she asked, looking into my eyes.

"Of course," I said. "It's just that I get restless after a bit. You understand, right?"

As a nurse, I assumed she would understand; every living thing got restless after being in one position for a long time, and it was a natural habit for them to move to find comfort.

"Sure, honey," she answered, shifting closer. She rested her head on my chest, and I put my arm around her and stroked her back.

"When should we head out?" I asked.

"It's probably best that you wait," Katie said. "That bullet wound should close up soon."

"All right," I said. "But we can't stick around for too much longer."

"I know," Katie said, getting up and walking to the bathroom. "Now, let's get you cleaned up, get all that blood out of your fur."

We had just finished showering, and when Katie cleaned around my wound, it was a painful and seemingly gruelingly long process, but the huge bloodstain was finally gone.

"Is there a towel hanging there, Chance?" she asked. I peered around the curtain and found a neatly folded towel on the rack by the shower.

"Yup." I nodded.

She slipped by me and stepped out of the shower, grabbing the towel and drying off. I stepped out after her. She turned around and threw the towel around my neck, yanking me toward her. I stumbled forward into an embrace. My nose was less than an inch from Katie's, and I looked into her eyes.

I couldn't hold myself back anymore, and I kissed her. We kissed passionately for about thirty seconds, then Katie collapsed backwards onto the floor. We were both overcome by a powerful feeling of passion that had led us well past the point of no return.

Finally, I just couldn't take it anymore, the feeling was so strong. My heart was pounding in my chest and I began to feel a great surge of energy throughout my body. I put my left arm under her legs and my right around her shoulders, and I stood, carrying her. We interrupted our kiss for the journey to the bed. I set her down on the bed, got onto the bed, then she pulled me down with her.

After engaging in relations, Katie and I were sitting on the bed, cuddling with each other. My shoulder still hurt, but it felt a helluva lot better than it did moments ago.

"Did you ever call Mike and Charlie?" I asked.

"Yeah, just to make sure," Katie said, "but they're still here. They've been 'vacationing.'" She made quote signs with her fingers.

"Hmm," I said.

"They're just waiting for us to get back to them," Katie added.

"All right," I said, "good. Should we head out this afternoon?"

"That's fine," Katie said.

"Okay, try calling them again to make sure," I said, getting out of the bed and grabbing my uniform from the side of the bed and putting it on. "I'll grab some lunch for us and we'll head out later. I'm starving to death."

Katie chuckled.

"Yeah, I'm hungry too," she said.

"Love you, babe," I said leaning onto the bed, and we exchanged a kiss. "I'll be back in a bit. Don't go anywhere."

"Trust me," Katie said, "I'll be waiting here for you."

"Okay then, I'll see you later," I said. I exited the room and made my way down the hall.

I felt so good. I didn't know whether it was from what we had done earlier or the passionate love I felt for Katie. Either way, I felt great. I seemed to have the whole world in the palm of my paw. I just wanted to start singing.

I had quickly run to the street market, where I grabbed some exotic fruits and vegetables and some beef and noodles for a special pasta dish I had just planned out. The fruits were more of just a side dish. I made sure to use my flashing device on everyone I came across.

Now this particular street market was in the Favela, which was run by drug lords. I would occasionally see a man carrying either one or multiple guns. As I began to leave, one of these armed men stopped me.

"Hey," he said in his native tongue, "what's with the costume?

"It's not a costume," I said.

"Really?" he said. "Well, what are you, may I ask?"

I began thinking, *Really, you don't know a fox when you see one?* Then I remembered. He either didn't think of me as a fox because I was almost six feet tall and standing on two legs, or this was Brazil, where one wouldn't find any red foxes.

"Well, I'm a fox," I answered.

"Oh." The guy just nodded and turned away. I could hear him tell another guy that I was a fox, whom I guessed was really the one who wanted to know. He was significantly younger than the guy who approached me and probably more curious. Just not willing to ask.

I finished shopping and took our rented motorcycle back to the place we got it from and paid for it, which was pretty expensive since we had it for well over a week. I was glad Mike and Charlie were the ones taking us to and fro, free of charge.

I got back to the hotel with my load and went upstairs to mine and Katie's room. I knocked on the door.

"Who is it?" I heard Katie ask.

"It's me, darling," I said.

She unlocked and opened the door.

"Hey, honey," she greeted. We gave each other a kiss.

"I grabbed some stuff for a recipe I just came up with in my head," I said, holding up the bag as I entered the room.

"Mm, hope it's good," Katie said.

"Trust me, you'll love it," I said. I went into the small kitchen and set the bags on the counter. "Did you call Mike and Charlie?" I asked.

"Yeah," Katie said, "but as soon as I hung up, I got so tired. And I felt a little feverish too. So I took a short nap."

"Oh yeah?" I asked.

"Yeah," Katie said. "Probably just morning sickness or something."

"So what did they say when you called?" I asked.

"They said the plane was being prepped today," Katie said, "and they'll be ready to go first thing tomorrow morning."

"Good," I said, "so we'll be able to spend another night together." I looked at her with a wide smile.

"I can't wait," Katie said, smiling back.

We had both prepared the ingredients and put them in the pot to cook. I was stirring them in the pot as Katie watched. I looked at her and raised my eyebrows, and she smiled and laughed. You should have seen us, it was like we weren't in the middle of trying to stop a destructive, hostile takeover of the world.

The thing about foxes was when a male came across a female, they would mate for life, with some exceptions, of course, like if one got killed or something.

I couldn't believe we were like worlds apart at first, then all of a sudden Katie was pregnant with my kids, and we were so in love with each other. Well, I didn't know at that time if she was pregnant or not because we would have to get the test done. Katie and I talked about it as we put the pasta recipe together, and we decided maybe we should take her to a doctor to get the test done.

"All finished!" I said.

"Mm, looks good," Katie said.

"You won't know until you try," I said.

We dished it up and sat at the counter to eat it. It wasn't bad for an inexperienced cook such as me, but it was good. As soon as we finished, it got dark, and we decided to go to bed.

The next morning, we woke up in the same position as two mornings ago. This time, she was first to get up. I got up after her.

"I'll tell you," she said, entering the bathroom, "I've definitely gotta be pregnant."

"What's wrong?" I asked. She sounded kind of blue. "Aren't you happy about it?"

"Of course I am," Katie said, "I just feel kind of sick, is all."

She opened the toilet lid, and leaned over it, obviously expecting to vomit. I looked in the mirror and decided to brush my teeth for the hell of it.

Foxes normally don't need to brush their teeth; as a matter of fact, the only species that needs to brush their teeth are humans, for they have the dirtiest mouth in the animal kingdom. I just decided to because I wanted my breath to smell good. I mean, sure, foxes have stuff in their saliva to defend against plaque, but there is nothing in the world to defend against bad breath, save it be made of strong mint.

Katie retched a bit, but didn't seem to toss her cookies. When she finished, she closed the toilet lid and came over to me.

I spat out the toothpaste and rinsed my mouth with water. Katie moved in front of me to wash her paws, and I wrapped my arms around her waist, my whole front side making contact with her backside. I rested my chin over her shoulder and gave her a kiss on the neck.

"Should we get out of here?" I asked.

Katie nodded.

Katie put on her jacket, I put on my uniform, and we both packed and left the hotel. We had to take a taxi to the airport, and from there, we had to walk out onto the runway to meet with Mike and Charlie. Katie was a little dizzy from nausea, but that was what happened when one got a girl impregnated. The first thing I told Mike was to take it easy because Katie was likely pregnant.

145

"Oh," Mike said with a chuckle, "having some fun in Rio, eh?"

I didn't even crack a smile.

"Are you okay?" I asked.

"Yeah," Mike said, "though some guys came on and knocked us out. I assume they were looking for you."

"When did this happen?" I asked.

"Yesterday," Mike said. "When we were prepping the plane."

"Hmm." I wasn't too surprised. When I ran off after realizing the bomb had gotten to the airport, Lance probably assumed I would head there.

When we got onto the plane, Katie and I sat in the table seat. As soon as we were in the air we moved over to the three-person bench seat so Katie could rest. I sat at the end, and Katie lay down, resting her head on my lap. She had taken off her jacket and used it as a blanket.

"You feeling okay?" I asked, giving her a kiss on the forehead.

"I'm super-nauseous." She groaned.

"Try to get some sleep," I said, in the most soothing voice I could. "It may help."

Katie turned on her side and nestled her head in my lap, placing her paw on my thigh and closing her eyes. I reached behind me and moved my tail to a comfortable position, for we were going to be that way for a long time.

I woke up. My head was leaning against the back of the couch and my mouth hung open. A little drool leaked out of the corner of my mouth. Katie's head was no longer resting on my lap. As a matter of fact, Katie wasn't even on the couch. I could hear her in the bathroom at the rear of the plane. She was spitting, probably just got done vomiting. She flushed the toilet and opened the already partially opened bathroom door and came out. She closed the door behind her and came over to the couch, sitting next to me.

"Had to throw up," she said.

"Oh." I wrapped my left arm around her and pulled her close. "I'm sorry."

"Don't be," Katie said. "I knew this would happen. It's completely natural."

I rubbed her head with my left paw and gave her a kiss on the forehead.

"We'll be in LA soon," I said soothingly.

She sighed.

12

We arrived in Los Angeles late that night. I picked up my Cutlass and we drove to Jeremy's apartment. We arrived at about midnight. I knocked on the apartment door with my right arm around Katie, and Jeremy answered the door.

"Hey, Chance," he said, "Quite a while since we've seen each other."

"Hey, Jer," I said, calling him by a little nickname I made for him. "Katie needs to get to bed pronto."

"She sick?" Jeremy asked, stepping aside and letting us in.

"She's pregnant," I said. "Most likely."

"Congrats," Jeremy whispered, and we gave each other a high-five.

"Guest room is still open," Jeremy said. "It's only me and Derek right now. We're playing cards in the living room if you want to join us."

"Thanks, but I'll be looking after Katie," I said. "Plus, I'm hella tired."

"Okay," Jeremy said. "I'm right down here with Derek if you need anything."

"Thanks, man," I said.

We walked past the kitchen to the stairs, and Derek and I exchanged a friendly wave. I walked Katie up the stairs to the guest room. When we got in the room, I laid Katie down on the bed and pulled the covers over her. I then softly patted her shoulder and went to the other side of the bed, then took off my uniform, sat on the side of the mattress, and looked out the window at the full moon, which illuminated the city of LA. I sighed.

"What's wrong?" Katie asked.

"Why are we doing this?" I asked. "Why were we created for the sole purpose to destroy when I see more good in life?"

"Some people can't see past their own nose," Katie said. "You're so much more than what people say you are, Chance. You just have to refuse to accept it, otherwise, it'll become reality."

I looked back at her, and she looked up at me. God, how I loved her so much. I laid myself next to her and opened my arms, and she scooted herself into my arms with her forehead against my chin and her cheek to my chest.

"I love you, Katie," I said.

"I know, baby," she said.

We eventually dozed off and fell asleep.

In the morning I woke up, and Katie wasn't in the position she was last night. She lay with her back to me and her uniform, which she hadn't taken off the last night, was now off. I reached over and put my paw on her shoulder. She turned her head and looked at me.

"What is it?" she asked.

"You all right?" I asked.

"I feel a lot better now," Katie said as she turned over, and we resumed our positions from the previous night. We snuggled in bed a while longer.

Eventually we got up and both went downstairs. Katie wore a neutral expression, evidently feeling a lot better. All three members of the family were in the front room, all sitting on the couches.

"Hey, Chance!" Tyson said.

"Hey, Ty," I said.

"How was Rio?" he asked.

"Well, to make a long story short," I said, "the bomb is headed for LA right now."

"Oh no." Tyson sighed. "What are you going to do?"

"We'll figure it out," I said. "ASIS has been tracking the bomb since day one so . . ."

"Well, that's good," Tyson said. "At least someone is."

"By the way," I said, sitting next to Jeremy on the couch perpendicular to the one that faced the TV, where Katie sat next to Ethan, "I never said sorry about the Porsche."

"Don't worry about it," Jeremy said. "It's not the first time something like that has happened to my reliable steed."

"Well, I could pay you back if—"

"Nah, it's cool," Jeremy interrupted. "It came back from the shop yesterday."

"Oh, that's good to hear," I said.

"So any good news from Rio?" Tyson asked.

"Well," I said, "Katie is pregnant."

"What?" Tyson said. "That's awesome, congratulations!"

Ethan leaned over and put his ear to Katie's stomach. She just chuckled and put a paw on his head.

"The babies haven't developed yet, sweetie," she said. "They'll be kicking in a few months."

Tyson just laughed at Ethan.

"Anyway," I said, "we're going to need some serious help if we're going to find that bomb."

"Well," Jeremy said, "Tyson and I were going to get some breakfast for you guys. We were hoping to surprise you when you woke up, but now that you're awake, you can come with us."

"Okay," I said, "I'll just get my uniform. Katie, you wanna come?" I asked.

"No, I'll stay here with Ethan," She said.

"Okay, well, have fun," I said. I ran upstairs real fast, grabbed my uniform, and put it on as I ran back downstairs. I gave Katie a kiss and told her I loved her, then Tyson, Jeremy, and I left.

We decided to take my Cutlass because of what happened last time. We decided to head to IHOP to pick something up and were just driving down the street and talking about my car on the way.

"You've got a sick ride, Chance," Jeremy said from the back seat. "Where did you get it?"

"It was just . . ." I paused, trying to come up with the right word. "Issued to me, I guess."

"Oh, so it was the spy network that gave it to you?" Tyson asked.

"ASIS," I said, "yeah."

"I noticed it was reinforced," Jeremy said.

"Yeah, it is," I said as I nodded. "Everything from the windows to wheels."

"Are the tires reinforced?" Jeremy asked.

"I actually don't know," I said. "I'll have to see."

"Well, either way, it's a badass car," Tyson said, looking in the rearview mirror. "But look at that car behind us."

Jeremy turned and looked out the back window.

"Wow, look at that Aston."

I looked out the back window through the mirror. Sure enough, there was an Aston Martin right behind us. A black Aston Martin V8.

"Hmm." I turned on my blinker and the black Aston Martin did as well. I turned right and he followed me.

"Okay," I muttered.

"Now I find that guy suspicious," Jeremy said.

"Yeah," I said as I took a sharp left without using my blinker. The Aston Martin did as well, almost getting clipped by a car, in which the driver honked his horn angrily.

"Head to that mall and park there," Tyson said pointing to a large mall ahead.

I drove all the way over there and stopped the car in a parking lot, which was fairly empty. I looked around and couldn't see the Aston Martin anywhere. I opened the door and stepped out to get a better view and walked around, trying to catch the scent of the exhaust. I could recognize the difference between the emissions of an American car and a European car.

I walked around, sniffing the air, my ears flicking to even the slightest noise. I walked through the rows of cars, sniffing and listening, when I heard a car door shut. I looked in the direction my ear had turned to. I heard footsteps approaching. Black dress shoes, judging by the sound of the soles. I was looking in the direction of the sound of footsteps and all of a sudden saw a familiar figure step out from behind a minivan.

"Hello, Chance," Jack said with a warm smile.

"Jack?" I said, almost smiling.

"In the flesh."

"What are you doing here?" I asked rather excitedly.

"I heard you failed in Brazil," Jack said. He kept his hands in the pockets of his long beige coat.

"Well, I—" I began to explain, thinking he was disappointed.

"No, it's okay," he said. "You shouldn't have gone off and tried to stop it. You couldn't have taken on the whole Lance division yourself."

"Well, Katie was with me."

"Chance," he walked up to me and put his arm around me. "Remember what I told you about Katie?"

"She's changed," I said. "She's pregnant with my kids, I'm sure."

"Really?" Jack said, his eyes widening in surprise.

"Yeah, we're gonna get her test done," I said.

"Okay, let's cut to the chase," Jack said. "I've got some good news and bad news."

"Oh, do tell," I said.

"The good news is we tracked the bomb and know the exact co-ordinates where it is," Jack said. He handed me a card with coordinates printed onto it.

"Great," I said as I took it. "What's the bad news?"

"The bad news is the bomb's already in Los Angeles," Jack said. "And Lance was right, it's in the most unsuspecting place of all. So you need to find those coordinates as soon as possible and get there pronto."

"How is that even possible?" I asked.

"I have no idea," Jack said. He looked around suspiciously. "But we have to get out of here, they're here."

"Who?" I asked.

"The Soviets," Jack said. "They've tracked you down here."

"Damn," I muttered.

I heard running footsteps approaching. I looked over and saw Tyson and Jeremy come to a halt, panting from sprinting over to us.

"Who the hell is that, Chance?" Tyson asked.

"This is—" I began.

"Jack O'Reilly," Jeremy interrupted.

Jack looked confused.

"Have we met?" he asked.

"It's me," Jeremy said. "Jeremy Stone."

Jack looked up to the right, in an effort to recall his memory.

"I took out that biological terrorist in the Republic of Congo."

"Oh," Jack said, "I remember now. Yeah, you're the one who took out the guy who was trying to spread the Ebola virus."

"The same." They shook hands.

"Nice to see you again, Jeremy," Jack said, "but we need to go. Chance?" He looked at me. "Where's your car?"

"It's right over—" I was interrupted by a rocket whistling by us and colliding with a nearby car, which was taken up in a massive ball of fire. We were all knocked down onto the pavement.

"Ugh, dammit!" Tyson groaned as he struggled to get back onto his feet.

"Get to Chance's car!" Jack shouted.

Jack, Jeremy, and Tyson booked it all the way to my car while I struggled onto my feet and followed. We got to my car and ducked behind it as unseen, ubiquitous enemies fired at us. I dove to the driver's side door and opened it, then pulled the lever and popped the trunk. The others were ducked on the other side of the car, and I grabbed my weapons bag and ducked down with them.

"Okay, guys," I said, opening the bag to reveal my weapons. I grabbed my CAR-15 and loaded in a magazine. "Choose your weapons. We're gonna have to fight our way out of this."

Then I realized I only had my Colt pistols and Skorpion machine pistols left.

Tyson and Jeremy grabbed one of each. Bullets were pinging off my car as they loaded magazines into their weapons. Jack just pulled out a pistol from his suit pocket and cocked the action. I got up, spotted a Soviet soldier, and fired at him. Dropped him. He fell, dropping his gun, which clattered onto the ground loudly.

Tyson got up with the Skorpion and spotted another soldier. He fired three shots. All entered the soldier's chest and he fell facedown. Tyson spotted two more soldiers. He fired three more shots, taking the first guy out, then rotated to fire three more shots, shooting the second in the head. His head kicked back, and he fell against the car.

I watched in astonishment at Tyson's shooting. As soon as the machine pistol clicked empty, he pulled out my Colt and began shooting. Every shot counted. A soldier was dropped with each. Then Tyson spotted a sniper, which I didn't notice until Tyson dropped him from a hundred yards with my pistol.

"Holy hell," I said as he began to reload both the Colt and the Skorpion. "Nice shooting."

"I never miss," Tyson bragged.

I heard a scream behind me and turned my head to see a Soviet charging at me. He was just a few feet away and swung his AK to hit me. I blocked his blow with my CAR-15, holding it up with both paws and blocking the butt of his rifle. I moved his gun away, swinging my gun to the side and brought the butt of my rifle to him. I swung hard, and the butt stock collided with his chest and he fell onto the ground, panting hard, trying to take some of the knocked out air from his lungs.

I paid no attention to the fighting taking place around me, and I suddenly heard the crack of an SVD sniper rifle. I instantly hit the ground as the bullet broke through several car windows and hit the Cutlass, where my head was a moment ago.

"Chance!" Tyson yelled, noticing that I had fallen.

I slowly rose to a seated position, and Tyson came over to me and put an arm around me.

"Chance, you okay?"

"Yeah," I said, "I'm fine."

"It's Nikolai," Jack said. "He's here, he's the one who shot at you."

"We need to get into the mall," Jeremy said. "The last thing the Soviets are gonna do is make themselves obvious in there since they're on US soil. We're heavily outnumbered, but in there we'll have a chance."

"Jeremy's right," Jack said. "If we stay here, we'll be surrounded within minutes. In there, they'll have to bring in small arms to conceal themselves."

"Yeah," I said, "but these guys are obviously Spetsnaz. They'll do anything."

"We either stay here or die!" Jack said.

"C'mon, guys!" Jeremy said. He began to run for the mall, firing the Skorpion at unseen enemies behind cars. Tyson followed, then Jack. I grabbed a couple of grenades and put them into the trunk along with my CAR-15, shut the trunk and the driver's side door, and followed them. I caught up with Tyson at the main entrance as he fired at a Soviet with the Skorpion.

"Can I have my pistol?" I asked.

He reached behind him and grabbed my Colt from his belt and handed it to me. I then grabbed it and unzipped my uniform and stuck it into the concealed pocket. I zipped my uniform back up, then entered the building with Tyson as he concealed the Skorpion.

"Where are the others?" I asked.

"No idea," Tyson said, walking alongside me. "They just entered the building and split up."

We walked through a crowd of people, who all looked at us strangely. I was looking around for any sign of the others, when I felt a tug on my tail and exclaimed then unzipped my coat and turned around with my paw gripping my pistol to see that it was just an African American teenager who had tugged on my tail.

"Yo," he said, "wassup with the costume?"

"I just like to wear it!" I said in an annoyed manner as I let go of my pistol and zipped my uniform.

"You a furry?" the kid asked.

"What do you think?" I asked back.

"I dread the day that becomes a worldwide thing," the kid said. "Then you guys will be everywhere."

"Maybe that's a good thing," I said.

"Hey, guys," the kid said, "come here. I found a furry wandering through the mall."

At that, another African American, kid who was quite muscular, came up alongside him, followed by a tall, lanky, pale, Caucasian kid.

"Well, well, well," the muscular kid said, "look what we have here."

"Beat it, you bunch of punks," Tyson said.

"Who are you calling a punk?" the white boy said.

"You, you pasty rascal!" Tyson answered. "Now beat it!"

The muscular kid began to approach Tyson with his fist raised but looked over to see a mall cop glancing at him.

"Whatever," the muscular kid said, "enjoy your time here, animal screwer."

I spotted a Soviet with a pistol on his thigh wandering behind the Little Rascals gang here before me. Not even ten feet behind them.

"Get, down kids!" I yelled.

The Soviet spotted me and shoved his way through the kids. The first kid and the lanky kid fell to the floor, while the muscular kid kind of stumbled back and regained his balance. The Soviet grabbed for his pistol, but I swiped his hand away with my paw and made for an uppercut to his chin, which he blocked.

I ducked as he swung his arm to deck me in the face and punched him in the gut while I was crouched. He was bent over from the blow, and I rose and punched him in the face, and he was knocked upright, and he stumbled back about a foot and regained his balance.

He made two swings at me with his arms. The first one I deflected; the second collided with my cheek. I nearly lost balance but regained it as the Soviet made his next move. He attempted another punch to the face, but I moved out of the way of his arm and grabbed it, locked his elbow, and bent him over, bringing his face down to my knee, which I brought up. He was knocked backward and fell onto the floor.

"Oh my god," the lanky white kid yelled, "them furries are government spies!"

157

"You ain't screwing around," the first kid said as he backed off.

"You're damn right!" I said. I looked down at the Soviet to see that he was still conscious and brought my foot down on his head, knocking him out cold. I watched the kids run off into the crowd that I had attracted the attention of.

"Sir." I heard a voice behind me and turned to see the mall cop behind me. "You and this man are going to have to come with me."

"Wait," I said, "you don't understand—"

"Save it," the mall cop said as he went to grab my arm.

"No!" I backed up. "You see this uniform?" I turned to show him my right side with the Australian flag on the shoulder. "I am ASIS!"

"In a fursuit?" The cop looked at me in a way of saying I was an imbecile.

"It's not a fursuit!" I said.

"Okay, so a talking fox who stands six feet tall?" the cop said. "You can save it for the judge now."

He went to grab my arm again, and I couldn't hold myself back anymore. I swung my arm outward and punched him right in the jaw. He groaned as he put his hand to the impact area, and I jumped up and spun around as I did a midair roundhouse kick to his face. He fell backward onto the floor, knocked out.

I looked around and couldn't find Tyson anywhere. He must have ditched so he could find me later, which was a tactic we had used in Vietnam that saved our asses so many times, but Tyson was nowhere to be found. The cop was regaining consciousness, and he groaned as he slightly rolled on the floor. I booked it for the escalator. There would probably be more cops on my tail soon, and I had to find everyone else and get the hell out of there. I ran up the escalator and pushed and bumped through people as I went.

"Excuse me, sorry, coming through," I said as I pushed through the crowd. I passed by the Macy's store and kept running, looking in each store I ran past to see if any of the others were in there.

I was running past a small jewelry store when I heard a roar and looked to see Nikolai coming at me at full speed. He swung his arm in a backhand and hit me so hard I flew through a window of the jeweler and crashed through a display counter. I was racked with pain. My skin, muscles, and bones hurt everywhere; it was almost too much to handle.

I was surprised at the fact that I was able to move, no bones broken or anything. I groaned as I struggled slowly to my feet. Nikolai came in, and all the people went running out screaming.

"No more games," Nikolai said in English. "Now you die."

I barely got to my feet when he hit me again. Another backhand swipe and I flew back and hit the wall, knocking some stuff off the shelves. He came at me again and punched me hard in the stomach.

"I'm going to enjoy this," he said as he grabbed me by the neck and pinned me to the wall.

I couldn't breathe. I struggled and squirmed, but his iron grip didn't budge. I looked around for something to use as a weapon. That was when I spotted the wound on his paw from when I had stabbed him there with a pen. I brought my arm up and hit it as hard as I could. Nikolai just exclaimed a little and tightened his grip.

I was losing all hope, but that was when I saw the knife tucked in his belt right under his uniform. I grabbed it and yanked it out. Before he could realize what was happening I stabbed him deep in the shoulder. He groaned loudly as he released his grip. I fell to the floor and coughed as I filled my lungs with air. Nikolai just kept groaning as he held his shoulder. His back was turned to me. I could end this once and for all.

I got up, but his ear flicked back as he heard me coming. He grabbed my arm as I went to stab him. Instead of the menacing expression I had always seen him wear, he now had an expression of fear and innocence as he strained to keep the blade from reaching him. I back-handed him hard in the face, and he fell on his back on the floor.

I wasn't going to have any more of it, and I pinned him to the floor. I held the knife to his throat as he braced himself for the kill, and that was when I spotted something fall to the floor. Something from Nikolai's pocket that floated down slowly and landed front side up.

It was a photo of whom I guessed was Nikolai's wife and child. His wife was a beautiful white tiger with dazzling blue eyes. She was laughing as her husband gave her a kiss on the cheek. She had their son held to her waist as he hugged her. I looked back to Nikolai and into his eye as he breathed hard in exhaustion and panic. His deep-brown noncovered eye. I looked back to the photo and looked at his wife's bright blue eyes and thought we weren't so different after all. Just like Katie and I, except our children hadn't been born yet. I studied their happy child in the photo.

I couldn't bring myself to take the life of another family figure and sighed as I released my grip on the knife, letting it drop to the floor. I got off Nikolai and sat on the floor next to him. He rose to a seated position, rubbing his neck with his paw, and he just studied me with his one good eye.

"Why didn't you do it?" he asked.

I remained silent with my eyes to the floor.

"You could have killed me and ended it all, but you didn't. Why?" Nikolai inquired once more.

I remained silent for about thirty more seconds, and I gestured with my head toward the photo.

"Your picture," I said. "I saw the picture fall out of your pocket and I just couldn't do it."

Nikolai looked toward where I gestured and grabbed the photo. He smiled and chuckled to himself.

"That's my wife, Veronika," he said, looking at the photo, "and my boy, Vassili. I named him after Vassili Zaitsev."

I just chuckled then sighed, my eyes still locked on the floor.

"I couldn't bring myself to destroy another family," I said. "I mean, what are we doing here? Why are we doing this?"

"Because humans say we're just animals," Nikolai said as he tucked the photo into his uniform pocket. "They say we don't value any life except our own, that we kill on instinct when needed, and so on."

"I wish I could prove them all wrong," I said, "but I've already destroyed enough families. Enough lives."

"The work of a spy is a dirty one." Nikolai nodded. "But you can't let that haunt you forever."

"There's no way," I said. "The last guy I did it to is after me now. Trying to start a nuclear war between our two countries."

"Hmm." Nikolai nodded again then looked at me, confused.

"You're American?" he asked.

"Well, no," I said. "I'm Australian, actually."

"But you're an American red fox," Nikolai said confused.

"Well, I was born and raised in Australia." I said. "Actually, born in England, then went to Australia and . . . yeah, it's complicated."

"I know how that is," Nikolai said, "I was born in the USA, actually. I was sent to the Soviets for God knows why. My first mission was in Afghanistan." He pointed to his eye patch. "That's where I met Veronika. She felt sorry about me losing my eye, and well, we've been in love since."

"How old were you then?" I asked.

"Sixteen," Nikolai said. "Veronika is actually a year older than me."

"How old are you now?"

"Thirty-one," Nikolai said.

"I'm twenty-two," I said, "but I've already messed up so much."

"Hey," Nikolai said, "you're only twenty-two. You still have time to do some right."

I just sighed.

"I've been messing up so much now," Nikolai said, "since I accidentally got Veronika pregnant when I was twenty-three. But now that she and I look back at that moment, we don't regret it. We brought Vassili into this world and we love him so much. He's seven now."

"Really?" I asked.

"Mm-hmm." Nikolai sighed as he got up and straightened out his Soviet jacket. "Well, I think I'll just call this mission a failure. Unless you're all right with being pronounced dead."

"Why were you after me?" I asked.

"Because you were the one who put that bomb in Ukraine and infiltrated our territory," Nikolai responded. He began to walk out of the store.

I sighed, then quickly reacted.

"Wait!" I said as he started to leave. "I need your help."

"Huh?" Nikolai was confused at this and wore an expression of stupor. "You need my help? I've been trying to kill you this whole time."

"But there's nukes all over the United States and the Soviet Union." I got up and stood next to him, straightening my uniform and shaking off the glass shards. He was so much bigger than me for he was a tiger and I a fox the size of the average adult human being. "They're gonna go off when Lance reaches his final destination."

"What?" Nikolai looked at me confusedly. "I was told you were responsible for the nukes."

"Well, unwillingly I was, partially." I brushed some glass shards out of my bushy tail. "But I made a mistake that Lance is trying to get back at me for. And he's the one behind all of it. If you can help me stop him, then—"

"Where is it headed?" Nikolai asked.

"I was just given coordinates, nothing else—"

"Chance!" Tyson yelled, running into the jewelry store. "I found the others. We gotta get the hell out of here." I noticed Jeremy with Jack leaning on him, walking by the door. Jack was clutching his chest.

"Oh, jeez," I said. I turned to Nikolai. "You got a way out?"

"Yeah." He nodded.

"Just follow the black car with the white stripes!" I said, and we all took off, running our separate ways.

"He's on our side now?" Tyson said, running alongside me.

"Sure looks that way," I answered.

"Holy hell!" Tyson said as we caught up with Jeremy and Jack.

"What's the problem here?" I asked, looking at Jack.

"He's been hit," Jeremy said. "He might not make it."

"Not with that attitude he won't," I said, wrapping Jack's arm over my shoulders and taking him off Jeremy's hands. We started walking hastily to the entrance of the mall.

We descended the escalator and made toward the entrance, getting looks from the totally unaware people who passed us by.

When we got outside, we crept around the cars, slowly making our way toward my Cutlass, making sure the place was cleared of Soviets. I was sure Nikolai had called them in by the time we got to the Cutlass. Jeremy and Tyson sat in the back, taking out the Skorpions and holding them on their laps. I strapped Jack into the front seat.

"Hang in there, mate," I said as he breathed heavily and clutched his chest.

I shut the door, went to the other side of the car, and hopped into the driver's seat and quickly started my car. I put the car in reverse, and the engine roared as I quickly backed out, spun around, and threw the car into first gear. I barely avoided another car as I sped out of the parking lot.

I pulled onto the road and sped toward the intersection, where the light turned red, and the cars on the perpendicular road started moving.

"Hang on, guys!" I said and gunned the engine.

Tyson and Jeremy yelled in panic and held each other as I swerved and dodged two cars and a bus, speeding through the intersection.

"I'm so glad this car doesn't have license plates," I muttered.

I looked into the mirror and saw a black Lincoln following us. I guessed it was Nikolai until a man leaned out the window and fired at us with an AK-47. Bullets pinged off the car's frame as he fired long, concentrated bursts at us. We were headed for a tightly packed intersection, so I merged into the left lane before we hit the divider; the black Lincoln followed, and the man kept firing.

"Dammit!" I yelled as a bullet pinged off my window. We reached the intersection, and a large truck was heading for us. I gunned the engine and made it to the other side of the intersection, but the Lincoln wasn't so lucky, however. The truck plowed through it like it was nothing, and the car just exploded into a million pieces. The guy leaning out the window was thrown out, crushed in the mangled window frame. That Lincoln didn't stand a chance against a Peterbilt.

"Good god!" Tyson yelled.

I slowed the car a bit, and the truck turned on the intersection, and followed us. I looked into the rearview mirror to see who was driving the truck, for it seemed strange that a large truck like that would just plow through a car at the intersection and follow us. I looked closely and saw that it was Nikolai. He must have noticed I was looking because I could see him wave. I waved back at him. We were in good hands now. Or in this case, paws.

We rushed back to Tyson and Jeremy's place and carried Jack in. Nikolai kind of disappeared somewhere, since the truck couldn't be parked in that parking lot. Jack insisted on walking on his own, but he was weakening and bleeding out. We insisted on calling an ambulance for him, but he refused. He didn't want any emergency services on our tails compromising the mission. Having been soldiers, Tyson and I had limited knowledge of paramedics, but Katie was a nurse, so we thought we were good.

Jeremy quickly unlocked the apartment door and pushed it open. Katie was cuddling little Ethan like her own son on the couch, while the TV played cartoons. She turned her attention to us and gasped.

"Oh my god!" she said. She let go of Ethan and got up, running over to us.

"We ran into some trouble," I said, laying Jack on the closest couch. "We need to get this bullet out of him as soon as possible."

Jack just moaned painfully.

"Hang in there, bud," Tyson said to Jack.

"I'll grab the first aid stuff!" Jeremy said. He ran up the stairs and went to the bathroom to grab the first aid kit.

"Chance," Tyson said, "get Ethan out of here."

"But, I can help . . ." I said.

"It's fine," Katie said, examining Jack's wound. "Just get him out of here. We don't want him to have to see this."

"All right," I said. I went over to the other couch, picked Ethan up onto his feet, and held his hand in my paw, leading him to the stairs and taking him up to the guest room, where all of mine and Katie's stuff were. I had Ethan sit on the bed, and I took off my uniform and put my pistols on the side table, making sure they were empty, actions open, magazines out, and on safety. I put on my black T-shirt and sat on the bed next to Ethan.

"How have you been, kiddo?" I asked, trying to take his mind off the events that had just taken place.

As a soldier, I was trained to do that. When one has gone through a traumatic experience and was panicking, it was best to take his mind off it by starting an everyday conversation.

"Good," Ethan said, only looking at me for a second.

"You all right?" I asked.

"Mr. Logan," Ethan said, "is that man gonna die?"

"Come here, son." I waved him over with my paw. Ethan scooted over, and I wrapped an arm around him and held him close in a comforting embrace. "Don't worry about it, okay?"

"Okay." He hugged me and leaned his head on my chest and I held him like he was my own child. I nuzzled his hair.

"There, there . . ." I pat his back.

"Mr. Logan?" Ethan said.

"Yes?" I asked.

"Why do people kill each other?"

I sighed and rocked him gently. "Because someone has to get greedy. He has to place himself above others, value his own wants over the lives of fellow members of the human race."

"Why?" Ethan asked.

"It'll always remain one of the world's greatest mysteries, child," I answered.

We sat in silence until we could hear Jack moaning loudly in pain.

Ethan started panicking, I could feel his pulse rise, so I held his head to my chest and covered his other ear with my paw.

"Shh . . ." I shushed soothingly.

We sat like that for a good forty-five minutes or so. Eventually, Ethan fell asleep, and I laid him in my bed and tucked him in. I went out to check, and Katie was closing the first aid kit. She looked up at me and shook her head sadly. She then came upstairs and whispered into my ear.

"He doesn't have long to live," she told me.

To be honest, I had to hold back my tears. He had been a great help to me. Like a mentor in the Arthurian quests I used to study when I was young. I looked at Katie, then gave her a big hug and a kiss.

I sat on the couch across from Jack, tapping my tail expectantly, waiting for him to move, talk, even if it was a little sigh. I waited for hours,

166

until eventually, it grew dark. I didn't rest, sleep, or even drink water. Everyone went to bed. Katie tried to persuade me to go with her, but I refused in the best way I could. I gave her a kiss good-night and went back to expectantly waiting for Jack to show any sign of life.

Tyson had taken Ethan out of my room and put him in his then went to his own bedroom. Pretty soon it was just Jeremy and me. Jeremy called Derek and later came over and sat by me.

"Nothing?" He handed me a glass of water.

I didn't take the water. I just sat there and slowly shook my head.

"You should get some sleep, Chance," Jeremy said, resting the glass on the coffee table and getting up to go to his room.

"Jeremy?" I said.

"Yeah, Chance?" he said, standing by me.

"Why am I even here, Jer?" I asked, not taking my eyes off Jack. "I was bred to do nothing but kill. That's all I've ever done."

"I think you're here for something more, Chance," Jeremy said. "Before I retired from killing, I thought the same thing about myself. And look at me now."

I sighed as I processed what Jeremy had just said.

"And you don't do nothing but kill," Jeremy continued. "I mean, you helped Chanel feel a bit better by cuddling with her, Katie is pregnant. Or you think she is. And you did all that only in the short time you've been here."

"Thanks for reminding me I need to get Katie tested." I cracked a short smile.

"Well, maybe you can do that tomorrow," Jeremy said, starting to walk away. "Take your mind off of all this. I'm gonna get some shut-eye, and you should probably do the same. The brain handles better on at least eight hours of sleep."

"I've stayed up for thirty-six hours straight," I said.

"Okay, suit yourself." Jeremy chuckled and went upstairs to his room.

"Good night, Jer," I said and kept my eyes on Jack.

I watched and waited. Hours, which seemed like days went by. I didn't give in to sleep. I sat there, not even getting drowsy, whether it was because of the worry for Jack or just me, waiting for him to move or show any sign of life. Finally, at around one o'clock in the morning, he moved his head to the side toward me.

"Chance," he uttered.

"Jack!" I sprung up and got on my knees beside him, grabbing his hand and holding it in my paws.

"Chance," he said again, "I'm not gonna make it."

"No," I said, rubbing the back of his hand, "don't say that. Every-thing will be all right, you'll see."

He shook his head and looked into my eyes. "There's something I gotta tell you before I go."

"No, you aren't going anywhere," I said.

"I'll be all right, Chance," he said.

"No." I shook my head, and tears began to sting my eyes and blur my vision. I looked down.

"You can't go." I sniffled.

"Chance," he said, "there's something I need to tell you now." I looked back up.

"It's come to my attention that you wonder why you were created. You wonder who created you and for what purpose, am I correct?"

I nodded.

"See Chance—" he groaned and grabbed his chest.

"Hang in there," I said soothingly, putting a paw on his forehead and still holding his hand.

"I was the one who had you created." Jack turned his attention back to me.

I was shocked.

"What?" I asked, loosening my grip on his hand.

Jack just nodded weakly.

"But why?" I asked. "All I am is some monster, bred for the purpose of killing. I've done nothing else."

This time, he was the one gripping my paw, and he did it in a serious manner, looking into my eyes as if peering into my soul.

"I had you created because I was inspired," he said. "Inspired by one who goes by Aaron Richards."

That name rang a bell at that moment, and I remembered seeing him on the hit list Jack showed me.

"Why?" was all I could say.

"A long time ago, Aaron saved my life," Jack said, taking a deep, shaky breath. "Aaron possesses qualities I've seen in no human, other than his appearance. And you are just like him, Chance."

"How so?" I asked.

"You're more makings of a man than most humans I know." He turned his head and looked up at the ceiling. "You put all that you love first, even if it means putting your life on the line. And rather than always knowing when to take a life, you always know when to spare one. And that's why I created you. To show the world that things aren't what they seem."

"But why did I go on all those missions, taking and destroying people's lives? Why did I go on that mission that got us all into this mess in the first place?"

"Stuff happens, Chance. "But you had to learn and grow one way or another." He started coughing.

"Jack!" I said, placing my paw on his bandaged chest.

169

"There's good in you, Chance," Jack said as he stopped coughing. "I've seen it in you since the beginning. You just gotta learn to find it in yourself and ignore the bull. Otherwise, you'll become what they call you. You'll be just like Lance." He turned his head to the side, facing away from me.

"Jack, no!" I said.

"You can—" I felt the life leave him, and he slumped. I let his hand drop to his chest.

"Jack . . ." I whimpered and rested my head on his chest and cried. I cried for a while, and after about a half hour, my ear flicked to the sound of a knock at the front door.

I got up and dried my eyes as best I could, walked over to the door, and opened it. There was Nikolai, standing in his leather jacket. He adjusted his eye patch strap as I opened the door and looked at me with his good eye.

"Hey, Chance," he said in his native language, "you okay?"

I just nodded. "*Da.*"

"Well, sorry I got hung up, but I had to try to call off my men," Nikolai said, taking off his jacket, which now had the red stars torn off the shoulders. He left on a black T-shirt, similar to mine except it had a faint *USSR* embroidered on his chest.

"I couldn't call them off," Nikolai said, shaking his head as he hung his jacket on the coat hanger. "I found out they're following your man Lance. I guess he's some kind of double agent."

"Good god," I whispered, putting my paws on my head and throwing them down to my sides.

"Anyway, after my little . . . failure, I guess, I was approached by someone. He called himself Erich. Asked if I knew Jack, and I just kind of said, 'A little.'"

"And?" I asked.

"Well, he gave me this card with an address on it. Not quite sure where exactly it is, but he wants us to go there tomorrow." Nikolai pulled out a small card, which I recognized as a special CIA location card, like the one that held the coordinates of where the bomb was going to be placed.

I took it, but instead of coordinates, it had an address on it.

"This Erich character also told me someone would be coming to us tonight. Well, soon, since it's the morning." Nikolai continued.

"Who?" I asked.

Nikolai just shrugged.

"Hmm." I thought for a bit.

"Speaking of which, how is Jack?" Nikolai asked, now in English.

I sighed sadly. Apparently, that was enough to get the message to Nikolai. He just nodded.

"I see," he said.

"We're on our own now," I said.

At that very moment, there was a soft knock at the door. The knock went from the bottom of the door and advanced up to the top.

Who in the bloody hell knocks like that? I thought as I approached the door. I slowly opened the door a crack, then upon seeing who it was, opened the door wide and looked him up and down, shocked.

"Ah, hello, pardner!" a fox who looked a helluva lot like me but wearing a brown trench coat and a wide-brim hat, said in a Southern accent.

I moved out of the way so he could come in, and I eyed him as he did so. He was taller than I and most likely older. About forty-five to fifty years old or so. His fur was a darker shade, and the black marks on either side of his snout were more broad than mine, indicating he was born in a place where the sun shone brightest.

"You must be the one Erich told me about," he said as he went to Nikolai and shook his paw.

"Who in the hell are you?" I asked.

"Oh," he said, taking his hat off and letting it hang by the string around his neck and rest on his back, then coming over to me and shaking my paw. "How rude of me. The name's Aaron. Aaron Richards."

I opened my mouth, but no words came out. I was confused.

"Don't hang your mouth open like that or you'll attract the gnat flies, boy," he said and wiped his finger on his nose and sniffled. This guy was a stereotypical American from the South, swear to god.

"But I thought you were dead," I said.

"Now where in the Sam Hill did you pull that from?" Aaron asked.

"Jack showed me a CIA hit list," I said.

"Oh, I'm sure the old guy was just covering my tracks," Aaron said, taking his hat and hanging it on the rack, then taking off his coat and hanging it up as well. "Them pissy sons of bi—"

I lowered my voice to a whisper and interrupted him, "You may wanna tone down the language, mate. There's a little kid here."

"'Kay, Aussie," he said, unstrapping a gun belt from his waist that was full of bullets and two old style .357 Magnum revolvers. He now stood in front of me wearing not a single article of clothing. "Sorry about that."

"It's fine," I said. "Just make sure it doesn't happen again."

"Agreed." Aaron nodded. He looked around the room, slapped his paws, and rubbed them together. "Quite the place you've got here, sonny."

"Well, actually—" I started.

"Hmm?" Aaron turned his gaze to me.

"This place actually belongs to someone else," I said.

"Ah, understandable." Aaron nodded. His expression suddenly turned into a frown as he went over to the couches and sat in the one across from the one where Jack lay. Aaron just looked at him and shook his head. "Somehow I knew he'd go this way. But the work of a spy is nasty."

"It is." Nikolai nodded.

Aaron eyed him. "So you're the ruskie, eh?"

"Uh, y-yeah." Nikolai nodded.

"Sorry," Aaron said. "Erich didn't tell me any details."

"Perfectly fine," Nikolai said. "I'd just prefer you don't call me ruskie."

"That's fine," Aaron said. "My apologies."

"No need to apologize," Nikolai said as he just waved his paw.

Aaron brushed his tail and lay it next to him as he sat. He looked at Jack and shook his head.

"Never thought they'd get him, though," he said. "Damn Lance Division."

"What's with Lance Division?" I asked. "Why would they turn on the CIA now?"

"Well, Lance Division opposed Project Anthro in the beginning," Aaron said, "but they decided it might be useful to do all the dirty work the CIA itself wouldn't do."

"Why turn now, though?" I asked.

"Well" —Aaron rubbed his eyes— "Lance had confidence in you. He was trying to uproot the Soviet Union so he could rescue his family and safely bring them over to the US. Little did he know that the government knew that his family was being held hostage at that safe house, and you were given the shoot-on-sight order. Lance is trying to get back at both countries for what they did, the USSR for all they did and the US for trying to cover up the mistake they made. Mostly a mistake that ripped everything he loved from his life."

I just sighed and sat on the couch perpendicular to the one he was on.

"And he's specifically targeting you," Aaron said, "since you were the main operative."

"He assigned me for the mission, though," I said.

"Yeah, but he had no idea what happened. He thinks you're help-ing cover up what happened," Aaron said.

"I had no idea either." I shook my head.

"John sent me after you to Vietnam, but I was put with a differ-ent battalion. Far from the one you were in. I ended up going to east Cambodia, and well, Lance tried to get me transferred. After some time, I got shot in the back and was presumed dead."

"Hmm," I said, thinking.

"Anyway, as soon as they found out I wasn't dead, Jack secretly sent me back to the States and, I guess you could say, fired me from the CIA."

"Hmm," I repeated.

"Well." Aaron got up and looked at Nikolai, who obviously was confused as to what was happening and kept quiet. "We should probably hit the hay, whatdya say?"

"Yeah," I looked at the clock, which now read almost two o'clock in the morning. "We all need to sleep."

"I can sleep in here if you want," Nikolai said.

"Yeah," I said. "The room upstairs is occupied by me and Katie."

"Ah." Aaron wiggled his eyebrows at me. "You got yourself a lady, eh?"

"Whoa now," I said, holding my paws up.

"Nah, it's fine," Aaron said, lying on his back on the couch, "I got myself a wife. She's such a sweetheart, Emily."

I started going up the stairs.

"You know" —I stopped halfway up— "I never knew there were more like me."

"There's lots of us," Aaron said. "You just gotta know where to look."

He tapped a finger on the side of his head near his eye.

"Now get some rest," Aaron said. "We're meeting up with some other guys tomorrow."

"Okay," I said, continuing up the stairs. "G'night then."

"*Spokoynoy nochi,*" Nikolai said, lying on the other couch.

"Nighty-night," Aaron said.

Almost as soon as I got up to the top of the stairs, I heard Nikolai and Aaron whispering to each other. I just sighed, shook my head, and went to the guest room, where Katie slept. I went in and shut the door behind me. Katie's ear perked up, and she opened her eyes.

"Sorry, sweetheart," I whispered.

"Perfectly fine, hon," she said as she yawned, stretching her arm and then rubbing her eye. "I'd probably sleep better with you here to keep me warm." She smiled.

"Aw, honey," I said, smiling, and took my shirt off. "That's my specialty."

I laid myself down with her in the bed and pulled the covers over me, then held her in my arms as she snuggled up to me. She nuzzled my chest and rested a paw on my shoulder as I held her tightly in my arms.

"I love you," she said.

"I love you too, dear," I said. Eventually we both fell asleep in that position.

13

I awoke the next morning, my arms still wrapped around Katie, her head still resting on my chest, and her paw caressing my chest and running her fingers through my fur. Knowing she was awake, I gave her a kiss on the head.

"Morning, honey," I said.

"Good morning," she said, still rubbing my chest and keeping her eyes closed.

"How did you sleep, my sweet?" I asked, rubbing my paw up and down her back.

"Nice and warm," Katie said.

"Still tired?" I asked.

She nodded, leaving her eyes closed.

I kissed the top of her head. "Will you be all right if I go downstairs?" I asked.

She just nodded. I slowly got up and put the covers over Katie's shoulder, then my feet touched the floor, and I stood. I put on my black T-shirt and exited the room then heard Tyson, Jeremy, and Aaron talking in the front room. When I got to the banister by the stairs, I looked down to see Tyson and Jeremy sitting on the couch next to Aaron, who had Ethan sitting on his lap. Nikolai sat on the couch perpendicular to them.

176

"Yeah, I actually came before—" He looked up and noticed me. "Hey, there he is!"

He bounced Ethan on his knee a bit.

"What?" I asked.

"Oh, nothing," Jeremy said. "This guy Aaron has been telling us a bit about himself."

"Oh," I said as I incuriously raised my eyebrows.

I wasn't in the mood for breakfast that day after what had happened last night. To watch Jack, my mentor, pass to the other side.

Jack was no longer on the couch, and I asked where he was, and Aaron told me some officials came by and got him. I just sat in the living room as everyone else ate. Aaron didn't have much, expressing his avoidance of imposition. Katie came downstairs in a red-and-white California Angels T-shirt. At first she was shocked at seeing Aaron, but then he did some explaining. Katie came into the living room and sat on my lap, and I tapped my tail excitedly. Ethan came in after a bit, sat next to me, and wrapped his arms around my arm. I just kissed his head and kept my arms around Katie's waist.

"Hey, buddy," I said, smiling down at him.

"Hey, Mr. Logan," Ethan answered. For some reason, that reminded me we still needed to see whether Katie was bearing my kids or not.

"Katie?" I whispered in her ear.

"Yes, Chance?" she asked.

"I gotta go somewhere today," I said. "Would you come with me so we can get your pregnancy test afterward?"

"Sounds good." Katie smiled.

"All right." I kissed her neck and rubbed her belly.

"Mr. Logan?" Ethan asked.

"Yes?" I answered.

177

"How did you get Mrs. Logan pregnant?"

"Well, you see," I started, "I used a special magic, and I used it to put a baby inside Katie's tummy."

Katie giggled.

"Sure was," Aaron said, coming in the room. "It's called male magic."

He smiled obnoxiously as he leaned in the doorway.

"Aaron, shut the—" I looked at Ethan then back up at Aaron.

"Just shut your mouth," I said.

Aaron raised his eyebrows and tightened his lips to squelch a giggle.

"Ethan, if you're curious about where that magic comes from, feel free to ask."

"What did I tell you about talking inappropriately in front of the kid?" I asked.

Aaron snorted as he tried to keep a laugh down.

"Chance, where does that magic come from?" Ethan asked.

I just looked at him and shook my head.

"Hence the name, it's something that only guys have." Aaron looked at me, put his arm over his head and pulled up his nose, then stuck his tongue out at me.

"Aaron!" I jabbed a finger of warning at him.

"Okay, okay." Aaron held his palms up in surrender.

Katie was still on my lap, trying to squelch a laugh. I could just picture her thoughts being, *this is what I get for being in the same room with a bunch of guys.*

"Mr. Logan," Ethan asked, "what's he talking about?"

"Excuse me, honey," I said as I helped her up off my lap. I got up as she sat back on the couch, and I approached Aaron. "He's talking about these!" I kneed Aaron in the nuts, and he gasped and fell on the floor.

"Oh god," Aaron said as he groaned and knelt with a paw on the floor to stabilize himself and another paw on his crotch. "It's no wonder me and Emily could never have kids."

I just bent down to his level and whispered into his ear, "Don't humiliate me anymore or I'll kick your ass."

"Agreed." He groaned.

I just pat his back and went to the stairs and up to the guest room to get myself ready for the day ahead.

We made our arrangements to go, and Nikolai said he'd stay behind for this one. So just Katie, Aaron, and I went out of the apartment to the back parking lot, where Aaron had his black 1969 Ferrari Dino 246 GT parked.

"This is a two-seat car," Aaron said, opening the door, "so, Katie, you may have to sit on Chance's lap."

"Totally fine with me," Katie said, looking over at me and batting her eyelashes. *God, she's so hot.*

I nodded and took a seat in the car, then Katie came in and sat on my lap as Aaron shut the door behind her. I reached behind me and adjusted my tail, then wrapped the seat belt around us both and buckled it, then wrapped my arms around Katie's waist. Aaron got into the car and took off his hat.

"Ready to go?" he asked as he put his hat behind his seat and started the engine.

"Yup," Katie and I answered in unison.

"All righty," Aaron said, putting the car into gear. "Let's hit the road."

He backed out of the parking space and drove out of the parking lot and onto the road. We drove in awkward silence for a good half hour until Aaron broke the silence when we hit the freeway.

"So, uh," he started, "these guys we're going to see are all the way in San Francisco. Staying at some old pile of crap warehouse at the bay."

"So," I said, "where did you get this Dino?"

"Hmm?" Aaron took his eyes off the road and looked at me for a second. "Oh, this." He turned his attention back to the road and gestured to the steering wheel. "It's not a real Dino." He shook his head. "It's just an armor car styled after one. There was only a few of these cars ever made, but this one is just an armor car issued to me back in '69."

"Oh, so that means my car isn't really a Cutlass?" I asked.

"Hehe." Aaron chuckled. "You got the Oldsmobile, huh?"

"Yes." I nodded.

"Yeah, no," Aaron said, "yours isn't a real Cutlass. It's a CIA armor car."

"So that means I don't have a real Beetle." Katie said.

Aaron chuckled again. "I should've known someone like you would get the pill bug car."

"Excuse me," Katie scoffed, "it's a nice car."

"Cute operatives get the cute cars, my dear," I said, kissing Katie's neck.

"Psht." Katie shook her head and cracked a smile.

I ended up falling asleep, regardless of how loud the car was, but with me sandwiched between the soft seat and Katie's warmth, I fell asleep. On top of that, Aaron's car handled really well. One of the smoothest car rides I had ever been on. Whenever the car went over a bump in the road, the sport shocks smoothly absorbed the impulses as if we were floating along the road. The pistons inside the enlarged V6 engine ran smoothly, never missing or skipping.

Just as I woke up, we were driving onto the beginning of the iconic Golden Gate Bridge.

"Hey, Sleeping Beauty," Aaron greeted upon seeing me open my eyes. "Welcome to San Francisco!"

"Oh," I said with a grunt, trying to adjust myself in my seat. "How long was I asleep?"

"Oh, a couple of hours," Aaron said. "Katie's asleep now, if you haven't noticed."

"Oh god," I said, groaning in discomfort. "How much longer? I gotta piss."

"Eh, not too long," Aaron said. "Maybe about ten minutes from the bridge."

"Not too bad, I guess," I said.

Aaron just nodded, keeping his attentive brown eyes on the road.

We crossed the long Golden Gate Bridge and Aaron took the car down by an old run-down part of the harbor. We drove along the bay for about ten minutes until we reached a gate that had a No Trespassing sign posted on it. Aaron stopped the car in front of it and got out, then took a key ring out of his trench coat pocket and flipped through each individual key as he approached the gate. Katie woke up and stretched her arms.

"Hey, hon," I said.

"Hey." She yawned.

I gently squeezed her, and she held my arms around her waist.

"Sleep good?" I asked.

"You know it." She nodded.

"Good," I said as I watched Aaron unlock the padlock on the gate and open it. He walked slowly back to the car and got in.

"Okay," he said putting the car into gear, "let's move!"

We drove through the old gate and into an area full of ugly warehouses. Aaron drove slowly and turned a corner, driving toward the largest warehouse there, then stopped and parked the car right in front of the ugly-ass, sorry excuse for a structure. It may have looked good when this city was first settled, but then? Of course I'm just making an exaggeration, but you get the idea.

Aaron turned off the car and got out. "C'mon, you two," he said as he shut the door and started toward the rusty door of the building.

I unbuckled the seat belt and let Katie out then followed her. I shut the car door behind me and walked side by side with Katie to the rusty door in front of which Aaron was standing. Aaron pounded on the door with his paw curled into a fist, and we waited. Behind the door, I heard voices but couldn't make out what they were saying. Even my sensitive ears couldn't quite hear through that big metal door.

I then heard footsteps approach the door and heard the lock click, then the door opened, and standing there was a cheetah, an anthro cheetah, and I recognized him from the hit list that Jack had shown me. It was Erich.

"Ah," he said, raising his eyebrows upon seeing us, "hello, there."

"Greetings," Aaron said. "You must be Erich."

"Yes, sir," he said, speaking in a Dutch accent. "The one and only Erich."

"There's lots of other people named Erich, dude," Aaron said.

"Well, how many of them are cheetahs?" Erich said, stepping aside and letting us in.

"Well, shoot," Aaron said, walking in, "got me there, sonny."

"I'm Chance," I said, stopping in the doorway in front of Erich. "This is my girl, Katie." I wrapped an arm around her.

"So you're the Australian," Erich said as he grabbed my left paw and shook it. "Pleasure to meet you two."

"Pleasure is ours," Katie said.

"No," Erich said, looking at her and winking. "A beautiful female such as yourself can make anybody's day."

Katie giggled in apparent flattery, and I figured Erich was flirting with her, so I made my statement so he wouldn't get any ideas.

"Yeah, well, whatever we're here for, could we make it fast? We need to get Katie's pregnancy test."

"Oh?" Erich said. "She carrying your child?"

"Yeah," I said, "if she's even pregnant."

Erich grinned. "You lucky son of a gun," he said in Dutch.

"Cut it out, would ya?" I said back in his native language.

I led Katie into the building, and Erich showed us to a section called the so-called family room, where there was a couch, three recliners, and a TV. Behind the couch was a Plymouth Superbird armor car, white with a red flash along the side. The red flash broadened at the rear of the car to the tall tail on the back of the car.

On the other side of the Plymouth was a 1973 Nissan Skyline. Black with a red stripe running down the middle of the top.

Sure I was Australian, but of all cars in the world, the ones I admired most were American muscle cars. But as I looked and saw those two cars side by side, all I could think was *badass*.

In front of the cars was a counter with various tools and such, where a wolf with black fur was sitting on a stool and sharpening a katana. He looked up at me. I expected him to sneer at me menacingly, stereotyping him for what he was doing at that time. Instead, he cracked a smile, lifted his paw, and gave a little finger wave. I gave him a funny look and gave him a finger wave back. He just snorted and continued sharpening his sword.

"Everyone," Erich called, "come in here! We have some guests!"

Within seconds, I saw a flash of white come flipping from the banister and land on the floor before me. It was a beautiful female white wolf with almost florescent blue eyes. Strangely, the two wolves didn't wear a single article of clothing.

"So just tell your name and age, guys," Erich said. "Introduce yourselves."

"My name is Faolan," the young white wolf said. "I'm sixteen."

183

"My name's Keanu," the black wolf said, still sharpening his sword. "I'm eighteen."

Both wolves had strange names, but to my surprise, they spoke unaccented English, and they were both surprisingly young too.

"Well, I'm Chance, and I'm twenty-two. And this is my girl, Katie," I said, putting my arm around her shoulders.

"I'm nineteen," Katie added.

"Well, you guys know I'm Erich," Erich said. "I'm thirty years old." He looked around the room. "Where's the third?" he asked.

"Kay?" Faolan called. We waited in awkward silence.

"He's nocturnal," Erich whispered to us, "so he likes to sleep during the day."

We heard a doorknob jiggle then footsteps, and I watched him come out. I recognized him instantly.

"I'm up, I'm up." Kay yawned, rubbing his eyes as he came into the family room.

"Kay!" I shouted excitedly.

Kay darted his eyes toward me.

"Chance!" he shouted as he spread his arms for a friendly hug, which I instantly ran into, and we hugged.

"Good lord," Kay said, "I thought you were gone forever in London."

"I had a bit of trouble," I said.

We ended our embrace and stepped back. Kay kept one paw on my shoulder.

"I take it Jack found you," he said, "which is why you're here?"

"Yes," I said. "I also had a little visit with John."

"Lance?" Erich asked.

"Oh, yeah." I looked back at him and nodded.

"What's the guy like?" Faolan asked.

"He's arrogant," I said, "stubborn, almost childish."

184

"Ha ha." Keanu laughed.

"I've met the bastard many times," Aaron said. "I had worked for him at one point."

"So did I," I said. "I never realized what his true objective was, though. I made one mistake, or to be more specific, the US made a mistake, and the USSR and US alike are both gonna pay dearly for it unless we act now."

"Which is why we had you guys come here," Erich said. "These two young'uns are American but spent the last few years training in Japan, which is where they came from." He gestured to Faolan and Keanu with his head.

"I suppose we better explain the situation to everyone, now that everyone is here," I said.

"You know more about this than any of us do," Erich said.

"Okay," I said, "you guys may want to sit then."

After I had gone to the bathroom and relieved myself, everyone was sitting on the couch as I paced back and forth in the middle of the circle of seats. Katie kept a smiling face on, looking at me and batting her eyelashes at me as I explained everything from John's main objective, which led to my mission in 1968, and what happened all the way up to that moment. I explained every detail, which took about an hour or so, and Katie ended up falling asleep. Honestly, I didn't blame her.

Faolan sat patiently and listened attentively, as well as Erich and Kay. Keanu was getting restless, though, and would groan as he looked at the clock every couple minutes. At one point, I lost my cool and snapped at him to knock it off and listen, and he stopped his groans and inaudibly looked at the clock.

I finally ended my explanation, knowing it was dark outside, since there were some spots with cracks and holes where sunlight leaked through while it was still up. Now there was just empty blackness where the yellow light had once leaked through.

"Hmm," Faolan said once I finished, "never thought that was the reason he was so pissed."

"Well," I said, "that's why." I just shrugged, not knowing what else to say.

"Kinda childish, dontcha think?" Keanu said.

"Yeah," I said with a nod, looking at the ceiling in thought. "I guess you could say that."

"But how do we stop him?" Kay asked.

"Good question," I said. "I have the coordinates to the dropping point for the bomb. All we have to do is seize it and dispose of it. Getting the bomb is all that matters."

"And how will we do that?" Faolan asked.

"Don't worry," I said, "finding out what to do once we find out where it is is a specialty of mine."

"I take it you don't have a real plan." Kay commented.

"Yeah," I answered, "not really."

I told everyone what was going on with Katie, and we agreed to leave right away. We had planned what we would do next, and in a half hour, we all piled into the cars. Aaron, Katie, and I got into Aaron's Dino, while Keanu and Faolan got into the Skyline, while Kay and Erich got into the Superbird. Aaron turned on the car and turned it around. He drove slowly, looking into his mirror, evidently waiting for the others.

"Chance," he said, still looking into the mirror while slowly driving.

"Yeah?" I answered.

"Just want you to know you're doing good, bud," Aaron said. "You got further than I, or anyone else ever did. Keep it up, and we may just win this."

I saw the light from the headlights of the cars behind us shine on the interior of the Dino through the back window, then Aaron sped up a bit more and led the convoy to the road.

14

Aaron led the convoy all the way to the veterinarian, where at first I was a bit confused and asked why he didn't take us to a normal hospital. Aaron just explained that that place was just for humans, and this place would most likely deal with Katie, since they knew animals. We got out, and I warily escorted Katie in while Aaron told everyone else to stay in their cars.

"Hurry up," I heard Keanu say. "I gotta piss!"

I reached into my pocket to make sure my flasher was in there, but it wasn't. I frantically searched myself and cried out in panic.

"What the hell's your problem, dude?" Aaron asked.

"My damn flasher is gone!" I said.

"Relax," Katie said, "just use mine." She calmly reached into her leather jacket pocket and pulled hers out and handed it to me.

"Thanks, sweetheart," I said, giving her a big kiss on the cheek.

"You know, Chance," Aaron said as we walked to the main entrance, "one of these days, you're gonna have to forget the flasher. You're gonna have to reveal yourself to the people you've sworn to protect, and they'll realize who you really are."

"But it's not this day," I said.

"True," Aaron said, "but just take into account that one day, possibly soon, you'll have to. I know I've revealed myself to many people."

I just shrugged, and we entered the small, single-floored building.

"Um . . ." the desk clerk said upon seeing three anthropomorphic foxes enter the lobby. "C-Can I help you?"

"Yes," Aaron said, taking off his hat and holding it in both paws as he leaned into the counter to talk to her. "Pregnancy test for her." He pointed at Katie.

"Name?" the desk clerk asked.

"Katie," Aaron answered.

"Okay," the clerk said, taking out a clipboard. "Fill out the stuff that applies to her, and the doctor will be here in a few minutes."

"Thank you, ma'am," Aaron said, taking the clipboard. He walked over to where Katie and I were sitting and sat down.

"Crud," he said, suddenly getting up and setting the clipboard down then walking to the front desk. "Forgot the pen," he said to the desk clerk, as if she even cared. He came back over and handed the clipboard and pen to me.

"Why are you handing it to me?" I asked.

"Buddy," Aaron said, "I don't know jack about your girl, Katie. However, you know her inside and out."

I couldn't help but smile and chuckle.

"What?" Katie asked.

"Oh, nothing, sweetheart," I said. I began to fill out the sheet. I got a little more than halfway through it when the doctor came in. I could tell he was a bit startled upon seeing us.

"Uh . . ." he looked at his clipboard. "Katie?"

"That's me," Katie said, getting up and walking to the doctor, who had an even more shocked expression as she approached him.

"Wh-who are you with?" he asked, stammering.

"Just a sec," I said as I finished the paperwork.

I then got up and followed the doctor and Katie to the examination room. I had to wait outside of the room, so I decided to go back to the lobby and wait with Aaron. He sat there, reading an auto magazine silently as I sat next to him. We sat in awkward silence for a while, when I looked at Aaron and got an idea. A somewhat cruel prank idea to get back at him for humiliating me earlier, if I do say so myself. I walked to the desk clerk.

"Excuse me, madam," I said.

She looked up at me. "Yes?"

"I need to make an appointment for Aaron," I said quietly, gesturing with my head back at Aaron.

"For what?" she asked.

I could picture myself like Sylvester the cat from Looney Tunes, fiendishly rubbing my paws together as I played out my newly formulated mischievous plan. I whispered to her, and she nodded.

She handed me paperwork, which I filled out at the desk, making estimations about Aaron since I didn't know much about him. When I finished, I sat back in my seat next to Aaron, who had his face still in the magazine and had apparently not heard a single word I said. Or didn't pay any attention. I waited about two minutes. Another doctor came through the door and into the lobby.

"Aaron?" he said.

Aaron suddenly made a confused expression and looked at the doctor then at me. I just pointed to the door indicating for him to go, and he put down the magazine and walked to the doctor. They went through the doors, and at first all I heard was mumbling, then I heard Aaron raise his voice.

"What?" he shouted loudly.

He burst through the door and looked at me, then pointed at me, probably implying he'd get me back. I waved him on with my paw, and he went back through the door, and I just laughed to myself as soon as he was out of sight. Not long after, Katie came through the door with the doctor right behind her.

190

"Well," the doctor said, "she's pregnant."

"Oh, thank god," I said as I kissed Katie on the lips after she sat next to me. "Do you know what gender he or she is?"

"No," the doctor said, "but it's not just one."

"What?" I said.

"You're having twins," he said.

"Oh wow," I said excitedly, kissing Katie again, more passionately this time.

"Wait, how do you know that?" I asked curiously.

"We just found that two were fertilized in there," the doctor said.

"Oh yes!" I said to Katie, hugging her. "I love you, honey."

"I love you too, Chance," Katie said, hugging tightly back.

"Hehe." The doctor chuckled. "It's funny you guys do this, because humans are always pissed when the girl is pregnant."

"Okay then," I said. "It's not our problem that this generation of humans hates repopulating, but we gotta go."

"Wait, where's Aaron?" Katie asked.

"Oh yeah," I said as the doctor walked out of the room. "He's getting an exam. You know . . ."

Katie just wrinkled her nose.

"I did it, though. I gave him the appointment." I tried to squelch a giggle but had a hard time. "I couldn't help it. I thought it'd be hilarious."

"Okay then," Katie said.

"We'll wait here until he gets back," I said.

"You heard Keanu," Katie said. "He's gonna end up pissing himself."

"I know," I said, when suddenly, speak of the devil, Keanu burst through the door, wearing nothing but his Kevlar vest.

"Sorry, guys," he said, "but my bladder is about to explode." He walked over to the desk clerk. "Is there a bathroom in this place?"

"Um . . ." she pointed toward a hallway on the other side of the desk. "In that hallway."

"Thank you," Keanu said and ran in the direction of her finger.

I heard her mumble to herself. "What the hell is going on here? A goddamn furry convention?"

I never knew why these so-called furries kept getting brought up, for I didn't even know what the hell a furry was then, but whatever.

After a while, Aaron came bursting through the door then leaned against it, reinforcing it to keep anyone from pushing through.

I laughed.

"Have fun?" I asked.

"No time to explain." He moved hastily toward us. "We gotta get out of here."

He pulled us out of our chairs and pushed us out the doors to his Dino. He opened the passenger door, shoved me in, then pushed Katie onto my lap and shut the door behind her.

Keanu came running out of the building to the Skyline, hastily opened the door, and climbed in, shutting the door and turning the car on. I turned to Aaron with a wide grin on my face as he got in and shut the door behind him and started the car.

"So how was your appointment, Aaron?" I asked, eager to hear his reaction.

"Well," Aaron said, throwing the car into gear and beginning to drive out, "at first it was uncomfortable. But it's actually not as bad as you think. You should try it sometime."

"What?" I said. "Hell, no. I thought it would make you uncomfortable, and I was getting you back for making me look like an imbecile."

"Oh come on," Aaron said as we pulled out onto the street. "I was being sarcastic. Do you really think I enjoyed that?"

I smiled. "That's what I was waiting to hear."

We made it back to the apartment pretty late. The sky was pitch-black, and the streets were illuminated by yellow-orange street lights. We pulled into the parking lot of the apartment building, and Aaron parked his Dino, then Keanu parked the Skyline next to it, and Kay parked the Superbird next to them.

Katie and I got out of the Dino. Faolan was brushing and straightening the fur on her tail as she stood by the Skyline. In a pretty damn good mood, it looked like. She was always a high-spirited, energetic she-wolf. When I looked at her in later times, it was like she was a daughter of mine.

"God, that was a long drive," Faolan said, stretching her arms out. She had on a Kevlar vest similar to Keanu's, but for a feminine figure.

"No kidding," Keanu said, getting out of the driver's side of the Skyline.

Kay scoffed as he got out of the Superbird in unison with Erich.

"Kids." He shook his head. "Can't handle sitting in a car even."

"Hey," Keanu snapped. "Watch it, Kay, or you'll be the pincushion for my new steel."

"Shouldn't have got him those throwing knives, Kay," Erich said.

"Cool it, guys," Aaron snapped as he got out of the Dino. "Sheesh, it's like babysitting all over again."

"All over again?" Erich chuckled. "I couldn't see you babysitting."

"Oh yeah," Aaron said. "I did. Don't remind me about it, though."

"Quiet, guys," I told them. "There's people trying to sleep here."

We went into the building, through the lobby, and ascended to the floor where Tyson and Jeremy's apartment was. We reached the end of the hallway, and I knocked on the door softly. We waited a bit.

Keanu, Kay and, Erich bickered quietly among each other like children when I heard footsteps approach the door from the other side.

Soft footsteps. I guessed it was little Ethan coming to see who was at the door.

I heard the lock click, and the door opened. Sure enough, there was Ethan, looking up at us.

"Uh," he uttered. "Jeremy?"

"What is it, Ethan?" Jeremy said, walking into the front room. He noticed all of us and stopped in his tracks. "Oh, it's gonna be a full house tonight."

"It'll only be for tonight," I said. "We're moving out tomorrow morning. The last bomb should be there by then."

"Well, what if it isn't?" Jeremy asked.

"I don't know," I said, "but trust me, there's a higher chance of it being there than it not being there."

By the time we got there, it was around 8:00 p.m. By the time everyone established where they would be sleeping for the night, it was about 8:30 p.m. Nikolai was in the living room with Kay and Erich. Keanu, Aaron, and I would be in the front room, since I wanted the females to have a comfortable place for the night, so I let Faolan take my place in the bed with Katie. I could imagine them gossiping all night, but I guess that would be a bit stereotypical of females, but . . .

"You sure you're comfortable with Faolan sleeping with your girl?" Keanu asked me, taking off his Kevlar armor and setting it on the floor as he lay on the couch.

"Well, yeah," I said. "Why? She lesbo?"

"She tends to be a chatterbox," Keanu said. "To a talkative guy like me, it doesn't matter. But I noticed that Katie is pretty quiet."

"Once she gets going, she's pretty talkative," I said.

"Well, I've known Faolan all my life," Keanu said, "and I have the biggest crush on her. But she told me she has a slight crush on you."

I just wrinkled my nose. "She's only sixteen . . . seventeen?"

194

"Sixteen," Keanu said.

"Well, jeez," I said, "but Katie's my girl, and I make it pretty obvious."

"Yeah," Keanu said, "and you also got Katie pregnant."

"Yeah," I said, "and I wasn't ever planning on populating the world with folfs, either."

"Say wha'?" Aaron said, lying on the second couch.

"Folf," I said, lying on the third couch, "cross between a wolf and a fox."

"Where do you come up with half of the things you come up with, Chance?" Aaron asked.

"Excellent question," I answered. "Now shut your damn mouth and go to sleep."

"Okay, okay," Aaron said, rolling over so his back was toward me.

"Now that's a skill that few have," I whispered to Keanu, "getting Aaron to shut the hell up."

Aaron just grumbled to himself, and Keanu shook his head with a forced, half-crooked smile and shut his eyes. I fell asleep not long after.

Everyone woke up at about 7:00 a.m., and we got ourselves ready to go. Jeremy insisted we eat something, but I didn't want all of us to eat him out of a home, so I politely turned him down.

My weapons, except my Colt pistols, were in the car already, so I cleaned and loaded my .45s and put them into my belt holsters, which I put around my waist. I then put on my ASIS uniform, zipping it and straightening it out.

Katie put on her brown leather jacket, wearing only that and a white tank top underneath.

Faolan and Keanu helped each other put on their armor, then they strapped on their katanas and loaded up on shurikens (throwing stars), then put on Kevlar knuckle gloves and arm cuffs with three spikes on each.

Kay and Erich had dark-gray jackets. Kay's had an American flag on the right shoulder, and Erich's a Dutch flag. They said their weapons were in the Superbird and that I'd really like them. I'm easily impressed by guns, if you hadn't noticed by now.

We were all just finishing up getting ready to go when I heard the phone ring, and Jeremy went into the kitchen and answered it.

"Hello?" he said.

I heard some indistinct chatter over the phone.

"Mike?" Jeremy said. "What happened?"

I walked into the kitchen and stood right next to Jeremy as I listened to Mike faintly explain what happened.

"Lance Division," Mike said. "They were here just a little bit ago. We were preparing the plane to pick someone up in Chicago, and they came and attacked us."

I took the phone from Jeremy.

"Mike," I said, "do you know why they attacked you again?"

"Again?" Jeremy asked in an alarmed tone. "They were assaulted before?"

I nodded as Mike took a breath and continued.

"They tried knocking us out again," he said. "But I somehow didn't fall unconscious, and I saw them pull a big box from the cargo bay."

My eyes widened in realization. The Lance Division had smuggled the bomb on the plane. But why? And how?

"Mike," I said, "are you and Charlie okay?"

"I'm fine," Mike said. "But Charlie suffered a bad head injury and is being taken by the paramedics."

"How long ago were you guys jumped?" I asked.

"Like an hour ago," Mike answered. "If it helps, I heard them say something about heading to Anaheim and a big wreck on the freeway that's causing long delays."

"Do you know where in Anaheim?" I asked. "Do you know?"

"No." Mike sighed. "They said nothing about that."

"Thanks for calling, Mike," I said.

"I just did because I was sure it had something to do with what you were doing in Brazil," Mike said. "Whatever it is, you gotta stop it."

"That's what I'm about to do," I said. Mike hung up, then I did.

"We need to move right now," I said.

15

We got into our cars, but with a bit of separation. Tyson, who decided to come along, got into the Superbird with Kay and Erich. Katie went with Keanu in the Nissan. Nikolai went with Aaron in the Dino. That left just me and Faolan. She seemed a bit excited, though I hardly was since Keanu told me that Faolan had a crush on me, regardless of the fact that I loved and was with Katie. I kept my eye on her.

She got into my Cutlass a bit jumpy. I gave the location card to Kay, who would lead the convoy. His car had a positioning system just like mine.

I got into the driver's seat and started it. Everyone pulled out of the parking lot and got onto the road, and I was the last in the convoy. I followed Aaron's Dino closely, and all seemed well until we got to a traffic light. The rest of the convoy left us behind, but there was no way for me to communicate with them, so we stopped, and I grunted in frustration. Faolan and I just sat in silence until she decided to break it.

"So" —she cleared her throat— "Australian, huh?"

I just nodded. She was flirting; I could tell. At least trying to.

"What's Australia like?" she asked.

"It's hot," I replied nebulously.

"Oh." She nodded. "Hot guys come from hot places, right?"

198

Out of my peripheral vision, I could see her look me up and down. In the mirror, I watched a black Lincoln come a little too close to my car.

I then just looked at her. She looked at me and smiled, biting her lip. She was waiting for something. I thought I'd use my tactic of bringing someone up then bringing them down low. I leaned over the seat as if I were going to kiss her passionately on the lips. She grabbed my cheeks and held my head there for a while until I gently pulled away.

"Katie's my girlfriend," I said, smirking devilishly at her.

Her smile turned to a frown as soon as I said that. She was obviously upset by my gesture, but what could I say? I loved doing that.

The light turned green, finally, and I started to move the car across the intersection when a black GMC Suburban flew out in front of me. I stomped on the brakes, and the Lincoln hit my car, bumper to bumper.

I groaned as two more Suburbans pulled up to my Cutlass. Horns honked and people shouted as a bunch of armed men got out of the SUVs, all wearing LD uniforms and carrying either a twelve-gauge shotgun or an MP5 sub-machine gun. I locked my door and nodded at Faolan to do the same, which she did.

"Step out of the car, Mr. Logan," a man holding a Colt pistol to my window said.

I looked at him coldly.

"Out," the man said. "Get out of the car or we'll spray it up."

"Faolan," I said, "don't do it."

She just shook her head and opened her mouth, obviously too scared to speak.

"Don't comply," I said. I kept my paws on the wheel.

"Last chance," the man said as all the gunmen cocked their guns. "Step out of the vehicle and surrender yourself."

"Don't do it, Faolan," I said. "Trust me."

She was panicking. She was a little too young to be doing this, in my opinion.

"Fire!" the man shouted to the gunman next to him.

"Duck!" I shouted as the gunmen sprayed up my car with bullets and buckshot. Faolan screamed as I held her down, but I had to keep her held down because if anything were to give out, the windows would be the first.

"Ah!" Faolan screamed. "Help!"

"Stay down!" I shouted over the gunfire. That was when the driver's side window gave out after a shotgun blast hit it dead on and shattered to pieces, showering us with bits of glass.

I yelled, not really thinking straight.

I reached over, threw the car into reverse, and stomped on the gas pedal with my foot. The back tires screeched as they skidded on the asphalt then caught a grip on the road just as the back side window and the passenger side window cracked simultaneously. The back of my car collided with the black Lincoln again and shoved it aside in a vigorous manner.

I threw the steering wheel to the side, and the car swerved at a full 180 degrees. I then threw it into first gear and hit the gas. The car burned out again and sped off as the LD troops piled into their Suburbans and swerved around to pursue me. I looked in my mirror and saw them gaining. I didn't quite know how that was possible, but it was happening.

I looked around in a frantic manner for something to help get them off my tail, whether it was part of the car or something in the car. I looked in the rearview mirror and saw a little hatch on the back seat that led to the trunk, which was where my weapons bag was. I turned to Faolan.

"Faolan," I said, "you need to go through that hatch in the back seat and get my weapons from the trunk!"

"What?"

"Just do it!"

She unbuckled her seat belt and slowly crawled to the back seat of the car. Her tail kept getting in my face, and I was trying to drive, I kept having to swat her tail away, but it would just go back in my face.

Bullets started pinging off the car's frame. Not to mention the cracks from the bullets on the windshield obscured my view.

"Dammit!" I shouted in extreme frustration. I circumvented a slow car, and Faolan hit her head.

"Ow!" she yelled. "Careful, for crying out loud!"

"Sorry," I said as I looked for a way onto the freeway as we fled from our pursuers. We were steadily losing ground between them. I heard bullets ping off the back as one of the gunmen in the lead Suburban leaned out of the passenger side window as he fired his CAR-15 at us. These guys weren't about to quit soon.

I turned the wheel and drifted onto the main road parallel to the freeway, and the Suburbans followed my lead in a hostile manner. The passenger in the lead SUV kept right on firing at us.

"Damn," I muttered, looking at Faolan in the rearview mirror. "Hurry!" I told her.

"I'm trying!" she yelled with her head through the hatch and her rear end in the air.

We came upon a bus driving the speed limit on the road, and I sped up to it. I passed the bus and maneuvered my car onto the shoulder, then shifted down a gear and slowed down. As soon as I was behind the bus, I moved the car back into the other lane, right behind the lead Suburban. Bullet holes exploded through the back window of the large vehicle as the men inside started firing at me. The men in the Suburban behind me fired at my car as well. I was surrounded.

I shouted as the web like cracks on my windshield obscured my view, and I could hardly see anything. I swerved the car over and hit the bumper of the Suburban in front of me. The driver lost control and went off the road, still at full speed. He couldn't slow it in time before he collided with the concrete base of a light post, and the whole front end of the SUV was caved in at the extremity of the impact.

I looked around for the ramp onto the freeway and found one. I took the round ramp onto the freeway. My car started to slow as we rounded the entrance ramp, and one of the two remaining Suburbans hit my car from behind, causing a huge jolt that bumped Faolan into the front seat, on her back with her legs in the air. She held my weapons bag in her arms, which I was relieved about.

"Hand me one of those Skorpions!" I told her.

She sat upright in the seat and complied, opening the bag and pulling out one of the automatic handguns. I took it and pulled back the action, loading a bullet into the chamber. Faolan did the same with the other gun. We got onto the freeway, barely missing a civilian car upon our entrance.

"What now?" she asked.

"Ready for this?" I asked.

"For what?" she asked.

That's when I jerked the wheel, and my Cutlass skidded and turned completely around, the front bumper touching the Suburban's. I hit the cracked windshield as hard as I could with my gun and it broke to pieces, finally giving me a clear view. On instinct, I fired at the windshield of the Suburban, Faolan followed my lead and we sprayed the whole windshield.

The driver's head jerked back as a bullet collided with it, and two bullet holes exploded on the passenger's chest. He fired his CAR-15 uncontrollably, and under all the gunfire, the windshield gave out and shattered.

Faolan took a grenade out of the bag, pulled the pin, and tossed it through the now opened windshield.

I jerked the wheel again and turned the car back on course as the Suburban exploded and swerved into a cinder block, causing it to roll a few times. The large SUV was nothing but a dented hunk of metal by the time it stopped rolling. We were well past it by then.

"Chance," I heard Kay's voice. "Where the hell are you?"

Faolan pushed a button on the dashboard.

"We just got onto the freeway. We got caught up with some of the LD." She replied.

"Are you kidding me?" I said, seeing that there was a way of communicating with the other cars, and I wasn't even informed.

"What?" Faolan said, looking at me as if to say, *What did I do?*

"Why was I never informed about that?" I pointed at the button on the dash as another volley of lead started pinging off the car. The back window gave out and shattered to bits. My car was screwed at this point.

"We're on the freeway also," Kay said. "We'll wait for you to come by and give you a hand . . . or paw."

Faolan pushed the button. "Thanks!"

"Hope we come across them soon," I said, navigating through the nightmarish Los Angeles traffic. I looked back at the remaining Suburban, which was right behind us. The passenger fired at us through the cracked windshield of the SUV.

I maneuvered through the civilian cars, jerking the wheel back and forth with one paw and shifting up and down gears with my other. I turned a bit too late at one point and clipped a car, knocking off the side mirror.

I cursed under my breath. That was when I looked in the rearview mirror and saw Kay's Superbird speed up to the black Suburban that was right on our tail.

The window rolled down, and shots rang out. Bullets pinged off the Suburban's frame and shattered the window, then hit the driver. I could catch a glimpse of the passenger throw his arms up in panic as the Suburban swerved off the road and into a concrete divider. Kay swerved to avoid the spinning out of control Suburban.

"Holy hell!" Faolan said.

"How was the show?" Erich asked over the mic. He was evidently the one who took out the last SUV.

"Beautiful," I heard Keanu say.

"Great work," I said, with my finger on the button.

"Okay," Kay said, "you're gonna wanna take this next upcoming exit here."

"All right," I said, nodding as if we were talking face-to-face. "This one here?" I saw the exit sign.

"That's it," Kay said.

I nodded again and veered into the exit lane. I looked at the road signs.

"Where the hell are we?" I asked.

"We just got off Santa Ana Freeway," Faolan told me.

"Turn right onto East Katella," Kay said.

We rounded the exit ramp. When we got to the intersection, I should have looked right, for I had just begun to pull onto the road when Faolan screamed and a large class eight truck plowed into my car with such great force that it dented the side and shattered all the remaining windows.

"Ah, Jeez!" I exclaimed.

The truck kept going. An alarm started sounding in the car. My tires screeched as the truck pushed it sideways along the road at about forty miles an hour. Faolan didn't have her seat belt on, so she was shoved out of her seat and onto my lap, where she wrapped her arms around my neck in panic, and I kept one paw on the wheel and one arm around her waist.

"What do we do?" Faolan asked a bit shrilly.

"Um." I looked around and saw one of the Skorpions on the passenger seat. "I got it." I grabbed the Skorpion. More alarms blared.

"Chance, get out of there!" Kay said.

"Self-destruct in thirty seconds," a male voice in the car said.

I paused upon hearing that.

"Oh, come on!" I said.

I pulled back the action on the automatic handgun and aimed at the driver of the truck, obviously LD. I fired a couple shots at him, and he was knocked back, away from the wheel, and the truck began to slow a bit.

I still had no control of the car and we needed to lose the truck within the next fifteen seconds. I aimed way down and shot at the truck's tires. Most of the bullets hit either the bumper of the truck or the pavement. Ten seconds.

"Dammit!" I yelled as I fired more shots.

Five seconds.

I fired my last shot, which punctured the tire, and the truck swerved out of control and veered off the road, falling onto its side once it got to the ditch. My car finally came to a stop, I was still holding Faolan on my lap and gripping the Skorpion.

"Self-destructing," the car's voice said

"Oh hell!" I said and grabbed for the door handle, when suddenly, the roof of my car blew open and my seat was ejected.

Faolan and I landed violently on the shoulder of the road, and my car exploded in a ball of fire. I unbuckled my seat belt and let go of Faolan then stood and watched my car burn.

"No! My car!" I shouted.

I sensed someone's presence as they walked up next to me.

"Bummer," Kay said. I gave him a cold look.

"Chance!" Katie said, getting out of Keanu's car and running over to me. I opened my arms and received her, hugging tightly. I then looked down and saw that my bow with the special abilities arrows in their quiver had survived the explosion and landed about ten feet from me. I released Katie and grabbed them. The quiver had suffered some minor damage. Dented here and there. I looked at my car, which was now just a burning road obstruction, and sighed.

Me and Katie sat in the backseat of Keanu's car, and Faolan sat in the passenger seat up front.

"That was the craziest moment of my life!" Faolan said. "I mean, I've never been in a car wreck before! And I've never seen an explosion before!" She turned back to me. "Have you seen an explosion before? Of course, you probably have." She answered for me before I could even say anything.

"And that car chase, that was like the most intense thing I've ever been in! I mean, they were shooting at me! I've never been shot at before . . ." she rambled on and on.

Keanu was right about her being a chatterbox. I could see Keanu's reflection in the mirror, and judging by his frown and his slightly lowered brow, he was getting irritated.

I silently chuckled to myself and looked out at the road signs. We were on South Manchester Avenue, approaching the intersection with South Zeyn Street.

Keanu stopped at the red light. I looked around our setting, recognizing that we were in Anaheim. I'd been here once before. I wondered if there was any significance to Lance's position here. If he really wanted to do some damage, it probably would've been ideal to go north some and place it in the heart of Los Angeles or something. Somewhere with high population and an ideal stopping point for tourists, but I, being raised in Australia all my life, didn't know jack about most stopping points in the United States.

Was there something in Anaheim that made it popular? That attracted a lot of tourists? I looked out the window as I digested these thoughts. We started to move when I read the next road sign. Manchester had turned into Disney Way.

Disney? I thought. *Disney as in the movie company? Maker of movies such as "Mary Poppins"? Well known for the cartoon characters such as Mickey Mouse,*

Donald Duck, etc.? I processed this in my mind and came to a conclusion as soon as it hit me. *Of course! How could I forget? Disneyland is located here! So in a way, this place is more than ideal for the placement of the last bomb. There would be plenty of Americans from around the country and tourists from around the world there. Would other countries react to the fact that an American did all this and turned the world into chaos and try to remove the "threat" of the United States? Or would Lance just be pronounced a terrorist? Or would gain all the power he wishes to avoid justice?*

I thought about it more, one possibility leading to another.

Kay led the way and turned right onto Harbor Boulevard. We drove a little way when I heard Kay over the radio.

"Now, if you look to the left, you will see our destination," he said, as if he were the tour guide on a London River tour boat.

I looked to the left and didn't see anything at first, but we kept driving. I shrugged and looked out of my window to the right when I heard Keanu exclaim.

"You have *got* to be kidding me," he said.

I looked to the left again and could see the roller coasters, the unmistakable structures, the amusement park rides, and finally the castle of that one unmistakable place.

"Disneyland?" Faolan said, sitting up and taking her feet off the dash.

"Why the hell would Lance come here?" Katie asked.

"Tourism," I said. "Popularity, population . . ."

Katie gave me a look that was a mixture of frantic and horrified.

"We have to hurry," she said.

"Problem is," Keanu said, looking at me in the mirror, "he's probably got one entire area controlled by the whole freakin' LD in there, probably all hired as staff."

"Yeah." Faolan turned in her seat and looked at me with those innocent blue eyes. "And how will we get in unnoticed?"

Good question. Then I remembered what Tyson had told me in Vietnam when he was trying to convince me to live in the state of California.

"Yeah, there's the beaches in San Diego, Los Angeles, Oakland. Why you could get a job at Disneyland as the Robin Hood costume."

That last part was the key. I heard plenty about this new movie Disney had just released and looked at Katie. Just get her a Maid Marian costume and me a Robin Hood costume. I even had my bow and arrows, which would be my weapons. It would work for Katie and me, but to get the others in would have to require an entirely different plan.

"Press the button, would ya, hon?" I asked Faolan. She turned around and pressed the button, and I spoke. "Guys, pull into the parking lot and meet with me. I think I've got a plan."

Katie gave me a nervous look. She may have known what I had in mind.

16

Katie and I had managed to sneak inside the hoity-toity theme park through a maintenance entrance, and we sneaked around the area, looking for our disguises. Katie and I had both mastered the element of stealth through our training.

Katie and I had split up to more effectively find something. After making my way through the park for some time, I quietly and carefully moved through the trees in the garden area. I had left my ASIS uniform behind, so I wore just my black T-shirt and belt, though I still felt a bit exposed regardless. There were some spaces between the treed areas, divided by walkway, which were difficult to cross since I couldn't have anyone see me.

I hid behind a tree and waited then looked around and saw that nobody was coming, so I had begun to make my move when a little kid came running around the bend.

I cursed to myself as I hid behind the tree again. I heard more approaching voices.

"Slow down!" the presumed mother of the kid said. I heard the presumed father chuckle and mutter something.

"Man, it's hot out here!" a teenage girl said. She wore a green T-shirt that was way too big for her over a striped black-and-pink long sleeved shirt and jean shorts.

That green shirt was just what I needed, the perfect ex machina that had appeared so suddenly as to provide for my current, seemingly insoluble predicament. Now that I had found this piece to my disguise, the only problem at that given time was how I was going to get it.

"Honey, why don't you take off that ugly green shirt?" the mother said as she came around the bend. She was pushing a stroller with a toddler in it.

They all stopped, and the teenage girl took off the oversize green T-shirt and tried to tuck it into the little undercarriage of the stroller. They began moving again, the girl walking ahead.

"Hon, slow down," the father said, lingering behind the mother. "Not all of us are as young and energetic as you are."

That was just a cover-up of the fact that he was fat. I guessed the green T-shirt was just a hand-me-down from him since it was significantly oversized for his daughter, who looked to be a bit taller than me. They rounded the next curve in the walkway, and I waited a bit impatiently for the old fat ass father to get around the corner. By then, I felt hopeless that they had all gone out of sight, taking that green shirt with them.

Fat bastard, I thought in my annoyance. *But that's America for you.*

I made sure the coast was clear and began to move across the walkway when I just happened to look down and spot the green T-shirt. Apparently, it had fallen out of the undercarriage of the stroller just to give me relief with an add-on to the ex machina. I picked it up, wondering if it actually would work out for my disguise.

As I looked it over, I suddenly heard more voices approaching, so I quickly darted to the patch of trees on the other side. I hid within some bushes and continued to look over the shirt as the voices passed by. The shirt was hideous and even had a large purple peace sign on the back of it.

210

Disgusting. But I had to make do with whatever I got. My sensitive nose caught a scent. I sniffed the shirt, and it smelled strongly of perfume. A feminine, flowery smell.

"Good lord," I said to myself, "where's Old Spice when you need it?"

I took off my belt and quiver, then put on the shirt anyway after turning it inside out. Like I said, I had to make do with whatever was available. I put the belt around my waist, around the shirt. It was a little medieval looking, except one thing. I tore the shirt a little to make a V-neck down my chest. *Better.* I continued my way through the patch of trees.

On the other side, I encountered a little sales cart, which I ducked behind. The thing was loaded with souvenirs. I looked over the cart, with my nose barely over the cart's surface. I looked it over while the sales guy wasn't looking. I looked up and happened to spot something. A tan feathered hat. Actually, about a dozen of them hanging from a rack.

"Hmm," I thought aloud.

I slowly went to grab it when the sales guy started to turn around, so I had to dart my paw down out of sight. He looked at the cart, then up at the trees, then turned back around and faced all the people passing by. I went to grab the nearest hat again. That was when a little kid and his father came to the cart, so I had to drop my arm again.

"Anything you want, son?" the father asked, looking at the cart.

"Um." The kid put a finger in his mouth then pointed at a feathered hat. "That!"

The sales man grabbed the hat that was nearest to me, and I quietly grunted in frustration.

"This?"

The kid nodded eagerly. The father handed the salesman some cash, and he returned the change. The man and his son walked away, the son skipping excitedly with his new medieval feathered cap. I watched them go and sighed at the sight of the father picking up his son, hugging him, and carrying him to their next destination.

At that moment, I began to wonder how my relationship with my children and Katie would be, but I snapped out of it. I had to focus on the task at hand. I peered back over the surface of the cart. Bad move. The salesman was looking right at the cart and spotted me. I ducked back down.

"Hey there," he said softly, slowly moving around the cart to the side I was on.

Dammit, I thought, *what now?*

He slowly came around the corner of the cart. Evidently, he thought I was a regular fox or a dog; otherwise, he wouldn't even think of coming close to me. As he peered around the corner of the cart, I grabbed him and vigorously pulled him down. He looked up at me with an expression of surprise and horror.

"Sorry, man," I said, giving him an expression of sympathy.

I hit him hard in the head, and he was out cold. I laid his unconscious body aside, peered over the surface of the cart, quickly grabbed the next closest feathered cap, and ducked back down. I examined the cap. It was made of poorly sewn, cheap material, and the feather was a plastic-like material that felt almost like a real feather, but not quite.

I put it on, hoping it wouldn't fall apart, since it felt as if it would. I quickly scampered back into the trees and adjusted my costume disguise in the bushes then made my way out to the next walkway. When I saw that nobody was coming, I moved out of the bushes and started casually walking on the walkway. I looked down at my shirt, adjusted my belt, and hoped to god that my disguise would be convincing enough to anybody who may pass me by.

I heard voices headed my way. If I really needed to know if my disguise would work, now was the time. I took a deep breath, boosted my confidence, and kept right on walking down the walkway. I saw a young man, his presumed girlfriend, and a tagalong guy come around the bend. They all saw me.

"Oh, my God," the girl said, "your costume is so cute!"

They stopped in front of me, and I in front of them.

"Can we get a picture?" the young man asked.

I made like a costume and kept my mouth shut in the same smiling expression and nodded.

The girl squealed excitedly, ran to me, and hugged me.

"Such a soft costume too!" she said.

I hoped this would be over soon as the young man handed the tagalong the camera and stood next to me. I put my arms around them both, keeping on the same expression.

We waited for a bit, and the tagalong finally took the picture. I let go of them both, and the young man went to retrieve his camera. The woman gave me a hug and a light kiss on the cheek. I tried my best to behave the way a guy in a Disneyland costume would and put my hands on my cheeks, shaking my head in a sort of bashful manner. She just giggled and walked over to the others, and they all moved along.

"Enjoy your time here!" I called as they turned their backs on me.

I began to walk away as they turned around and answered with thanks. I made my way to the authorized personnel gate, where I told the others to wait.

I had to stop for hugs and pictures along the way, and to be honest it was a little awkward. If Katie were with me at that moment, it probably wouldn't be so awkward, but I just kept moving. I did eventually run into Katie, finally. She had on a dress with a bit of cloth around her head like a medieval maiden. It was perfect. I led her toward the gate and complimented along the way.

"Where did you get an entire dress?" I asked, the biggest grin on my face.

"Oh," Katie said with a shrug, "I found the place where all the princesses' dresses are. I took some things from different dresses."

"Ah," I said. "Nice one, sweetheart."

I leaned down for a kiss, and she kissed me and we held paws as we walked along.

"Thanks, hon," she said. "You look really cute in that outfit."

"Thanks, baby," I said, kissing her cheek. "You're really pretty in that dress."

"Thank you, honey," she said.

We finally made it to the gate after a while and opened it from the inside. Faolan was the first one through.

"Oh my god!" she said, walking up to me. "So cute, I just wanna kiss your cheeks!"

I rolled my eyes.

As far as I knew, everyone had weapons on them. Kay and Erich carried concealed Beretta 9 mm pistols; Keanu and Faolan had their katanas and throwing projectiles plus some mystery weapons used for emergencies; Tyson had an Uzi, which was provided by Kay; and Katie had her custom Walther PPK, which I hadn't been aware of her having until that moment. I just had my bow and quiver full of special use arrows.

"Everyone here?" I asked and looked at everyone.

"Where's Nikolai?" Kay asked

"Hold up, comrades!" Nikolai shouted from the other side of the gate before I could say anything. He ran in, jamming a magazine into his tactical Kalashnikov AK-47.

"Just filling up," he said, holding up the AK and pointing at the magazine.

"This lunatic better be here," Keanu said with a sneer.

"Well," I said as I shrugged, "I've worked with ASIS for a long time. I haven't known the intel to be wrong."

"Don't worry, Chance," Faolan said, grinning at me, obviously swooning. "Mistakes are made. Nobody's perfect."

She winked at me and blew me a kiss. I just frowned and huffed.

"Okay, guys," Tyson said, "enough of the chatter. We gotta find these bastards and stop them quickly. We're running out of time."

Tyson had always been one to goof off, but when there was a sense of urgency at the task at hand, he had always been one to suddenly turn serious and take charge.

"The little human is right," Nikolai said. "Knowing the US intelligence agency, they'll make it as quick as possible, so they may be moving out in less than an hour or so."

"Little human?" Tyson glared at Nikolai.

"Anyone is little compared to me." Nikolai smirked.

"Yeah," Kay said, "and knowing the LD, they probably will clone to smuggle the last bomb out."

I nodded in understanding.

"They most likely will."

Kay took out a radio and handed it to Tyson.

"Care to do some scouting?" he asked.

"Sure thing," Tyson said, taking the radio and beginning to walk off.

"Uh, Tyson?" I called his attention.

He turned around and looked at me.

"You may wanna lose the gun." I pointed at it with my folded bow.

"Trade me," Kay said, waving him over. Tyson came back over and handed him the too-large-to-be-concealed Uzi, and Kay gave him his 9mm pistol.

"Don't lose that," Kay said.

Tyson nodded and began to walk off, concealing the weapon.

"And Tyson," I called as he groaned impatiently and turned to me. "Just try to look like a tourist."

I gave him a little two finger salute and waved him off. He walked out of the scene, and we waited.

We had waited just under a half hour before Tyson radioed Kay and told him where the LD was. He said they were disguised as maintenance personnel at the castle. The only reason Tyson could tell was because he caught a glimpse of one of the LD operatives' CAR-15s as he was grabbing some tools. Both had concealed pistols on their tool belts.

I guessed the castle would be where they were gonna make the delivery. Those "maintenance guys" would be the ones making the transfer. That was a common tactic of the LD. Having people inside a certain place disguised as staff, guards, maintenance personnel, plumbers, electricians, etc. It was commonly referred to as "tunneling" since it was like the "mole in the agency" type thing.

Kay sent Katie and me to go ahead and find Tyson since we were the ones with an acceptable disguise. We made our way toward the castle, Katie and I with our arms linked together as we walked. We stopped every now and then for pictures with the oblivious guests of the theme park.

Katie and I were just walking along when I was suddenly pulled aside into a secluded corner. I saw it was Tyson before I could react. I was about to say something when Tyson put a finger to his lips.

"Shh," he softly shushed. Katie came to our secluded corner.

"What is it, Ty?" she asked as she knelt down next to us.

"The castle is just over there," he whispered as he pointed to the tree line and indicated going over. "That's where the LDs are." He got up and motioned for us to follow him into the trees.

We followed him through the dense plants and came to a sidewalk divide, which we crossed when nobody was around, then through more trees until we reached the water. Across the water, we could see the castle. A bridge led from the entrance of the castle to a roundabout of Main Street. As I scanned the scene, looking for the supposed LDs who were there, Tyson's finger blocked my view as he pointed toward the roundabout. I looked in the direction of his finger, and he was pointing at a truck. Obviously an LD, armored five-ton painted yellow and with a fake company name on the door.

"You've gotta be kidding me," I whispered, shaking my head.

"That's only one of them," Tyson whispered. "The other one will be here soon. I heard the LDs talking while I was acting like a tourist. They already have the bomb apparently, but it's going somewhere else."

I nodded.

"And if we can't stop it, the whole world is gonna break out into World War Three."

"Why would they come here just to make a transfer?" Tyson asked.

"This is the last place anyone would think to look," I answered. "Even if things got out of hand, nobody would wanna make a scene."

"We have to stop them here," Katie added. "They can't be allowed to move past this point."

"We gotta get the others over here." I nodded to Tyson, who handed me his radio and took off back to where the others were.

I felt Katie give me a kiss on the cheek.

"I love you," she said, as if she were saying, *In case we don't make it.*

As soon as everyone arrived, we strategically positioned ourselves around the castle. Kay, Erich, and Nikolai divided up and waited on either side of the castle. Tyson acted like a tourist reading a map and not looking where he was going.

We found the so-called maintenance guys at the entrance of the castle. They had a big cart, which had the four-foot-by-four-foot crate containing the bomb in it. How they expected they would get away with this, I had no idea, but apparently, it was working.

Anyway, Tyson would begin moving as soon as the truck arrived, and he would stall them in whatever way he could just past the gate, giving Keanu and Faolan time to rope down from the top of the castle and approach them from there. Kay, Erich, Aaron, and Nikolai would flank from the sides. Katie and I would wait on the other side of the castle, and we would approach through the gate, and as soon as we had them surrounded and outnumbered, we could stop them in their tracks; hence, foiling Lance's plan.

Seemed like a perfect plan to me, though I had never devised any plans in my whole career. I was just assigned to stick to and follow them, but Kay, who had plenty of experience with devising plans and tactics, seemed to approve of my idea and went along with it.

From my standpoint with Katie, on the other side of the castle, we had a perfectly clear view of the LD operatives in the gate, waiting with their cart. Sometimes people would get near them, and they'd lead them away, saying something about harmful chemicals and waiting for a truck to take them away to arrive. We waited for close to a half hour before I finally saw the distinctive armored five-ton pull up to the roundabout with its bed canopy removed and different chemical canisters in the back so it would look like a truck meant to move that kind of stuff around.

I held the radio to my mouth and pushed the button.

"Ty, you're up."

Tyson, with his eyes on the map, began walking across the bridge toward the castle gate. The LDs secured the crate on the cart and began to move. I watched the LDs and Tyson meet about halfway on the bridge. I called Tyson a bit too late to move and we lost the element of them being just past the castle gate so they could be flanked easier. My sensitive ears caught most of what they said.

"Hey," one of the LDs snapped, "watch it!"

Tyson jumped as if startled and to avoid the oncoming cart. The man pushing the cart tried to maneuver the cart, and the crate fell off. I cringed, thinking it may go off.

"Hey," the other LD said, "careful! We're carrying harmful substances here!"

"Uh, I'm sorry," Tyson said in his own fake African-Indian-sounding accent. "I'm just not very familiar with this place."

"Well, you should be familiar with this," the first LD pointed at his shoulder, where a black-and-yellow patch was sewed onto his suit. "That means we handle dangerous chemicals in every language except Braille."

"Well," Tyson said as he shrugged confusedly, "I'm sorry." His voice cracked.

One of the LDs muttered something and bent down to pick up the box, the other helped.

"Need help with that?" Tyson asked, bending over, placing his hands on top of the crate and shoving it down.

"No, we don't!" the first LD got up and lightly shoved him away with his gloved hands. "What if I told you this is liable to explode?"

"I'm sorry," Tyson repeated, "I didn't know. I just wanna help."

"Well, where the hell are you from," the second LD asked bitterly, "Canada? Now beat it!"

I saw the ropes drop from above the gate, and Faolan and Keanu slid down slowly and stealthily as if they had read my thoughts, for I knew it was time to move. I began walking toward Tyson and the LD operatives. I motioned for Faolan and Keanu to stay put as I walked past them and kept right on walking.

I was about three feet away when one of the LDs saw me. His eyes widened as he recognized me, and he reached to his belt and drew his suppressed pistol. I spun around, roundhouse kicked the pistol from his grip, and grabbed his arm. I chopped at the inside of his elbow, forcing it to bend, and I pulled his forearm behind his back, bent him over, and brought my knee up to his face. He quickly stood upright just to fall backward onto the cement.

The other LD had already drawn his pistol and had it aimed right at me, but Tyson grabbed the pistol from behind and yanked it away. A muffled shot rang out, then another. The operative elbowed Tyson in the gut with his free arm, and Tyson let go.

By then I had made my move and was in range to strike the guy when he saw me coming. He made an effort to punch my nose, but I moved my head aside and slapped his fist away. I then grabbed at the wrist of his armed hand and hit his hand as hard as I could, forcing him to drop the pistol to the ground. I was a little too occupied to notice the other LD getting up from the ground, until Tyson moved to him and kept him occupied.

This man was bigger and a lot stronger than me and the other guy, so he was a bit difficult. He had managed to hit his mark right on my nose, which caused me to let go of him and fall back, my sight blurred with forced tears. This large-stature man loomed over me, about to finish me off, and that was when I swept at his leg behind the knee, and he was forced onto his knees. I got onto my two feet as quickly as possible and jumped into the air, kicking him in the face with both legs, and he fell back hard. I landed on the ground, taking my own share of pain.

Tyson had just knocked his victim to the ground with his fist when I heard the clicks of rifles loading. I looked around and saw a large number of LDs, all with their rifles trained on Tyson and me. In the front-middle of all of them stood their boss.

"I knew I'd find you here." Lance chuckled, grinning his devilish grin. "Let's just say I came prepared to pick up the package."

I slowly got onto my feet.

"Lovely costume, by the way," Lance gestured at my attire. "You look exactly like the Robin Hood from that children's cartoon, except there's just one problem . . ."

He stepped toward me.

"You won't be the victor of this story," he said with a voice as cold and deep as his stare. "Nottingham is going bye-bye. In this case, America." He smirked.

I wished I could just skin his face off right then and there, but there were several men with their guns trained on me. I looked around at the people who circumvented us, avoiding getting in the way of what they may have thought to be police work.

"You won't get away with this," I said. "I'll die before I have to see those bombs go off!"

"Correction," Lance said, holding his finger in the air. "I need you alive when the bombs go off. I've taken some desperate measures to keep you alive. You're not dying."

I glared at him. He just smiled and touched my nose with his finger.

"Take this one into custody," he said as he turned to walk away toward a black Lincoln waiting for him. "I don't want him to miss this. You may kill the others."

He opened the rear passenger door of the car, giving me one last evil grin, and sat in the car, closing the door.

As the Lincoln drove away, the men all trained their rifles on Tyson. One of the disguised LDs had his pistol against my head. I was now helpless at this moment. I was either going to watch Tyson get shot right on the spot, or I was gonna see him get taken away so he could be executed in a secluded place. I swallowed. I felt like there was a pit in my stomach, and my pounding heart had risen to my throat. I tried to utter his name as one of the men held a gun to Tyson's head.

Suddenly, a throwing knife was sunk into the man's chest, and he fell to the ground dead, or critically wounded. Faolan suddenly flipped over the crowd of men, her katana drawn, and she swung it at the nearest man. It cut from his shoulder and across his chest, and he fell to the ground.

Keanu came from the direction of the knife with his katana drawn, and he swung it at a rifle that was pointed at him. Shots were fired. Keanu kicked him down and turned to his next victim. I watched in awe as these young wolves demobilized the seven or eight men who had had us surrounded with absolutely nothing but their fighting skills and their blades. I heard my radio go off.

"Guys," Kay said, "we got company."

I looked at the roundabout, and more LD trucks pulled into the scene. However the hell they got them into the park, I had no idea, but the LD could do anything.

I looked at the crate that contained the bomb. I knew that I couldn't carry the crate and get away from these men fast enough; however, there was a critical component about the size of a soda can inside that the bomb couldn't work without. It held the transmitter/detonator that armed it once it was put in its designated target area and would be ready to go off on the push of a button. The reason Lance could only set them in specific areas was because they were only effective to a certain range, but Lance had created a chain of bombs transmitting one to another so all would go off once he hit the button on his remote once he was somewhere in the Central United States or central Soviet Union.

I quickly got up, shoving aside one of the LDs as I ran for the crate, and I fell to my knees by it. I fumbled around the crate with my paws for the button to open it, and once I located it, I pushed down on it with my finger and quickly tossed aside the lid. I peered in the crate and searched through the wires, explosive, and nuclear energy for the soda can transmitter. Once I found it, I grabbed it and yanked it out of its place and booked it to the castle gate.

Tyson, Keanu, and Faolan drew their attention from the LDs to me and followed me. Kay, Erich, Nikolai, and Katie were all standing at the castle gate.

"Chance," Erich said, "what are you doing?"

"I've been trained to use and handle explosives of all kinds," I said, quickly halting in front of them. "This is a critical component to the bomb, and if they don't have it, then the bomb can't go off."

I held up the transmitter.

"Oh yeah," Kay said, "that's a Sprite can."

I squinted at him, confused.

"What?" I said. "No, it's a transmitter."

Tyson interrupted me.

"Chance, you need to move. We got LDs coming into the park," He panted. "Whatever you got there, they can't have it. You gotta move."

"Sprite can is just a nickname, by the way. Now we gotta go, honey," Katie said, grabbing my arm and running with me.

"We'll keep them occupied!" Kay shouted after us. We ran past a building, and I heard a few shots ring out. We were all lucky it was late afternoon and there weren't as many people here. Katie and I reached the Mad Tea Party ride just as we saw a few undercover LDs headed our way, so we had to make a detour through the small labyrinth of spinning, orbiting teacups.

I was ahead of Katie and could hear people making loud comments about us. Some people gasped and gave startled screams, seeing a bunch of armed men chasing us onto the ride, who stumbled and tripped over the uneven, rotating surface. Some collided with the spinning teacups.

"Central Intelligence Agency!" one of the operatives shouted, letting everyone know who all these men with weapons were.

I was at the other end of the ride when Katie had tripped over her dress.

"Chance!" she shouted.

I turned around and saw her. An operative had his gun pointed at her and was ready to fire. I quickly dropped the Sprite can transmitter, unfolded my bow, and reached back to my quiver, drawing a standard arrow. I then quickly aimed toward the operative, drew, and released. The arrow sailed through the air and hit the gun that was aiming at Katie. He was forced to bring his gun up in the air, accidentally squeezing off a burst of about four bullets form his CAR-15.

The people around us gasped and screamed. Some were awestruck at the shot I had made unintentionally. I was hoping to hit the operative, but that worked. I then grabbed Katie's paw, picked up the Sprite can, when another operative came at us with his weapon ready. I grabbed his gun and twisted it from his grip and, at the same time, throwing him onto the ground. In a moment, Katie and I were about to be flanked entirely, so I looked around for the tallest tree, grabbed an arrow fitted with a rope and shot at the top of the tree. The arrow stuck firmly in, and I folded up my bow, clipped it to my belt, and held onto the rope.

"Grab on, honey!" I shouted, and as soon as she did, we took a running start, and we were lifted off the ground as the rope swung up, carrying us upward.

The problem was, I didn't exactly know where. As the rope began to swing back, I panicked and lost my grip and, on instinct, tried to grab something, which just happened to be Katie's shoulder. I was sure we were toast as we fell, but much to my surprise, we landed on something not very far from where we fell. I sighed in relief as I realized we had landed on a structure meant to look like a cottage.

"Hey, Katie?" I asked. "Would now be a good time to ask you something?"

"Yeah?" Katie said as she got on her feet and straightened out the dress.

"So I've been thinking a long time about what you said about settling down and all back in Vietnam."

"And?" Katie looked at me with her eyebrows raised in apparent anticipation for my comment.

"Katie, my love," I said, taking her paw, "will you marry me?"

"Oh, babe," Katie said, putting her free paw over her heart, "I thought you'd never ask. Especially at a time like this."

Suddenly, bullets pinged off the cottage roof, accompanied by sounds of suppressed gunfire.

I then lost my balance and slipped off the roof, landing on my ass on the ground.

Katie fell after me, and I caught her in my arms as she was about to fall right onto me. I smiled at her, and she smiled back when I suddenly noticed another operative coming. He swung his rifle at us, and I rolled, shoving Katie over with me as he barely missed us.

"Could've at least chosen a more romantic setting to ask a question like that." Katie continued, almost laughing.

"Where'd you wanna go for our honeymoon?" I asked as I blocked another hit from the operative's rifle butt with my bow. "France? Spain?"

"Why not?" Katie said. "Maybe go back to Rio."

I swung the operative's rifle away and brought my bow back up to his face, knocking him on the ground.

"Sounds perfect," I said, grabbing Katie's paw again.

We took off and made a run for it. We had the surroundings on our side, since there were people everywhere, and they could not fire due to the risks of wild shots.

We ran to the parade route toward a large blank building and passed by a ride entrance with little boats and a small river that seemed to flow into the building.

We turned right onto a different road that went around the building. I could hear the LDs right behind us as we ran. I saw a door on the side of the building.

"This way!" I veered off the path and headed for the door. At the moment, I arrived at the door I panicked. There wasn't a hinge on it. Just a lock.

"Oh no!" I shouted.

"Here," Katie said.

She pushed me aside and took out her own little lock-picking tool, then stuck it in and worked the lock. I could hear the men getting closer, and I urged her to hurry.

"I'm trying!" she said. Then, there was a click. "Got it!"

She managed to pull the door open, and we went in. It was dark, and I couldn't see a thing. Being a fox, I usually could see in the dark, but only if there was some light to reflect. I fumbled around and felt my way through the dark until my foot stepped on air, and I fell into water.

"Chance!" Katie shouted.

I surfaced and gasped for air as I flailed my arms around, feeling for a ledge or something to grab on to. I finally felt one and held onto it, coughing. I felt Katie put her paw on mine.

"You okay, hon?" she asked.

"Yeah." I coughed and looked around in the darkness. I realized I had lost my feathered cap in the water. "Where the hell are we anyway?"

I heard a boom then voices enter the building. The LDs had blown the door open with a charge and were inside. There was some chatter, and commands were shouted, then there was a click, and lights turned on. The lights weren't the only things that turned on, though, as there was also one iconic thing that turned on. Known for bugging the living crap out of people.

Little robotic people moved around as they cycled the song "It's a Small World" in the colorful room split by the canal.

"You may as well just kill me now!" I shouted.

Katie helped me as I climbed out of the water and onto the ledge.

"Over here!" one of the LDs shouted. We began to run and maneuver through the robots and props.

"Stop right there!" another shouted.

The "It's a Small World" song in that annoyingly high voice cycled over and over again as the robotic kids cycled their movements.

"Jeez," Katie commented, "of all places we had to come upon!"

"No kidding," I added.

I heard some shots echo through the building. Some stray bullets hit the poor singing robot kids. One's head exploded, and sparks flew out right next to me. I shielded my face from the pieces and sparks and exclaimed out loud. There was indistinct shouting as the armed men stormed the building.

"We should cross the water!" Katie said.

"You're right!"

We needed to get away from the LDs, and the only clear way was across the water. Katie ripped off the headpiece of her costume and jumped into the water, and I jumped in after her, and we both began swimming hastily across.

By the time we had gotten halfway across, the LDs had caught up and began firing at us. Bullets splashed into the water around us as we swam faster. Katie suddenly exclaimed in pain. She had caught a bullet in her shoulder blade and struggled in the water to keep her head above the surface.

"Chance!" she screamed.

"I'm coming, Katie!" I shouted, swimming faster.

I saw her head disappear under the water as I swam to her and grabbed her, holding her with the arm that had the paw holding on to the Sprite can as I pushed through the water with my other arm.

Suddenly, I felt two bullets hit me. One exploded through my chest just under the collarbone, barely above my lung. The other hit me on the side, below the armpit.

I shouted, groaning as I pushed to the other side through the water that was turning cloudy red with our blood. When we made it, I held on to the ledge and helped Katie up, and Katie turned around and helped me out of the water, and then, I felt a bullet from a .45 pistol go through my ear, leaving a hole. I yelled in pain as I put my paw to my ear.

I had now already taken three bullets, and I was losing mobility and was probably doomed to bleeding out soon. Katie held my paw and pulled me to safety as we moved into the next room, which was another section of the ride. Both of us stopped and took a little breather. Both of us in pain from taking bullets and exhausted from running and swimming.

"You okay?" Katie asked, holding me as I knelt to rest. I hugged her waist and leaned my head against her belly, panting heavily.

"We have to get out of here," I panted.

In the faint light, I could see another door quite a distance from us, but it was open. There was probably a maintenance guy in the building or someone who heard the commotion or something, but that was our ticket out.

"I gotta get you out of here," I said, looking up at Katie. "You're carrying our child. You need to get away from this."

"I'm not gonna leave you, Chance," she said, looking down at me and stroking my head.

"You have to," I said. "You need to be safe."

"I'm gonna stick with you, honey," she said. "We've been together from the start, and I'm not gonna leave you."

228

"Well, we need to get out of this building," I said, weakly getting on my feet. "There's an exit door over there." I pointed to the open door.

Katie nodded.

"One more swim, hon," she said.

She pulled me to the water, gently slipped in, and began to swim to the other side. I followed her lead, getting into the water and swimming after her. Once we got to the other side, we helped each other out of the water and moved through the props to the exit until we made it outside. We were now behind the building and made our way to the west side of the building. My radio crackled.

"Chance?" Kay asked. "You all right?"

I took the radio from my belt and pushed the button as I held it to my mouth.

"Yeah," I answered. "Katie and I are good."

"Where are you two?" he asked.

"Behind the worst damn ride in this whole park," I responded bitterly.

"Oh," Kay said understandingly, "I got it. We're headed your way now."

"Meet us on the west side of it," I responded again.

Kay said, "Got it. You still got the transmitter?"

I held it up and examined it. After all that, I hadn't dropped it, much to my surprise.

"Affirmative," I answered.

"Nice work, Chance," Kay said.

"Thanks, mate," I said. I grabbed Katie's paw and led the way through the alleyway.

We had made it to the northwest section of the park, exhausted of all energy and soaked to the skin. We did get some looks from the few people there, but at this point, Katie and I didn't care. Those people most likely thought we were just more costumes.

We waited about five minutes for Kay. In the meantime, Katie eased my stress by holding my paw in hers and placing her other paw on my chest, looking lovingly up at me. She smiled. I smiled back. Katie always knew how to calm me down since that day in Vietnam, which to this day I remember so vividly. Such a picturesque memory I'll never lose.

"Chance!" I heard Faolan's young voice as she came running to me.

I could see Keanu roll his eyes, and I did the same as Faolan wrapped her arms around me, wagging her tail back and forth. She pulled back, and I looked at her. She had a minor gash on her forehead and a big cut on her cheek, presumably from one of her knives or something. Both leaked blood and stained her fur.

Keanu approached after Faolan. He had more cuts and gashes on him that were hard to detect through his black fur until he got close.

Erich had lost his sunglasses and had a bullet wound on his arm just above the bicep, and blood leaked from his mouth, staining his chin fur.

Kay had cuts on his forearms and a bullet graze that tore his sweatshirt and exposed his bleeding wound plus a gash on his forehead just above his right eye and one below his left eye.

"You guys look like you've been through hell," I said, moving Faolan aside.

"Yeah," Kay said with a wince, "we barely got them neutralized. Erich and I took bullets."

"Where's Nikolai?" I asked, realizing he wasn't with them.

"Nikolai and Tyson got separated," Kay said and shrugged, "I guess the LDs got them."

"Aaron got lost as well," Erich added. "He was trying to make an escape plan when we found out we were surrounded and just . . . disappeared."

"I hope none of them have been killed," Katie said softly.

The park wasn't quiet. There were all sorts of noises produced by the machines of entertainment and their occupants, but I thought I could hear guns going off. Either that was Nikolai, Aaron, and Tyson, or my exhausted mind was just playing tricks on me.

"Anyway," Keanu interrupted the noises, "we gotta get out of this damn park before they find us again."

"Yeah," I said, nodding, "we gotta find an exit."

"Only one I can think of is by the hotel," Kay said, "by the parking lot where we left our cars."

"Yeah," I said, "we need to hurry."

"Not only because they'll get to us," Kay said, "but I paid for parking, and it's racking up my debit."

"Good enough." Erich looked over at him with an eyebrow raised.

"Let's move," Keanu said. "We're also burning daylight."

We all agreed and started making our way to the hotel.

We had faced no opposition on our way to the gate, and we were just passing by the Rivers of America. We avoided going near the castle or the Main Street roundabout since we suspected the LDs would still be there.

"Hold up!" Kay said, looking at a map he picked up. "I think we're lost."

His ears drooped as he confusedly studied the map, turning it in his paws.

Our ravaged crew stopped walking.

"You're reading it wrong," Erich said. "You always do!"

Kay's ears flattened in annoyance as he glared at Erich.

"Gimme that!" Erich snatched the map from Kay and looked at it. "Yeah, we're in Frontierland. We need to go that way." Erich pointed.

I turned my back on them and let out a deep sigh as I watched a steamboat chug by on the river. I seemed to marvel at it as it went by when my eye caught something at my feet, and I looked down at it. It was a feathered cap, like the one I had lost, but this one was flattened from someone stepping on it, though.

I crouched and picked it up, then standing, I fixed and adjusted it with care until it was in the best shape I could get it and placed it on my head, straightening the feather. I noticed Katie had been watching me, smiling at me. I gave her a smile and opened my arms for her, and she moved into them.

"You look adorable in that costume, dear," she said as we embraced each other.

"You look lovely, darling," I said.

I looked straight ahead and noticed a little kid a slight distance from his parents, staring at us. Marveling at us. From his eyes, the actual Robin Hood was right in front of him, and he couldn't help but stare. I gave the kid a warm smile, and I was suddenly distracted as Keanu's strong voice interrupted Kay and Erich's argument.

"Chance," Katie said into my ear, "you should break up the argument."

"Yeah." I nodded and sighed. "I love you, darling," I added, letting go of her and looking at her.

"I know, hon," she said, looking up at me. "I love you too."

I headed for the bickering group and shoved Erich away from Kay, then shoved Kay.

"Guys!" I shouted. "Break it up, for god's sake!"

"Yeah," Faolan said, stepping forward in front of us all. "We need to keep moving, 'cause if you haven't noticed, the LDs are still here, looking for us, and the sun is starting to set."

I looked past Faolan and saw the distinctive men in black uniforms running for us.

"Guys!" I shouted and pointed.

Faolan and Keanu acted quickly and took off. Our reflexes weren't so fast, and the rest of us didn't react quickly enough as several operatives came from all directions and completely surrounded us, all with their rifles trained on us.

"Well, the fox hunt stops here," the one in command said, stepping forward, and unlike the others, dressed in a black suit.

"I'm Dean," he said. "I'm second in command to John. And he instructed me to take you two alive." He pointed at Katie and me.

"Now you guys" —he looked at Kay and Erich— "he told me to kill you, but I wouldn't do that here in a Disney themed amusement park full of children, so I'm gonna give you a chance to make like the other two and get out of here before things get messy." He stared at them with such a look that was like sarcastic happiness.

"Chance," Kay looked at me. "What do we do?"

I hung my head. Thoughts raced through my head. There was no way we were going to stop this now, no way we were going to foil Lance's plan, and the world was going to get torn apart in nuclear warfare, and we couldn't stop it. Whether we all died or not, we failed. I dropped the transmitter to the ground and slowly, regretfully put my arms up in surrender.

"Chance . . ." Kay said sadly and weakly.

"Wise choice." Dean smiled.

He pointed at the transmitter, and one of the operatives bent down, picked it up, and handed it to Dean's waiting hand. He kept that sickening smile as he examined the transmitter.

"Such a strange world we live in," he said, looking up at me. "The things that are always valued most" —he eyed Katie— "are always so

233

easily lost. No matter how hard you fight for it." He turned his back on us and took a couple steps forward.

"That's the price you pay," he continued. "It just goes to show how sadistic fate can be. Just look at Lance. He valued his family and his country." He turned back to us, looking at me with a cold stare. "And he lost both. A tragic night in '68. Chance remembers clear as day, don't you, Chance?"

I couldn't bear it. My vision was blurred as tears filled my eyes and rolled down my nose.

"Yes . . ." I answered weakly.

"Oh, what was that?" Dean put a hand to his ear. "Speak up. I don't think everyone here heard you."

"Yes," I said a bit louder.

Dean raised his hand in the air.

"You guys are just monsters," he said, giving all of us a look, "killing machines. Bred by and for the government to do the dirty work. To kill. That's the animal instinct: mate, feed, kill, repeat." He stepped back toward us and brought his face just inches from mine.

"You guys are as much of monsters as the government that created you," he said. "Project Anthro was supposed to end this conflict with America and the Soviets, but like all plans, it ended taking a wrong turn and making it worse. Like all experiments, there was a mistake, a flaw." He looked at the others again then back at me, his face just inches from mine.

"And as a result," he almost whispered, "the whole world will feel the pain of losing everything they hold on to so dearly. Everyone will know what it's like to lose the *one thing* they hold so dearly." My heart began to pound with adrenaline. I was getting pissed off at this guy.

"And it's all on you," he said to me.

I couldn't hold myself back. I brought my paw curled in a fist to his nose as hard as I could, and he shouted as he stumbled back on the ground, and the transmitter flew from his hands. I watched it go up, and I stepped in the direction it was flying.

Kay punched the operative nearest to him, drawing his attention away from me.

Katie tore off her dress, exposing the brown leather jacket, and she and Erich did the same as Kay. I caught the transmitter in both paws as everyone fought behind me and turned back to them, just as Dean stood and regained his balance.

I was so pissed at him I put my left paw behind his head and hit him repeatedly with the metal transmitter in my right paw. I then bent and spun around, sweeping his legs out from under him with my leg, and I loomed over him, breathing heavily, full of rage.

"You're just a killer," Dean said weakly, blood all over his face as he looked up at me. "And that's all you'll ever be."

I wrinkled my nose in disgust at this asshole, and I kicked his head hard, knocking him out cold. I looked up just in time to see Erich get hit with the butt of a rifle and fall back into the water.

"Erich!" Kay shouted.

He stepped to the operative that hit Erich and punched him hard in the jaw just as another operative behind him aimed his rifle at Kay.

I quickly unfolded my bow and took out an arrow, drawing it and letting go. The somewhat wild shot hit the operative in the shoulder near the chest, and he squeezed off a few shots. One of the bullets hit Kay in the back and exploded out of his chest where his heart was, and he gasped, bending forward, then falling to his knees, then onto his back.

"Kay!" I shouted. "No!"

I drew another arrow and aimed at the operative who had hit Erich into the water and sent an arrow into his back. I aimed at the operative next to the one who had shot Kay and fallen to the ground and let an arrow go. It hit him in the chest, going between the armor plates on his vest, and he fired a burst in a death grip and fell back on the cement.

I ran to Kay and knelt next to him, dropping my bow and the transmitter onto the ground and holding his head in my arms.

"Kay!" I shouted, panicking.

"Chance . . ." he said weakly, looking up at the sky.

I felt the life leave him, and I screamed. I had looked up to Kay since we met in Vietnam, and we had been best friends since. And now, he was dead. I looked up at an approaching operative; behind him was another, putting Katie in handcuffs as she cried out.

"No!" I shouted.

I picked up my bow and went to grab another arrow when the operative reached me and brought the butt of his rifle to my head. All went black.

17

I regained consciousness slowly and opened my eyes to find that I had been stripped down to nothing but my black T-shirt and was sitting in a large warehouse. There was a dim light that filled the structure, just enough for me to make out the basic details, which was mostly rust, dents, and holes.

I could hear the slow creaking of turning fans and the groans of the lights slowly swinging from disturbances of breezes. I could also hear pigeons flying around the interior of the building in the rafters. Above all, I heard voices. The voices accompanied approaching footsteps. I gained my full, perfect vision just as Lance stood over me.

"Hello, Chance." He smiled, keeping his hands in his pockets. Instead of his black suit, he wore a light-blue dress shirt and khakis. "Finally awake from your nap, I see. You were out for almost thirty-six hours. You were hit over the head harder than I thought."

"W—" I stuttered as I tried to put my paws in front of me, only to find they were cuffed behind my back to a pole or pipe or something. "Where am I?"

"This . . ." Lance paused, throwing his hands into the air as more lights turned on, giving me a clearer view of everything. There were men loading stuff into the trailer of a specialized Mack 18-wheeler that was made to be a mobile command unit of some kind. "Is a warehouse in Denver." Lance finished. "In a couple hours, all of us will be safely in the plains of east Colorado just as the bombs go off in every major city in the United States and the Soviet Union."

I looked up at him, fully conscious.

"Where's the last bomb?" I asked.

"Oh, you realized it wasn't at Disneyland." Lance smirked. "It's right here. In this building. Denver was the last city I needed. I'm sure you understand. It's difficult to smuggle such weapons into the central area of any country, but I now have bombs in every city I need them in, and they'll go off at the touch of a button." He pointed to the trailer of the truck. "Oh, and I must thank you for getting the ball rolling on this. I don't know what I would've done without Project Anthro."

"Huh?" I stared at him, confused.

"Was I not the one who wanted this whole operation?" He crouched in front of me. "Was I not the one who proposed the bombs in the Soviet Union? The day the government covered up the death of my family that you had conducted?"

"That was a mistake!" I shouted. "Why the hell can't you just let that go?"

"This isn't only about that night in '68," Lance said. "I've been at this from the start. You delivering the bomb to Kiev so it could go to Moscow was part of the plan all along. I realized how big of a monster the US government really was long, long before you even got your third-grade education in Australia."

He stood up and slowly paced back and forth.

"I developed this plan to get rid of these monstrosity world powers and create only one world power to control the whole world." He stopped pacing and grinned at me.

"The only thing I was getting revenge on for my family was you. That's why I've done everything in my power to keep you alive regardless of the fact that all the anthros that took part in it, I had sent to Vietnam to cover my tracks. Since the day I found out about what you did, I did all I could to have you come back alive." He stroked his chin as if there were a beard.

"Why?" I questioned.

"Simple," Lance said. "So everything you love will be ripped out of your life, just like me. You'll finally know what that pain feels like."

I suddenly heard Katie scream. She was brought in from behind Lance as he smirked devilishly at me. She was shoved to the floor and fell to her knees, her paws cuffed behind her back. She had obviously been beaten a bit.

"Katie MacArthur." Lance tsked as he crouched next to her, grabbed her chin, and forced her to face him. "You went rogue on me, Katie. You disobeyed direct orders and, even worse, fell for your target. You were supposed to bring him to me, and now you're kissing and getting all lovey-dovey over him and helping him escape."

Katie moved her pupils so she didn't have to look at the fiend that held her by the jaw.

"Do you love Chance, honey?" Lance asked softly.

Katie remained silent.

"Katie?" Lance said, a bit louder in a berating tone. "I asked you a question."

"I do," she said, looking at me.

I was getting worried Lance would do something to her at this point.

"Funny," he said, letting go of Katie's jaw as she yanked her head away. "I thought love wasn't an *animal instinct*." Lance got up and crouched in front of me again.

"Tell me, Chance," he said in the same soft tone he used with Katie, "do you love her?"

I breathed heavily and answered, looking at her.

"I do," I said. "More than anything. More than life itself."

Lance laughed as he stood.

"Good," he said. "Good."

He suddenly drew his pistol and turned, aiming it at Katie, and shot her right in the gut. She gasped as she fell back onto the floor, bleeding.

"Katie!" I shouted. Tears flooded my eyes as I began sobbing.

Lance holstered his pistol and turned back to me, no longer smiling, but with his mouth straightened with seriousness.

"They say love is a powerful thing," he said, looking down at me as I cried. "But even the most powerful thing has a weakness that can break it. And not even the most powerful thing can save anyone or those they 'love' from death." He pointed at the now motionless body of Katie lying on the floor.

"This is only the start," Lance said. "Katie is just the first victim of my wrath. You think you're feeling pain now?"

He bent down and brought his face just inches from mine to the point where I could feel his breath as he spoke.

"Just think of all the pain you'll feel when you think of the millions of innocent cries of the people you failed."

An operative grabbed me from behind and held my paws back as a second one undid my handcuffs and put them back on my wrists, now not around the pole so I could be taken away.

"Take him to the truck. And give him a front-row seat."

"No!" I screamed in agony as they dragged me on my hind end to the truck. "Katie, no!"

"You really did love her," Lance said loudly as he headed for the passenger door on the rig.

He stepped up into the passenger seat of the truck and shut the door behind him.

"Katie, Katie!" I shouted. "No! Katie, please!"

240

I was dragged into the door of the truck, and it was closed before I could get a good look at Katie's motionless body, left behind by everyone on the floor. The two men picked me up and shoved me into a seat.

"Sit down and shut up!" one of them said, slapping the back of my head.

My eyes were filled with tears, which rolled down my cheeks as soon as they accumulated enough. I didn't know if Katie was alive or not as the driver of the truck started the engine and prepared to leave.

We had been on the road for a couple hours, headed eastward toward Kansas. There was a window opposite to the monitor that I had been seated in front of, and I had swiveled the chair around and watched the seemingly endless golden grassland pass by.

We had left Denver on I-70 and turned off to an empty highway to a small town called Seibert, just off a highway that linked an eastward chain of towns in that section of the state of Colorado. The highway had just merged into Rose Avenue in the town of Burlington, which is where we stopped to get gas.

As I sat in the seat, I happened to pick up my head and see a black-with-a-red-stripe Skyline. The only reason I didn't suspect it was Keanu's car was because I spotted Colorado license plates on it, along with tinted windows and a small spoiler on the back end. Though, it did remind me of Faolan and Keanu, and I wondered if they were okay or if they had even escaped the LD, then thought about Erich, who was pushed into the water and I didn't see him come back up, then of Tyson, Nikolai, and Aaron, who all disappeared. Aaron had seemed to not say a single word before he disappeared. I hoped everyone was okay.

I began to think of Katie, who could still be lying motionless on the floor of that old warehouse back in Denver. I sighed sadly as I hung my head again. One of the operatives, a young man not wearing his

armored vest or helmet and sitting in front of the monitors instead of going out and joining the rest, looked at me.

"Everything all right?" he asked.

"Yeah," I said weakly, "just a long trip."

"Uh-huh." The young man looked back at his monitor.

I looked him over.

"How old are you, son?" I asked.

"Nineteen," he answered.

"You shouldn't be doing this." I sighed. "You're still young. You
could be doing anything else."

"I just joined because I wanted some action in my life, you
know?" the young man said, glancing at me and shrugging. "I just . . .
wanted to fit in somewhere and be able to do what's right."

"Me too, kid." I sighed again. "But what Lance is up to is no
good."

"What are you talking about?" the young man sat up in his chair
and stared at me. "He's pushing to end the conflict with the reds."

"He's not going about it the right way," I said. "In, I don't know,
like ten or so years, the Soviets could have fallen and we could look back
at this conflict and just laugh about it and appreciate all the good it
brought, like the Space Race and the advancement of technologies . . ." I
studied the young man. "If you wanna do what's right, you have to know
what's right. War is not the answer; it's not right. But . . ." I looked out the
window. "Sometimes war is a necessary evil. Sometimes it's unavoidable.
But this" —I turned back to him and looked at him— "this can be
avoided. What you're doing. If you feel like something's right, you do it.
Don't give a damn about who's giving you orders. Focus on you. Because
if Lance happens to fail" —I shrugged— "he could get knee deep in ma-
nure and probably drag his cowhands into it."

The young man speechlessly turned back to his monitor as the other operatives, also not wearing their armor, came in through the door on the side of the trailer.

"Hey, Quinn," one of them said to the young man, "why didn't you join us, bud?"

"I'm tired as hell," Quinn answered.

The operative nodded and looked at me, noticing that I was looking at him. He stepped toward me and smacked the back of my head.

"What are you looking at?" He grunted. He opened a bottle of Budweiser and took a sip, going to the rear of the trailer and sitting in front of his monitor. I looked back out the window at that Skyline. The engine started, but the car just sat there. I sighed and thought about the others as the last five operatives, plus the driver and Lance, piled into the truck.

The driver started the truck, and we got back onto the main road again, and I watched the houses and small business buildings go by as we drove down the road. The truck stopped at a traffic light.

I looked down at the floor and twitched my whiskers when I suddenly heard the distinctive sound of a Chrysler 426 Hemi, and something caught my eye through the window. I looked out at the spoiler of a white Plymouth Superbird. White with a red flash on the side. My eyes widened. There was only about 1,900 ever built, and this couldn't be a coincidence. That was Kay's car. One of the others had to be driving it.

What could that mean about the Nissan at the gas station, though? Was it Keanu's car? Were the rest of the team gonna bust me out of here? I guess I'd find out soon enough. I smirked as the light turned green, and we started to move. We drove all the way to Old US Highway 24 and continued our journey eastward.

The other operatives were asleep, but Quinn had been sitting there, thinking for a long time. After about a half hour I couldn't help but ask.

"What are you thinking about?" I asked.

"Hmm?" He looked at me. "Oh, nothing. I was just blanked out."

"Mm-hmm," I said sarcastically and nodded as I looked out the window.

I sighed. If the others were really coming for me, I wondered when they would be here. I didn't see Aaron's Dino or the Peterbilt that Nikolai got in Los Angeles, but I wouldn't count on seeing that again. I heard a radio crackle.

"We'll be in Kansas soon," Lance said over the radio. "Soon we'll be getting back onto I-70, and we'll be letting the bombs go off. Just be ready to push the button in case something goes wrong."

I swallowed and wondered if he knew the others were possibly following this truck. As I sat there, I heard something hit the exterior of the trailer. It sounded not too large, but it was big enough to wake the operative who had smacked my head earlier.

"What the . . ." he said, getting up from his seat and heading to the window I looked out.

The other five operatives all woke up, and three of them followed the first one to the window.

"What is it?" one of them asked.

"I dunno," the first one said. "I thought I heard something. And those cars are pretty—"

There was an explosion at the back, and the whole back panel was taken out along with the two operatives who had been sitting in the back.

I jumped, startled by the explosion, and looked out the now open back and saw the white Superbird, followed by the black Nissan and even Jeremy's Porsche.

244

They did come for me! I almost smiled, but I was still handcuffed in the seat with four operatives right next to me. The one who had smacked me earlier turned to me.

"You!" He jabbed a finger at me. "He must have some kind of tracking device on him!"

"Are you kidding?" Quinn stood and moved between me and the operative. "Those are anthros! They would've tracked us down sooner or later!"

"We gotta get them off our tails!" the operative said, going to a phone on the wall of the trailer. He picked it up and dialed three numbers. "We need a chopper pronto!"

He hung up and grabbed an M16 off the weapons rack and held it up. One of the other operatives went over to him and took the rifle from his hands.

I noticed the truck started to accelerate, and the Skyline merged into the other lane to get alongside it. After about a minute, I heard a thump on the side, then smaller thumps that moved onto the roof.

"Hey," one of the operatives said, "one's on the roof!"

"Everyone, arm yourselves and get up there!" the first operative said, handing them all an M16.

One operative went out the back and climbed the side ladder up there. All that was heard was a burst from the rifle, and the operative was thrown overboard and hit the pavement. The Superbird swerved to miss his rolling body.

"Dammit!" the first operative said. "Quinn, stay here and guard the fox. Make sure nobody gets him or he doesn't escape!"

Quinn just nodded and drew his pistol. The rest of the operatives went up to take out whoever was up there. We heard thumps on the roof and gunfire, some scrapes and squeaks. Three went overboard on the rear and sides, then finally there was a big thump on the front end of the trailer.

I looked back at Quinn, who was looking up at the ceiling, listening to the noises.

"You gotta let me go!" I begged. "The whole world depends on it!"

"I have orders—" Quinn answered.

"Forget the orders!" I shouted. "What matters is what's right and wrong!"

Quinn looked up at the roof as footsteps moved across the top toward the rear.

"Do you even know what Lance is doing?" I asked.

"Of course I do," Quinn answered.

"Don't you have a family in one of those cities? Think about them! Think of all the innocent people who are going to die at the hands of Lance!"

Quinn stared at me in silence.

"Think of yourself," I continued. "If Lance's plan fails, then you'll be in just as much trouble as him. Take it from me."

Quinn swallowed.

"I'm begging you to let me go," I said helplessly.

He looked down at me in a stupor of thought, then put his pistol away and took out his keys, getting behind me and unlocking my handcuffs. As soon as I was free I stood and gave him a big hug.

"Thank you," I said.

"You're free," Quinn said, in a bit of a flustered and confused tone. "Now what?"

"Come with us," I said, "and I'll see to it that you don't get into any trouble in this. I'll see to it personally that you don't receive the punishment."

Quinn looked behind me at someone at the open rear of the trailer. I followed his gaze. Standing there was Katie, holding Faolan's katana. Her leather jacket had a big hole where the bullet had torn through, and she had a pistol in a holster strapped onto a belt that hung a bit loosely on her right hip. My eyes widened once I saw her.

"Katie!" I yelled and ran to her. I threw my arms around her and gave her a kiss. "I was so scared. I thought I lost you."

She smiled a bit. "I'm fine, honey," she said, "really. Erich managed to get me fixed up."

"Well, Quinn here just let me go right before you got here," I said, gesturing back at Quinn, who waved at Katie a bit awkwardly. I turned back to Katie.

"We gotta get you out of here," Katie said. I nodded just as the side door opened. The first operative came through with a big gash on his head that leaked blood down the side of his face.

"Quinn!" he shouted as Quinn turned to him. "What the hell are you doing?"

"I'm letting him go!" Quinn said boldly.

"Oh, are you now?" the operative said. "So now you finally have guts, huh? I gave you an order, Quinn!"

"This isn't about orders!" Quinn shouted at him.

The operative just scoffed.

"You've gone soft," he said as he then quickly drew his pistol and fired a shot through Quinn's chest. Quinn fell to the floor.

"Quinn!" I shouted.

Katie drew her pistol and loaded the operative with lead before he could fire a shot at us. I ran to Quinn and knelt next to him, putting his head on my lap.

"Aw, Quinn," I said to the poor, gasping, bleeding human I held.

"I'm sorry," he said, looking up at me, blood running from his mouth.

"No, Quinn," I said softly, "there's no need to apologize. You did the right thing, and I'm sure you'll make it."

"No." Quinn shook his head weakly. "I gotta destroy the contents of this trailer."

He weakly reached for an armored vest hanging on the wall, which I gestured for Katie to grab. She took it off the wall and lugged it over to me. I gently handed it to Quinn. He winced and breathed heavily as he grabbed a grenade from it, pulled the pin, and held down the lever.

"You gotta go now."

"No, Quinn," I said. "I can't leave you."

"No," Quinn said, "forget about me. Stop Lance. I'm nothing compared to the rest of the people who'll suffer if you don't."

"One person makes all the difference, Quinn," I said. I gave him a gentle kiss on the forehead. "I'll never forget you. And one day, the world will know what you did."

Quinn nodded as I gently set his head on the floor and stepped back toward the end of the trailer. Erich pulled the Superbird close to the rear of the trailer.

"You stop Lance!" Quinn said as he released the fuse on the grenade.

Katie took my paw, and we jumped onto the front of the car. I motioned for Erich to slow down, which he did.

As soon as we were about a hundred yards from the back of the trailer, the whole interior was filled with an explosion that knocked most of the contents out of the rear. Katie and I shielded our heads from the debris.

Erich leaned over and rolled down the passenger window, and Katie and I scooted over the hood and climbed into the car. As soon as I sat down, I noticed Aaron in the backseat.

"Where the hell have you two been?" I asked, berating.

"Oh," Aaron said, putting a finger to his chin as if he were thinking about what to say, "I was captured and nearly killed by several LDs who destroyed my car! If it hadn't been for Faolan and Keanu, I'd probably not be here!"

"Okay, chill out you guys!" Erich said. "Welcome back, Chance. You all right?"

"I'm fine," I said. "I need you to get alongside the truck."

"What?" Erich said. "No way. We only came for you. There's no way we can stop Lance at this point. He's got a helicopter coming."

"Someone in there just died letting me go so I could stop him!" I shouted at Erich.

Erich looked at me and sighed.

"All right. But you might get us all killed."

I took Faolan's sword from Katie and looked at Aaron. "You're coming with me!" I said to him.

"Okay then." Aaron sighed. Erich shifted up a gear, sped toward the truck, and matched its speed once the passenger window was beside the ladder.

I gave Katie a kiss.

"I love you," I said before I climbed out onto the ladder.

Aaron put on his wide-brimmed hat and clambered to the front and out the window, following me up the ladder. Erich slowed the car and followed closely behind the truck.

The Nissan slowed down by the ladder, and Faolan climbed out onto it. She followed the both of us, and the Nissan slowed behind the truck with the Superbird.

"Faolan!" I shouted over the rushing wind. "Go back!"

"I wanna help!" she shouted up to me.

I rolled my eyes and climbed to the top of the trailer. I got to the top with Aaron and looked at the front of the trailer to see Lance standing there, his shirt blowing in the wind.

"So you just don't know when to give up, do you?" he shouted.

"Not until I stop you!" I shouted back.

"Pretty naive for someone who's been running for the past couple of months!" Lance said approaching me.

I stepped forward to him and motioned for Aaron to stay back. Lance and I met at the middle of the trailer.

"Guess we'll have to finish this then," Lance said. "Man to *animal*."

"Don't call me that," I said with a growl, lowering my ears and glaring at him.

Lance just laughed and grabbed for his pistol.

"Chance!" I heard Faolan yell. She took out one of her shurikens, hurled it at John, and it stuck in between his chest and shoulder. He didn't flinch or even cringe. He just laughed some more.

"Oh, young operatives . . ." he said, yanking the shuriken out of his chest, aiming at Faolan, and firing a shot at her. The bullet pierced the Kevlar armor and buried itself in her stomach.

She gasped as she began to stumble back, but Aaron quickly grabbed her and held her, gently laying her down and crouching next to her. I was speechless. She was so young, but regardless, Lance had still shot her.

I turned back to him, and he looked at the pistol and shuriken and threw both overboard.

"Guess we'll see who's really the dominant species here," Lance said, holding up his fists. I took Faolan's katana from its sheath and stabbed it into the roof of the trailer so it wouldn't fall off.

"Humans have been screwing up this planet since they first came to be," I said. "It's time to put a balance to that."

I moved quickly over to him and threw a punch, which he dodged. He grabbed my arm and somehow picked me up off the roof and slammed me hard onto my back. He brought his foot over my head and went to stomp on it when I grabbed his foot and twisted hard.

He screamed in pain as he hopped on one foot, giving me a chance to get up. I put some distance between us as he bent down and massaged his twisted ankle.

"Woo!" Lance said, shaking his leg. "That was something. But, it's gonna take more than that to stop me."

I approached him again.

"How about for this?" I brought my knee up to his crotch as hard as I could, and he squeaked.

"That definitely did some damage," he said weakly. I uppercut his face and he fell back onto the trailer.

"Ah!" he exclaimed in pain.

I grabbed him by the collar of his shirt and picked him up, then brought my fist to his face three times before he finally punched my jaw. I released my grip on his shirt and stumbled back. He drew the katana from the roof of the trailer and came at me with it.

"Well, we already know which of us is the more gullible here," Lance said, walking toward me with it at his side.

"Foxes are one of the top smartest species, you know?" I said, regaining my balance and preparing for more.

"Not as smart as humans, though!" He strained as he swung the blade at me.

I ducked under his swing and chopped my paw behind his knee, forcing him to lose balance and kneel. He almost dropped the sword but grabbed it before it made it over the side of the trailer.

I punched his nose, and he sprawled back, still keeping a tight grip on the weapon. I got on top of him and started hitting him in the face repeatedly until it began to bleed. Lance blocked one last blow with the blade of the sword, and it cut my knuckles down the middle. I screamed in pain as I fell back off Lance and held my bleeding paw.

He began to approach me with the sword still in hand, and as soon as he got close enough, I hopped up and ran at him. My head hit his gut, and I threw him over my shoulder. He landed with a thud behind me, near the front of the trailer. This time he finally dropped the sword. I basically had him where I wanted him now. I approached him and picked up the sword, then as he got up, I swung at him, and it cut his stomach.

"Ah!" he screamed as he fell to his knees in front of me.

I held the sword to his neck, panting from exhaustion, and stood like that for a few seconds until Lance finally spoke.

"You think you've won?" he said. "What are you gonna do now? What could you do to convince me to surrender myself and my cause?"

He looked up at me with a bleeding-lipped smile.

"I—" I couldn't think of what exactly to say. "I'll kill you."

"Oh really?" Lance said, as he stood up, I brought the sword back, ready to stab him in the chest if necessary. "Even if you kill me, how can you possibly stop this? After me, there will be someone else. Then another, and another."

He reached into his pocket and took out the remote button for the bombs.

I was getting sick of it all. I stabbed at him with the sword, but he grabbed it by the blade and the skin of his palms split as the blade lacerated it. He shoved the sword at me, and the hilt collided with my nose and I fell onto my back. Lance quickly turned the sword in his hands, loomed over me, and ran the long blade through my shoulder and into the roof of the trailer. I was stuck.

I screamed in pain as I struggled and pushed on the sword, trying to get up only to meet more unbearable pain. I stopped when I could hear the *chop chop chop* of helicopter blades approaching. Lance sighed, putting a wide smile on his face and standing up straight as a black Huey approached from the side.

"Guess there's no stopping me now anyway," Lance said as the helicopter flew sideways in front of the truck, enabling Lance to walk over to it and step on. He laughed maniacally as he did so.

"Chance!" Aaron said, sliding to a stop after sprinting over to me and slowly yanking the sword out of my shoulder.

I groaned as he set the sword down and tried to get me on my feet.

"Aaron," I said, "just leave me. I'll figure something out. Just get Faolan off this thing."

"I—" Aaron began to speak, but I shoved him toward the rear, where Faolan still was.

"Get her off here!" I scolded. "She needs medical attention ASAP!"

Aaron just sighed and went over to help Faolan off the truck.

Erich pulled the Superbird alongside the ladder, and Aaron put Faolan in first then followed after her.

"So long for now, Chance!" Lance shouted over the noise as he looked out at me from the side door of the helicopter. "I'll see you when the fallout settles and the dust clears!" He held up the button, ready to press it.

I began to look around frantically for anything I could use to stop him. I looked at the sword lying on the roof of the trailer and thought I could probably toss it at him and take out his hand, but what if I missed? Or what if it wasn't fast enough and he pressed the button and every bomb went off in unison?

"Chance!" I heard Tyson yell.

I looked over to see him in the passenger side of the Porsche, and he tossed me something, which I barely caught. It was a bag with my beat-up pistol and two hand grenades. As soon as I saw the grenades, I pulled one out, pulled the pin, and let go of the fuse.

"See you in Hell, you son of a bitch!" I shouted at Lance.

I then threw the grenade, but I was way off on my aim and almost screamed in utter defeat as the grenade bounced off the bottom of the helicopter's fuselage. But as soon as it hit the hood of the truck, it exploded, sending the helicopter out of control and flying sideways right for me.

I acted fast and pulled the pin on the next grenade, cocked my pistol, and ran for the helicopter. Just as the helicopter and I met, I jumped through the opening, throwing the grenade into the cockpit, then fired all my rounds at Lance, killing him with every one of the shots. The helicopter passed, and I landed back on the trailer when the grenade inside the helicopter exploded and sent the aircraft spiraling to the earth, where it exploded into a massive ball of fire upon impact with the ground.

I smiled victoriously, but that smile was turned into a frown as I realized the grenade that exploded in front of the truck had apparently killed the driver, and the truck had been sent out of control toward the end of a guard rail. I definitely wasn't fast enough to act.

The truck's fuel was ignited, and it exploded upon impact. The trailer was thrown over the truck with me on it, and I screamed as I fell to the pavement. There was yet a bigger finale explosion. I was knocked unconscious as soon as I hit the ground.

18

I slowly awoke, lying on a soft surface and a blanket over my lower half. I heard a heart monitor beeping slowly at my left side, and I smelled the distinctive smell of a hospital room. As I realized where I was, I slowly opened my eyes, squinting in the bright light. My arms and legs ached really bad, and I couldn't even move my arms due to the IV needles stuck in my elbow joints.

On my left shoulder, thigh, and shin, there were patches of shaved fur with a sewed up scar in the middle of them. It was the same with my right forearm and thigh. I started to wonder what had happened to me when the truck crashed and exploded then looked around the room for anyone else. As I turned my head, I felt a sharp ache in my head and groaned.

"Honey?" I heard Katie say.

I looked over as best I could to a chair at my right, where Katie was sitting.

"Babe?" I asked. "Is that you?"

I then felt Katie wrap her arms around me and hug me tightly as she kissed the side of my neck.

"Thank god you're okay," Katie said.

"What happened to me?" I asked.

"You were knocked unconscious for almost a whole day again," Katie responded, letting go of me and moving into my view, sitting on the side of the bed. "I was worried sick."

"You American women are always worried sick." I said out loud this time.

"It's only because I love you, Chance," Katie said, smiling softly.

"Where are we?" I asked.

"A hospital in Kansas," Katie answered.

"What are these scars from?" I asked.

"You broke several bones when you hit the ground," Katie said. "They were so bad the doctors had to put in metal plates to hold them together."

"Well, I'm in so much pain now that I can't really even move," I said.

"Sorry, babe," Katie said, "you're stuck here for a little bit."

"How long?" I asked.

"Probably a few months," Katie said with a frown.

"Dammit," I said, looking back up at the ceiling.

"Look on the bright side," Katie said, "the little ones will be kicking by the time you get out." She rubbed her slim belly, inside of which our two kits were still developing.

"I'm looking forward to seeing them in person," I said.

"Don't worry, babe," Katie said, leaning down and kissing my head. "You will. Just be patient."

At that moment, the others entered the room, including little Ethan.

"Chance!" Jeremy greeted. "We're so glad you're all right! We were all getting so worried!"

"We all thought you were dead when we picked you up from the crash site," Tyson added.

"I'm good, guys," I said. "Just in a pretty massive amount of pain right now."

"I'm sure you'll be glad to know that Lance was officially pronounced dead yesterday," Erich said.

"I'm not surprised," I said.

"There is no way anyone could've survived a crash like that," Keanu said.

"I'd be damned if he did," Aaron added.

Upon Keanu speaking, I began to search for Faolan, who was shot in the stomach by Lance.

"Where's Faolan, guys?" I asked. That was when I noticed that Keanu looked down at the floor. I guessed she didn't make it.

"I'm sorry, mate," I said regretfully.

"No," Keanu responded. "She's fine. But as a result of the shot, she can't have pups. It damaged her uterus too much."

"I'm so sorry, Keanu," I said.

"Lance has paid for his actions," Keanu said. "It's done now."

After a while, we said our good-byes for the night, and everyone left me alone in my room. I eventually began to doze off and had closed my eyes when I heard someone's soft padded feet step into my room. I ever so slightly opened my eye, making it look as if it were still closed, to see whom it was. It was Faolan, weakly hobbling into my room with a big bandage around her lower gut, which she had placed her paw on.

She came over to my bed and sat on the side, while I kept my eyes closed and pretended to be asleep.

"Chance," Faolan whispered. I didn't respond, still pretending to be in a deep sleep.

"I just wanna thank you, Chance," Faolan said. "I know I was stupid and should've got off the truck, but you saved us all by what you did, even though you almost got yourself killed." She sighed and put a paw on my chest, slowly rubbing.

"I know you're with Katie, but . . ." she paused. "I love you, Chance. You're the kind of man anyone could only dream of. You truly do have more makings of a real man than any human I know."

She sighed again, then I suddenly felt her lips make contact with mine as she gave me a long, passionate kiss. As soon as she ended it, she sat back up.

"Stay strong, honey," she said. "Katie and your kids are gonna need you to be."

She then got back up and slowly exited my room, leaving me alone in the dark again.

I opened my eyes and thought about everything she had said. I had never heard anything like that from anyone, except for Jack, the one who had me brought onto this earth, but to hear it from someone else besides my mentor and, I guess, father figure made it really stick. More than ever before. But what seemed to make it stick even more was that she seemed to repeat exactly what Jack had once said to me. I suddenly felt light and warm inside and eventually fell asleep with a smile on my face.

19

Close to a couple months later, I was out of the hospital, healed enough to take my place in the world again. As I put on my now torn up ASIS jacket that would no longer even zip up. Katie told me on the way out that a place for us to live had been set up in the small town of Parker in Colorado. So we all said our good-byes to Jeremy, Ethan, Tyson, and Erich, who met us out front. Even Aaron had to leave. His wife was waiting for him back in Oahu, Hawaii.

Out of everyone, Ethan was the saddest to see us go our separate ways. In fact, he was in tears when I went over to him to say good-bye. So I asked him to come on a walk with me.

As we walked, I talked to him, trying to pull him together and help him feel better.

"It's okay, son," I said, walking next to him. "I know it's hard to see someone go, trust me. But I'll always be around. You, Tyson, and Jeremy are my best friends."

"You're like the dad I never had," Ethan said with a sniffle. "I don't want you to go."

He then walked over to me and hugged me tightly, wrapping his arms around my waist and hiding his face in my belly.

"Aww, kid." I hugged his head against my belly and rubbed his back. "I promise you'll always be able to see me. In fact, I still remember you guys' phone number, so I can talk to you whenever."

He looked up at me, and I smiled at him warmly.

"You're gonna be a great daddy to your puppies," Ethan commented.

I smiled flattered.

"You're a good kid, Ethan," I said. "One day you'll do something great."

We stood there in front of the hospital hugging for several minutes, before returning to the group.

"Well, Chance," Aaron said, putting a paw on my shoulder, "it's been one hell of a ride. And you definitely got farther than anyone else could've on this case."

"There wasn't even a case on it," I said.

"Exactly," Aaron added. "Well, I'm heading to the airport. Gotta get back to Oahu. And, Ethan, I'll see to it that you can come over and hang out every now and again."

"You'd do that?" Jeremy asked.

"Well, why not?" Aaron said. "Stuff like that costs nothing to me, so why not take advantage? Plus, I'm sure Emily would absolutely love to meet him."

"Any room for another?" Tyson asked.

"Oh, yeah." Aaron nodded. "Definitely."

"Don't forget that we'll be visiting you guys regularly," I told Jeremy.

"How about you, Nikolai?" Tyson asked. "What are you gonna do?"

"When the KGB finds out Lance was behind it all, the mission will close." He winked with his good eye. "And I may retire just so I can be around to raise Vassili with my wife."

"Well," Erich looked at the ground, "I don't have anyone to go to, so I may just go back to Amsterdam."

That was when I suddenly remembered what was in my pocket. I reached in and pulled out a wrinkled, partly faded card, but the text was still clearly visible, *Chanel A. Parker,* and a phone number on the front.

"Here, Erich," I said, handing it to him. "She's a human. She's a nice girl, and she *loves* animals." Erich looked at the card with his eyebrow raised.

"She hates her job too," I continued. "I'm sure she'd love an adventurous job with an anthro partner."

"I guess I'll give her a call then." He smiled weakly.

"She lives in LA," I said.

"Yeah, I guess LA will suit me fine," Erich said.

As I began to walk away, Erich handed me the keys to Kay's Plymouth.

"I'm sure Kay would want you to have it," Erich said.

Keanu and Faolan had requested to stay with us in Colorado, and of course, Katie didn't wanna say no. And I didn't want those young adolescent wolves out all by themselves with no help or support. As soon as everyone said their final good-byes, we all departed.

I took Katie, Keanu, and Faolan in the Superbird, and we began our journey westward to Parker. Katie wanted to sit in the back with Keanu, just so she could have someone with free paws to help her if needed since her pregnancy had begun to show. So that left Faolan in the front seat next to me.

I had no idea what to do next, driving on the open road with Katie and Keanu passed out in the back seat. Now that we had stopped a nuclear war from breaking out, what would we do now? I sighed, and that apparently gave Faolan a sign of my distraught.

"What's wrong, honey?" she asked.

"Nothing," I responded.

"You okay?" Faolan asked.

"Yeah," I said. "I'm just thinking . . . what are we supposed to do now? Society will probably never accept us."

Faolan sat up in her seat.

"I'm sure they will," she said. "If you look back in history, you'll find that many people have come to accept differences you thought they never would. Like, if you lived a hundred years ago, would you think you would ever see the slaves have equal rights?"

"I guess not," I said.

"It just takes time," Faolan said, "but they will. I promise."

We had moved into the house in Parker, a large high-income home owned by a nice lady named Beth, who was more than familiar with Project Anthro already. Beth ran her own private school at the house, which Katie volunteered to help Beth with.

By now, it was mid-1974, and Katie had given birth to our two kits, a boy and a girl. We decided to name our son Kay, after my best friend, and named the daughter Erika. I had begun a new job at a place called the CRF (Classified Relics Facility) located in the northern outskirts of Aurora, for it was the only kind of job someone like me could get. That very day, I was about to head to my first day of the job.

"Chance!" Katie called from upstairs, just as I was putting the CRF security uniform on in our room in the basement.

"Yeah?" I called back.

"Don't forget to kiss the kids good-bye before you go!"

"Trust me, I won't!" I called back with a smile. After putting all my stuff together, I headed upstairs and met Katie at the top. We exchanged a hug and a kiss.

"Love you, baby," I said, looking into her sapphire-blue eyes. The ones I had first looked into in Vietnam.

"I love you too," Katie said. "Be safe."

"Don't worry, honey," I said, smiling at her. "What could possibly go wrong? And where are my babies?"

"Living room," Katie said. I walked down the short hallway to the living room, where my two little kits sat on the floor with all their toys and playthings around them. I went to my daughter first and gave her a big kiss on the cheek.

"Bye-bye, Erika," I said. "Daddy loves you."

I then went to my son and gave him a kiss on the cheek as well.

"And I love you, Kay," I said. "See you guys later."

I then got up and noticed that Katie had been watching me. She was smiling widely at me and the babies.

"It's only been a couple of months, and you're already an outstanding father," she commented.

"Aww," I said, bashfully waving my paw. "Who couldn't love these two?"

"True," Katie said, wrapping her arms around my neck and looking into my eyes once more. "But you're still a great father."

We gave each other another kiss.

I had been driving for a couple minutes, listening to the classic rock station on the radio, when the next song began to play. It was "Bad Moon Rising" by Creedence Clearwater Revival, which I found to be a pretty fitting song at that moment. The mayhem we had faced for the past few months had finally, against all odds, ended.

Though the sixties and seventies hadn't been that great, when I look back at them now, I'm somewhat glad for all the events that took place in that time period and the good they had brought into my life. Like Jack had said, some things may have been bad, and I wasn't grateful for them then, but I had to learn somehow. I had made some major mistakes back then, but everyone makes at least one huge mistake in their life. But it was all said and done, and I had indeed learned from it. And I especially learned a lot from Jack, though I hadn't seen him much or even known him for very long.

As I drove down that open road, listening to that song, I thought of the future. Was Faolan right about the people of this society eventually coming to accept us? Would people finally put aside their differences and see the similarities? I wasn't so sure. There was still a lot to come. Many more years of conflict and war and all kinds of trouble would head our way. I had no idea at that time, but regardless of that as I looked in the future, I indeed could see a bad moon rising.

Made in the USA
San Bernardino, CA
18 October 2017